I0741183

Silver Verity
(Book 3)

By Lea Carter

ISBN 9780988599154

Cover illustration and design
by Daniel A. Manfredini

Learn more about the author at
leacarterwrites.wixsite.com/wholesomefantasy

Dear Queen Rebecca—thanks for being such a willing victim of my amateur efforts. It took us a while to get one of your stories told, and I hope you and King Hugh will have a long, happy life together.

Chapter I

I sighed and leaned heavily against a post in the stable yard. The one downside to arranging wedding gowns for Helen and Cassandra was that I was expected to attend their fittings as well as my own. After a morning of fittings, I was in a mood to see everything darkly. I was even beginning to be convinced that Hugh and I were never going to manage to see Father privately. We tried yesterday, but between our responsibilities and his, the appointment had deteriorated into a two minute exchange of greetings before we all rushed off to our next obligation. I repressed the urge to kick something in frustration. Time was growing short!

"You look positively gloomy," observed a kind voice, startling me out of my thoughts.

Sighing again, I turned to face my mother. "I am gloomy," I admitted, after making sure there were no ladies-in-waiting or stable boys lurking in the shadows. Then I noticed the way her fingers were interlocked. Her lovely pink gloves covered any potentially white knuckles, but I had used a similar nerve-restraining tactic often enough to be able to guess at how she must be feeling. "Walk with me?" I invited, tipping my head in the direction of the gardens. As our arms linked, I felt the taut muscles in hers. I did not completely forget the impending pirate battle, but I did focus my energies on my mother instead of on myself. I even roused myself enough to greet the various ladies we passed on the way.

"It must be quite a problem," I observed after we had reached the gardens and were again alone.

After a moment of flying in silence, she laughed. "Am I so transparent?" The laughter transformed her, making her seem as young as Gwyneth and as warm as sunshine. "It is really a simple thing," she said before I could respond, "but I cannot make up my mind!"

I was surprised by the faint desperation in her voice. "About what?" I prompted quickly.

"Where to take your father on vacation." She giggled nervously when she said it.

"Why," I started to laugh, "what a wonderful idea!" Her expression changed to mild mortification at my amusement and then relaxed when I finished my thought. "Tell me all about it, darling. Where are you thinking of going?"

We sat down together on one of the dainty benches. I loved watching her face as she animatedly described to me everywhere that she had thought of going. Each choice would be perfect…except for this or that. I used old cues in a new way today, watching her hand gestures to determine which of the destinations actually interested her. I was a little worried as to when they would actually be able to take such a trip, for I knew that the council had been in power for quite long enough. The monarchy had to be reasserted and while it was probably selfish of me to wish that Hugh and I could take a wedding trip before accepting the throne, I could not help myself. That was one thing I had associated with getting married since childhood.

"It sounds to me," I interrupted when she began suggesting destinations that clearly held no interest for her directly, "as if you should visit the Sky Fairies. Oh, not in the capital city of Regalis," I hastily amended. "A royal vacation in another tribe's palace is no vacation at all!" I squinted, trying to bring the memory of a particular map into focus. "However, I believe that the southern seaports are lovely this time of year."

Mother inhaled, an excited, girlish expression on her face. "Your father would love that!" she exclaimed. "He once told me that if he had not been born a prince, he would have run off and signed onto a windship."

I believe it, laughed my imp. *He would have made captain, too.*

"Now, Rebecca," a little of her age settled back into her face as she squeezed my hands, "tell me what is troubling *you.*"

I looked down at our clasped hands, so similar in shape and size—so different in terms of years and skills. Somewhere in the tall jungle-grasses a bird happily sang out that the weather was fine.

"I am troubled," I admitted, keeping my eyes lowered shyly. "I love Hugh very much…" I paused, struggling to put my feelings into words. It had all seemed so clear last night—and every night—since I had begun to wonder about it.

"Are you worried that you may love him too much?" she asked, tilting her head to one side so she could see more of my face.

"I know so little of love," I said, at last looking her in the eye again. "In me, it seems to blur lines that common sense drew long ago."

"It makes you feel things more intensely than you ever have before? Especially where Hugh is concerned? Especially," she watched me closely, "when he might make a mistake?"

I was too full of wonder and relief to answer with more than a nod. I had not been sure she would understand. But, understanding as she did, could she help me?

"I remember when you first learned to walk," she said, patting my hands lightly. "Like every child before you, you had a difficult time learning to balance. First, you mastered standing still; then, you conquered putting one foot in front of the other. Slowly at first," she smiled at the memories, "and not without your fair share of bumps and bruises. Now you not only walk, but because of Hugh, you can fly." She smiled as I blushed a little. "I remember, too, having the same questions when I got married. If I could give you some advice, it would be to not expect it to always be easy. You may fall," she winked, "and you may even bump heads. But someday, you *will* both fly."

I had to blink back a few tears to clear my vision. "Thank you, Mother."

"Of course." We rose together.

As she wrapped her arms around me and kissed my forehead, I knew that I would miss moments like this. I felt as light and free as a floating leaf. I was even able to set aside my worrying about the pirates.

"Pardon me," interrupted a male voice cheerfully, "have you seen the two most beautiful women-fairies… Why," Hugh stopped flapping and dropped to the earth as though stunned, "at last I have found you!"

Did you think I would let you lose me? my imp answered the light in his eyes as he stepped forward.

He greeted Mother first, bowing formally over her hand before presenting her with a lovely bouquet of late-blooming honeysuckle.

She gasped and covered her mouth with both of her hands. "For me?" she asked breathlessly.

"Of course," Hugh's eyes sought mine briefly before he added, "Mother."

I watched happily as she pressed one hand to his cheek, mouthed a 'thank you,' and flew dreamily away to put the bouquet in some water. Sweeter still to me was the expression of awe on Hugh's face as he watched her go.

"How did you know?" he asked me when he could speak.

I gently kissed his cheek and wrapped my arms about his neck. "You are going to make a wonderful son-in-law," was all I could say. To be sure, I had told him what Mother's favorite flower was when he asked. But he had *asked.*

"And husband?" he asked, drawing me closer.

"And king," I added.

He sighed. "You had to remind me. Come on," he drew back, "your father is waiting for us at the fencing area." Despite the serious conversation we hoped to have with Father, we smiled all the way there.

My smile faded a little when we arrived, though. Father was in the spaces, fencing with someone. My breath caught when I recognized his opponent.

"Rolf!"

"Easy," Hugh's grip on my arm tightened, holding me in place. "They are only practicing."

I swallowed my heart, allowing my head to take control again. As I calmed down, several things leapt out at me as obvious. Rolf was using a wooden practice sword instead of his own hand-crafted weapon; they both were. Father was pursuing the point very aggressively, as though testing Rolf's skill. Rolf was being…careful.

"Where did Rolf learn to fence?" Hugh asked, his tone a mixture of surprise and admiration.

"Jeffrey employs a master at arms on his estate," I shook my head, "but I have fenced with him. He could not have taught Rolf that style." I leaned forward, resting folded arms against the fence that surrounded the sparring area. My heartbeat sped up slightly as Hugh slipped one arm around me, leaning his other arm against the fence beside me.

Focus, encouraged my imp. *Your father fences with purpose.*

"Rolf has no military training?" Hugh mused aloud.

"No, none," I answered emphatically. I caught my breath when Rolf blocked, sidestepped, and lunged. Point—match!

Father saluted Rolf then surrendered his practice sword, acknowledging that he had lost the match.

"Methinks your father has his own idea of what we shall discuss," Hugh remarked, his breath stirring my hair.

Sorry, what were we talking about? asked my imp distractedly. Her distraction rescued me from mine.

"I do not think we shall enjoy it, either," I agreed. "This is most peculiar," I added, intentionally resisting the natural inclination to look up at him. "Jeffrey gave Rolf a sword of his own when he entered secondary school. It should still be balanced properly for him."

"Another mystery," Hugh sighed. "Smile,"

he reminded me as Father turned in our direction.

I could see just enough of Hugh's face to watch the corners of his mouth quirk up in his best 'company' smile. My own smile was instantly genuine. His determination to make the best of difficult situations was just one of many things I loved about him.

Father waved at us, then summoned Rolf. Rolf's face instantly went pale underneath the color that fencing had brought to his cheeks. Father draped an arm about Rolf's shoulders and gently urged him in our direction. When they reached the fence, we exchanged anxious greetings.

No sooner had we finished bowing and curtsying than Father remarked, "Rolf has found something he would like to show you."

I felt more perplexed by the moment as we all flew to the library window, Father carrying Rolf as easily as if one of them were thirty years younger. We filed in silently, but I jumped a little when the latch snapped closed behind us. My suspicions were confirmed when Rolf carefully checked all of the windows and doors before he shot a nervous look in Father's direction.

"Go on," Father instructed simply.

Obediently, Rolf climbed up on one of the lower cabinets and drew the map out of its hiding place. After he had reached the ground again, he turned to face us.

"I heard from one of the stable boys that the

post had secret panels and hiding places," he said, his tone apologetic. "No one else thought they would put one in the library, but I wanted to be sure." His voice faded and he stood there, uncomfortably waiting to hear his fate.

I had no immediate response. I briefly considered laughing aloud at the idea that our security measures had been so easily circumvented. Of course, the situation was too serious for that. How to proceed, then? This was no private diary, no trivial wish list that could just be replaced and forgotten.

"Have you shown this to anyone?" Hugh asked gravely, taking the map from Rolf's unresisting fingers.

Rolf shook his head, a miserable expression on his face. "Just Grandfather," he corrected himself promptly. "He already knew about it."

In trying to watch all three of them at once, I nearly missed the flicker of emotion on Father's face. Something else was amiss.

"Rolf," I said as gently as I could, "what are you not telling us?"

He looked up, eyes wide. "How did you know?" he asked.

"Woman's intuition," I answered, remembering a conversation I once had with Mother about being observant.

Rolf sighed and began twisting one of the buttons on his cuff. "My mother has that, too," he said, clearly missing the irony of his statement.

Hugh's face twitched, but instead of laughing, he set the map on the table. "We shall have to find another hiding place for this," he said, temporarily dismissing that concern. "Now," he put one hand on Rolf's shoulder. "You were about to say something important."

"I want to go," Rolf said after several moments of internal struggle.

I blinked. I could not help it. The thought of Rolf at the pirate battle (anywhere *close* to that battle) made the hairs on the back of my neck stand on end.

"Well done, Rolf," Father said approvingly. "Now, tell them why."

Hugh was exhibiting signs of mild panic as he folded his arms and gave Rolf his undivided attention. Clearly he had not expected this development, either.

If it had been difficult for Rolf to tell us about finding the map, this appeared nearly impossible. At last, after more soul-searching, he said quietly, "I want to record it."

"Like Tyler?" I asked, beginning to understand.

Rolf nodded. His eyebrows lifted a smidge, indicating hope.

"Rolf," Hugh began, then paused. Hugh could see Father, but Rolf could not. And Father was signaling for an indefinite answer. "We will have to think about it," Hugh said at last.

My stomach twisted uncomfortably when

Rolf smiled. I had read many adventure tales growing up and was still woefully unprepared for the experience of actually being kidnapped. I knew that Rolf had read about pirates, from military logbooks and Tyler's history—but it would be different to be directly involved in a pirate battle.

"Go tell your parents we would like to see them, please," Father directed Rolf.

I sagged into a convenient chair as soon as the door had swung shut behind Rolf.

"And what are *you* not telling us?" Hugh asked, turning sharply toward Father.

"Arabella will never agree," I added weakly.

"We have not even been able to decide," Hugh added in a calmer voice, "if one of us should be present."

"If one of you goes," Father said mildly, "you should both go." He let that sink in for a moment before returning to Rolf's situation. "Both of you look at Rolf and see a young boy-fairy. Rebecca, sometimes you have difficulty realizing that he no longer needs to take a nap each day. He is *sixty-eight* years old."

I considered the statement unhappily but could not dispute it. Left to my own devices, I would probably always think of Rolf as 'young.'

"Hugh, your vision is a little clearer," Father continued. "Tell me, have you never met a boy-fairy Rolf's age that was already making his own way?"

Hugh frowned darkly. "I have seen many younger," he answered, "but none that turned out well."

"Fair enough," Father nodded. "But it will take all of us to convince Arabella, if she is to be convinced. Rolf does not want to be a soldier. He has no thirst for violence or romantic notions about 'adventure.' However, he is a natural born historian."

Hugh and I looked at each other.

"There will be a hospital windship," I suggested. "I could go along and keep him safe."

"And who will keep you safe?" Hugh asked, softening a little.

"I thought that was why you were going along," I teased, reaching up to put a hand on his crossed forearms. I felt his muscles tighten when someone knocked on the door.

"We are agreed?" Father asked.

"Why?" Hugh asked, turning to face Father again. "This gala is a momentous time. There are dozens of things to record, from a royal wedding to the coronation of a new king. Why do you think he should go into battle?"

I sensed a very private distress in the question. Hugh had never told me how old he was the first time he got into a fight. I had never asked.

"Not into battle," Father corrected patiently. "Into his own life. He has demonstrated wisdom and courage today." He added pensively, "We all know that courage is a peculiar virtue, easily stunted."

"Particularly," I said, my past experiences with Arabella and Rolf coming to mind, "in a young man-fairy who has been told he is fragile."

"If he is to learn faith in himself," Father said slowly, "it should be while he is still young—while there are those about him to pick him up if he falls."

Silently, Hugh went to answer the door. Arabella and Jeffrey entered but did not sit down at once. Jeffrey positioned himself behind a chair, arms folded. Arabella turned habitually to Father.

"What has happened?" she asked directly. "Why do you all look so serious?"

Father put a comforting hand on her arm and led her over to the table, where he held a chair for her.

"You may want to come closer," Hugh told Jeffrey. Without waiting for a response, Hugh flew over to the table and began unrolling the map. He weighted the corners with a couple of books and my fan. Quietly he explained, "For some time now we have been monitoring a pirate build-up on the sea. We have reason to believe," he paused, "that they are planning a cunning attack."

"You have a plan to stop them?" Jeffrey interrupted, paling as he quickly calculated the significance of the symbols for our fleets and the pirate fleet.

"We do," Hugh answered reassuringly. "But you must understand that this," he put his hand on the map, "is a secret for a reason. With the exception of a few key military officers and necessary civilians, only the five of us know about it. And Rolf."

I was watching Arabella closely when Hugh mentioned Rolf. For a moment, neither she nor I breathed. "Arabella," I leaned forward and got her attention. "Rolf found the map himself," I told her.

After a short pause Jeffrey tapped the map and asked, "Rolf found this?" Shaking his head and smiling he admitted, "We never could hide anything from him, not even his achievement awards."

"He also keeps secrets well," Arabella interrupted, hands folded tightly in her lap. "He would never have told anyone about this. Why are you?"

"We want," I said, preempting Father and Hugh, "to take him along as an official historian." I locked one of my legs around the leg of the chair I was sitting in to keep myself from going to her when her face paled to match the colour of her ivory gloves.

After a much longer pause, Jeffrey asked, "By 'take him along,' you mean, take him into the battle?" His tone made it apparent that he thought we were insane, however temporarily.

"It has never been royal policy to endanger an historian," I said without thinking. Then I added, "He would observe it from the same hospital windship I will be on."

"You really think it is safe?" Arabella asked dully.

Father and I exchanged glances. Even if this was best for Rolf, something nobody could claim to know of a certainty, it raised very real concerns for Arabella's health.

"Yes," Hugh answered firmly.

Arabella stared at him wordlessly. Jeffrey straightened away from the map.

"Enlistment age for the fleet is seventy," Jeffrey thought out loud. "But they usually have years of academy training."

"I mentioned that to Rolf," Father interjected. Folding his arms he asked, "Have you fenced with him lately?"

Jeffrey looked embarrassed. "Between the girls and the estate, I have not had much time for Rolf lately."

"I take it you have?" Arabella asked insightfully, canting her head to the side as she looked up at Father.

"Just this morning. He took me by surprise more than once," answered Father, something of pride in his tone.

Arabella nodded. "We had a guest last winter, a Wood Fairy named Bradshaw. When we got snowed in, he sparred with Rolf every day.

I believe Rolf picked up some…unusual techniques from him.”

If Father's expression is any gauge, that is an understatement, remarked my imp in mild amusement.

“Arabella,” Jeffrey said, “we could at least think about it.”

I was not unaware of the strain in his voice when he spoke. In an effort to remain neutral, I concentrated on imagining a bland shade of gray.

Hugh waited patiently, aware of the tension but ignorant as to the full cause.

At last, Arabella spoke. “We will have an answer by morning,” she promised.

Father rolled up the map and tucked it inside his vest. After giving my shoulder a quick squeeze, he gently kissed Arabella's forehead. He may have murmured something to her before he left, but I was not sure.

I had a strong desire to wrap my arms around Arabella and just hold her. She looked so fragile sitting there, the afternoon sun adding gold tinges to her silver hair…then Jeffrey stepped forward. Taking her hands in his, he kissed them tenderly.

Hugh took me by the arm and we retreated quietly. When the door to the library closed behind us, I took a deep breath.

“I think we missed lunch,” Hugh said gently. “Shall we investigate the kitchen?” Still holding my arm, he led me away.

Our visit to the kitchen was brief but

rewarding. We left laden with packages of food and slipped through a few shortcuts to a private place I knew.

It would have taken more than a vase of flowers to turn the abandoned watchtower into an eating nook, but the blank stone walls and rough floors were irrelevant to us. I stretched a fresh leaf table cover over the rickety table that Hugh pulled from one corner of the room. He then set the packages down and I began sorting through them. Cold meat and biscuits, a leaf-bag of juice, even a bit of cherry cake for desert—it was a veritable feast!

Hugh's stomach growled as he dusted off a box and a pail for us to sit on. "I have been meaning to talk to you," he winked at me, "about giving Cook a raise."

"I should tell you about Arabella," I responded after I had poured the juice into the metal cups Cook had provided. It was not very subtle, I admitted, but it was what was uppermost on my mind.

Oh for a quiet meal! sighed my imp.

"Are you sure?" Hugh asked, his tone suggesting that he was interested but unwilling to press me for information.

I nodded and set the empty juice bag aside. "When Joanna died, everything changed. Arabella…stopped being a child and started being afraid." It was not without difficulty that I found words to explain something that had, up till now, simply been understood by everyone who needed to know.

"No one could blame her for a flying accident," Hugh objected, carefully seating me on the sturdy pail. He kept moving as he took up the bags and divided the food between us.

"No one did," I shook my head and put half of what he had given me back, knowing it was more than I could eat. "She says she woke up— that hearing so many fairies talking about how short life is, how unpredictable it is," I brought both hands forward, palms up in a gesture of surrender. "She began to believe it."

Hugh took his seat slowly. "It takes a lot of courage to love," he said, cutting open a few of the biscuits. "Arabella loves her family. She and Jeffrey will make the right decision."

I felt a rush of warmth at his compassionate response. Suddenly, I had to kiss him. Rising I circled the table and put my hand on his cheek. "I have to go," I told him, then leaned forward to kiss him goodbye.

"I look forward to kissing you hello someday," he murmured when he could. He caught my wrist as I lifted off. "Take this," he deftly closed a package of food. "Dinner is still hours away."

"Thank you." Taking the package with my free hand, I gently tugged at my other hand, which he still held captive.

With a sigh, he pressed a kiss to my palm, curled my fingers over it, and released me.

Chapter II

Two days later, I stood motionless in my mother's chambers. My small audience consisted of Madame Grey, Claudette, Mother, my sisters, and Angela. Queen Dianna had returned to Florcena to gather the rest of her household for the royal wedding.

"I wish you were not going away just now," frowned Madame Grey as she fluffed the skirt on my wedding gown.

"I will only be gone a day," I said reassuringly. "And you will need the time for the other fittings. Only three weeks left you know," I added teasingly.

Stepping back to assess her creation for any fatal flaws, Madame Grey favored me with an amused smile. "All three gowns will be ready in time," she stated calmly.

"Of course they will," I agreed. For the rest of the fitting the conversation stayed strictly on the subject of the wedding. If it began drifting elsewhere, Mother or I brought it firmly back.

You should be resting, my imp stated flatly. *Sleeping in a horsefly wagon is impossible and you know it.* She was right.

Hugh, Rolf, and I would vanish from the gala crowds immediately after dinner, not to be seen at the West Post until the morning after next. We would spend most of the night in a rocking, bouncing wagon on our way to the shore rendezvous point. If we were more than a few minutes late, the hospital windship would leave without us.

"Is it too tight, Your Highness?" Claudette asked, approaching to unfasten the gown for me.

"No, not at all. Why do you ask?"

"Oh, nothing," she hesitated. "It is just that you were frowning."

"Ah," I smiled, impressed with her enduring commitment to a wedding gown that was as comfortable as it was beautiful. "I fear my thoughts were on other wedding preparations. If I frowned," I shrugged a little, "it was merely in concentration." I made haste to exit the room once I was back in my regular frock. Mother detained Gwyneth on some pretext that I did not quite overhear, but it was enough that I got safely away. How glad I would be when the secrecy was over!

"Rebecca," Edward hailed me from down the hall. "We have something of an early wedding present for you," he announced cheerfully, approaching with a blushing Helen on his arm.

"How nice," I smiled, relieved to spend even a moment with two fairies who knew the bulk of the truth. In fact, Edward would be leading a raid on the ant hill at about the same time that the hospital windship reached its position in the Mists.

"It is very little," Helen said apologetically,

holding up a bag for me to see.

Upon accepting it, I was surprised by the weight. "Shall I open it now?" I asked, smiling for the benefit of the passing fairies.

"By all means," Helen smiled back, looking more excited than I had ever seen her.

Thoroughly curious by now, I loosened the string at the top of the bag and looked in. The fumes that came out nearly knocked me flat. I would have been annoyed if I had not recognized the scent from my classes in medicine. I could never have made the stuff myself, but I knew how powerful a healing potion it was.

"Thank you," I said, hastily sealing it again. "Very much."

"May you never need it," murmured Helen as I hugged her.

"She gave me a batch, too," whispered Edward as I kissed his cheek. "Once a doctor…" he shrugged.

Looking at them, I wondered if I should change my mind. Anybody could lead the attack on the anthill; it did not have to be Edward. Major Daniels had practically volunteered. While Edward had spent the most time there, there were such things as detailed maps. I drew in a shaky breath. If I tried to change a thing, Edward would literally kidnap me until after it was all over.

"Your eyes are watering," Helen said, tucking a handkerchief into my hands. "Lovely day,

Highness," she added more loudly, signaling to Edward that it was time to leave.

Surreptitiously I dabbed at my eyes. Thankfully crying was a perfectly normal response to receiving a special gift. Anyway, what was I doing standing there crying when I should be checking on Rolf? The lad might pack anything from a quill to a crossbow without really knowing what he was doing. Particularly if Arabella helped, which I felt certain she would.

Daniel and Steven were with the senior on a special tadpole harvesting and would be gone overnight. It would be too late for them to worry by the time they realized there was ought to worry about.

I paused at the door to Rolf's room. When they agreed to let Rolf accompany us, Jeffrey had privately promised me that he would take care of Arabella; I had promised him that I would take care of Rolf. A cloud of gnats whirled about in my stomach whenever I thought about it, and they all asked the same question—what had I gotten myself into?

"Ready for inspection?" I asked as I sailed gaily into his room.

Arabella looked up from where she was straining to buckle a packing strap about a bulging saddle bag.

"Just in time," she panted, straightening away from it. "You always had a knack for making these things work."

Eyeing it doubtfully, I nevertheless flew forward to try. "I may be out of practice," I told her as I set the medicine bag down. "It has been a long time since we went camping together."

She made a quick face at me and pushed a damp curl out of her face. It was unlike her to perspire unless absolutely necessary. I tamped my worries down into the back half of my brain, aware that I would get further faster if I used the front half of my brain instead.

"You know," I said, trying to lift the bag, "Rolf will have a hard time carrying this by himself, even as strong as he is. Do you suppose he would be willing to part with a few of these things?" If Rolf had been there I would have found a different excuse, but I felt sure he would not mind me using him to help his mother.

"Why," she crossed her arms, "I suppose he would." Her voice sounded a little strained.

"Excellent," I quickly spilled the bag onto the floor. If she got mad at me, it would take her mind off the battle.

"Rebecca! Oh," she wailed, "it took me an hour to make all that fit in there!"

"I thought so," I wagged a finger at her. "You let Rolf talk you into packing for him!" It was not true, of course, but it gave her the benefit of the doubt.

"You know better," she huffed and bent to pick up the four pairs of socks that had rolled over to her feet.

"We will only be gone two nights," I pointed out as I knelt down beside the pile of things. "He will not need three shirts or three pairs of britches." Swiftly I set all but one shirt and one pair of britches aside. I could not help chuckling as I continued sorting. "This reminds me of when Mother used to pack our camping bags."

Arabella visibly relaxed at the comparison of her actions to Mother's. "The senior made us carry them just the way they were," she remembered aloud, reaching down to remove an unnecessary item. "And then went through every item with us before he let us eat dinner."

I winced at the memory of how my back had ached and we laughed companionably. I kept working while Arabella watched. Once I had removed all the redundancies and a few articles I knew they would have on board, I began packing what was left.

"Will he need his sword?" Arabella asked, her face white but her voice steady.

"I am taking mine," I answered as directly as I could. "And my crossbow."

"If you may need a weapon," she quoted the senior, "make sure your own is available."

I nodded. "Exactly."

"I am not as afraid as I thought I would be," she said after a moment. "Rolf has his own sword because he knows how to use it. He is not helpless." There was a little spark of fire in her eyes that was uncharacteristic of the cautious sister I knew.

"He is also not alone," I stated in the nature of a promise. In a moment, the work of repacking was done. "There is one other thing that he will need," I said as I cinched up the straps. "Be in this room at about twenty to the dinner hour." I would say no more than that, though I smiled until my cheeks ached. More importantly I took her on an errand—something that would get her away from Rolf's room.

"Are you quite sure this has to be done now?" she frowned skeptically as we closed Rolf's door behind us.

"The sooner the better," I confirmed. "My excuse for being absent tomorrow is thin enough. Hugh's must be water-tight, or someone may question them both!"

"I do not see that it will have too much of an impact," Arabella said distinctly as we exchanged nods with an ambassador's wife. "Hugh may be the future king, but Father is quite capable of managing for two days without him."

Marveling at her seamless switch into our cover story, I sighed. "I know, and if he must go on an errand, I would prefer it be while I am absent as well. I do so hate to be away from him."

"I am convinced of the urgency," Arabella said more quietly, squeezing my arm gently, "for you would never say anything like that unless you had to!"

"Like what?" I asked, confused.

"That you 'hate to be away from him,'" she quoted me. "You probably feel it, you might even *think* it, but you would never *say* it."

Laughing, we went on our way. Every time we got the chance, we dropped another gem of gossip where a guest could scoop it up. If it all worked according to plan, our efforts would serve to support the idea that Hugh had arranged some fabulous present for me and would be gone two days fetching it. Mother, Father, Edward, and Alfred were also engaged in reinforcing Hugh's story—and mine—as casually as possible. At least my excuse had the benefit of being mostly true. Rolf and I *were* going off together. Whether we slept on a windship or in a leaf-tent had no bearing on the fact that we would know each other much better by the time we got back.

"You should go check on the girls," I suggested after a while, when she began leaning on my arm instead of just holding it.

"You are sure you can do without me?" she asked, sounding happy but tired.

"Never," I smiled and kissed her cheek. "But if we keep it up much longer we shall excite more suspicion than we allay." Pointing her in the direction of the stable yard, I gave her a gentle push.

I feel sure Arabella believes you are planning to elope, chuckled my imp as we watched Arabella fly slowly away. I roused myself enough to smile when I heard Alfred hail me.

"Rebecca," he called cheerfully, "how well you look today."

I kept smiling though I knew why he wanted to talk with me. As the official liaison between the military and the Royal Family in these last stages, there could only be one reason. We linked arms and flew sedately toward the Royal Family's chambers, apparently two friends chatting.

"We have made the final arrangements," he told me. "It is anticipated that the odds will be in our favor."

"Are you counting fairies or cannons?" I asked in a low tone of surprise. It seemed impossible to me that we could hope to match a heavily armed pirate fleet. More wings might simply mean more targets for the pirates.

"Both," he answered firmly. "The Sky Fairy commitment alone is overwhelming."

I thought that over carefully. Sky Fairies had their own style of windship, combining aggressive maneuverability with stunning speed. They were not as sturdy as the Wood Fairy vessels which the other three tribes used, but it took little effort to imagine Sky Fairy windships darting out of the range of pirate cannons while a heavier fleet vessel moved in to deliver a punishing broadside.

"Then there is hope," I surmised, admitting my fear with that positive remark.

Alfred drew me out of the regular traffic in the hallway. "I am no military expert, Rebecca, which is part of why I agreed to remain here and keep an eye on things," his smile was more bitter than usual, "but I believe, Highness, that we will succeed in wiping the pirates out and bringing safety to Fairydom again."

I put my hand on his arm, waited until he looked me in the eyes. "Alfred, you have been and will be indispensable to the successful resolution of this concern. Also," I carefully removed my hand from his arm, "in keeping this situation confidential, you have made a tremendous sacrifice." It was a new experience, having to reassure Alfred that he was doing enough. "I think you should tell her right after dinner tonight. Before it becomes public knowledge."

"And when she asks if I am going to…" he paused, lowered his voice to a normal level then continued, "be in attendance?"

"It will be with trembling in her voice and fear in her heart," I told him sincerely. "She has no desire to lose you." I hoped, from the thoughtful expression on his face, that he believed me. I kept hoping when he bowed slightly and left through the nearest window.

Fear takes many shapes, my imp reflected. *Fear of public opinion, for life and limb…*

Alone again, I flew slowly in the direction of my room. I wanted to add the medicine bag to my things, if only so I could get away from the odor for a while. During the flight I reviewed a mental checklist of things that had to be done before I left 'tomorrow morning.' I had already separated out a few reports from last night's work that Megan could deliver after breakfast tomorrow. I had also packed everything that I was sure I would need including, as my imp pointed out with a smile, a spare set of clothing.

"Highness," called a low voice from one of the windows.

I was so startled that I nearly called for a guardsman! One kidnapping in a lifetime was quite enough for me.

"Master Collins," I sighed in relief.

"Shhh," he admonished. "Is young Rolf about?"

Gathering my skirts, I shook my head and flew over to the window. "He is busy on the target range."

"Ah, good," he grinned boyishly and beckoned for me to come closer. "I have it." He handed a package through the window to me.

Lifting the cloth wrapping, I gasped with pleasure. I had never seen a brand new history book before. "Master Collins," I breathed, "it is exquisite!"

Every new Historian received a leather bound logbook filled with sheets of fine paper. Master Collins knew nothing of the pirates, but had enthusiastically supported the idea of making "young Rolf" an Historian. As my fingers traced the Royal Silver Fairy crest, embossed in the center of the leather cover, I shivered a little in anticipation of all the future history that would fill these blank pages.

"I will be sure that Rolf knows you made it yourself," I told Master Collins, wrapping the book back up.

Master Collins' broad face nearly split with his smile. "When will the ceremony be?" he asked eagerly.

"Not until after we return from our trip," I answered, my delight a little dampened at the realization that Master Collins would not be present at Rolf's unofficial-official induction tonight.

"It is a good thing, you taking such an interest in the lad," Master Collins said.

I put my hand lightly on his. "We all need someone to take an interest in us. You have been a good friend to him. Thank you."

He flushed a little with pride, tipped his cap, and flew away.

Wrapping my arms about the book, I started for my room again. Lunch was in less than an hour. Dinner was a lifetime away. Breakfast would be delivered to my room early tomorrow, where Megan could eat what she wanted and take the rest back to the kitchen. My mind resumed the list until Angela came to get me for lunch.

"You seem so far away," she frowned as she helped me clear the papers I was working on.

"I am just thinking about tomorrow," I answered as I lay aside the last book.

"Everybody is talking about it," she smiled back. "Quite a triumph for Rolf!"

"I…how do you mean?" I asked, on guard at once.

"Taking him camping, without Arabella." Angela looked as confused as I was. "I remember you saying that it would be good for him…" Her voice trailed off.

I set my quill on the desk. "There is something I must tell you." Taking her by the hand, I led her over to the settee. It had just occurred to me that I might not return from my 'camping' trip. "I cannot explain all of it, but you must promise me you will not tell anyone what I am about to tell you."

"I promise." Her answer came without hesitation.

"Rolf and I are not going camping. We are going to a very secret meeting." I hesitated. "I wish there were more I could tell you."

She put her warm hand on top of my cold one. "You are afraid."

"I am afraid," I hesitated, "that you will worry."

"You never were very good at deception," she smiled. "You could not even tell Miss Patricia that her multi-colored dress looked nice. You had to say you liked the beadwork."

I laughed. "That was a very garish orange, you must admit."

Her smile gave way to a serious expression.

"If it were not dangerous, you would not worry that I will worry."

"Angela," I said firmly, "you promised and I meant anyone—especially Sean."

She sighed. "Very well. But we will both come to find you if you have not returned by tomorrow evening."

"Agreed," I smiled.

Chapter III

Rolf was not thrilled when Hugh and I suggested that we go through his baggage with him.

"Oh," he said carelessly, "Mother is packing for me. She used to go camping, before she married Father. I am sure it will be fine." His tense posture suggested the exact opposite.

I started to move, then stopped. I hid one hand behind my back and made a tight fist out of it, throttling the urge to put my arm about his shoulders. My maternal instincts prompted me to protect him in much the same way that I believed his maturing masculine instincts made him put himself between his mother and any potential embarrassment for her. In short, he was old enough to make up his own mind.

"Rolf," Hugh said seriously. "Rebecca helped your mother pack your things. We just needed an excuse to take you to your rooms."

It was more blunt than I would have been, but it certainly got Rolf's attention. There was something 'man-to-man' about the way Hugh spoke, even about the way he looked directly at Rolf while speaking.

Rolf relaxed visibly. "Very well," he agreed.

I tucked one hand behind Hugh's arm and one behind Rolf's arm. I truly felt as though I had two escorts, instead of one escort and one nephew. I believe that difference was apparent to everyone in the small crowd assembled in Rolf's rooms. At the very least, Arabella leaned a little harder on Jeffrey's arm.

Father stood by the window, the cloth-covered history book in his hands. Like all the men-fairies present, he wore a ceremonial jacket and gloves in honor of the occasion. "Rolf Warner," he said. "Stand before me."

Rolf obeyed. Not many fairies could have withstood the gaze of so many eyes without knowing why. Rolf's confidence may have been more in the amiable intent of the group more than his own being, but it was still satisfying to see.

"I, Prince Nathaniel, of the Royal Silver Family, have the honor of bestowing upon you, Rolf Warner, the title of Royal Historian. Your family and friends, those who are aware of the history that is currently being made, have gathered tonight to witness your appointment. Allow me to present you with your first history book."

Rolf seemed to grow taller as his grandfather laid aside the wrapping cloth and handed him the gorgeous logbook. He held it for a moment, choosing his words.

"I accept the appointment, the title, and this book. I, Rolf Warner, vow that the history I keep shall be accurate and unabridged, in the tradition of our best historians."

There were several minutes of subdued celebration following his declaration. Hugh wrapped his arms around me and we watched as Rolf was alternatively hugged and slapped on the back. Mother gave him a handsome set of quills to match the inkwell that his parents gave him.

Hugh discreetly kissed my hair then whispered, "I love you."

"What did I do?" I asked, resting my head against his chin.

"You had the good sense to have a family as wonderful as you are," he responded.

Scamp, chuckled my imp.

It was our turn to congratulate Rolf next. Already the others were filtering out the way they had come in. The senior and Major Daniels left through the window to complete their evening circuit about the post. Mother and Father slipped out Rolf's window and in theirs, waving to Hugh and I as we flew toward the garden.

I had to laugh once we landed. It was all too silly, in a wonderfully refreshing way. Hugh laughed, too. We laughed all the way into dinner without bothering to worry about why. Whether or not we had arrived in the garden unobserved, more than one young couple could attest to our leaving it.

Mother and Father entered at the same time we did, but through a different door. Somehow we restrained ourselves enough to exchange bows with them and fly sedately to our table.

I had but one regret when my dinner plate was set before me. I wished I had remembered to ask Cook for soup tonight.

"You are not hungry?" Mother asked when she noticed that I was just picking at my food.

"I am, actually," I spoke freely as our table partners were all privy to the truth, "but we have a long ride ahead of us and I am not quite sure I want to be full."

Arabella turned a pale shade of green at the thought of the swaying, bouncing horsefly wagon and reached for her water goblet.

"I never thought of you as having a weak stomach," Hugh frowned.

"Ordinarily, no," I agreed, cutting another small bite of meat. "I have never travelled quite this way, though."

Hugh smiled and kept eating. Clearly there was nothing wrong with *his* stomach.

Rolf frowned down at his plate. As an active young man, he had a healthy appetite and was already close to cleaning his plate. Clearly my remark had struck a chord in him though, for as I watched he began eating slowly. He also regretfully refused when the servant offered to replace his empty plate with a full one. He ate dessert with equal reserve, but had a second helping when Hugh did.

It seemed years before Arabella began hinting that it was Rolf's bedtime. She made the usual motherly noises about early nights before early mornings and so on. No one seemed to notice when Hugh and I slipped away into the garden at about the same time. I truly enjoyed the few moments of peaceful moonlight between the dining room and the stable yard. Hugh gently kissed my hand and released it as we approached the woodbins where we were to meet Rolf.

"Psst," Megan called from the shadow of an empty stall.

I obediently flew over to her and she quickly helped me out of my dinner gown. There was no time to lose, for the wagon could arrive any moment.

Hugh eyed the riding suit I had been wearing under my gown and dryly remarked, "No wonder you looked so uncomfortably warm!" He had already removed his fancy evening jacket to reveal a plain brown shirt beneath it.

I exhaled and lifted my braid to let the evening breeze cool me. "You have no idea!" I retorted in a low tone as I handed my crown to Megan.

Rolf appeared just then, carrying what looked like a garment bag. Holding up the bag he explained sheepishly, "Mother said we would all have to change…"

Hugh rescued him with a chuckle. "Not too much change," he advised, throwing an arm about the young man-fairy's shoulders as he led him to a sheltering wall. "We like you the way you are."

Megan clucked softly as she added Hugh's jacket to the laundry bag she was carrying. "Lad has a case of hero worship, looks like."

Hugh reappeared almost instantly, carrying Rolf's dinner clothes in one hand and his crowns in the other. "Be sure no one sees you go," he warned Megan as she nestled the crowns on top and tied the bag.

"Reminds me of when I was courtin'!" With a laugh and a shake of her head, she flitted away.

Sometimes, my imp mused, *I wonder about her.*

The shadows swallowed her whole just as I heard the sounds of a wagon approaching.

"Hugh," I put my hand on his arm, worried about Rolf. It was odd enough having a wagon leave after dark, but having it stop by supposedly empty woodbins might tip the whole scheme.

"If we have to, Rolf and I can meet you outside the gates," Hugh told me firmly. "Do not miss that wagon."

"I…alright." I watched as he flew quickly to where Rolf was changing. I trusted Hugh.

My imp wanted to insist we all stay or go *together*! My common sense realized that would just cause trouble. Besides, there was a chance that Hugh could somehow get Rolf out here in time if I did not delay him with useless dramatics.

The wagon buzzed closer, the horsefly's green eyes flashing even in the dimly lit and otherwise empty stable yard. I wet my lips. Inside the stable yard, where the driver kept the horsefly reined in, it would be no trick at all to get into the slowly moving wagon. Outside, he would call for speed. There would be plants of all sizes and shapes that raked the wagon with stiff finger-like branches, sweeping off anything that was not fastened on.

I began moving as soon as the driver's box was past the wall I had been hugging. When I reached the wagon, I lifted the canvas cover and dropped inside, landing softly on the cargo of limp grass blades. To my relief, the canvas lifted again almost at once. Hugh deposited Rolf inside then rolled in himself.

"I think I found our packs," Rolf said in a hushed, pained tone of voice.

I clapped a hand over my mouth to prevent a relieved laugh from escaping.

Hugh tossed something to Rolf. "Put that on," he told him in a whisper. "Then go to sleep."

I could not really see in the dark wagon, but I could tell that Hugh was searching for me. Putting out my hand, I touched something warm. His fingers closed over mine and he came to sit beside me. His lips covered mine in a brief but exhilarating kiss.

"That is for being sensible," he whispered into my hair.

As noiselessly as possible, I shifted around so that my head was lying on his chest. "If you want to sleep," I whispered, "I will wake you when I get tired." I was probably being a little overcautious, but I had no intention of sleeping past our intended destination.

"No need to set a watch," he leaned back against the wall of the wagon, gently carrying me with him. "The driver will alert us when we are getting close." We rode in silence for a long time. I heard Rolf squirming around a little in the sweet smelling grass blades, but mostly I was aware of Hugh's chest rising and falling with his even breaths. It was the break in that rhythm that woke me.

"What is it?" I murmured.

He was holding the canvas up enough to see out. "I smell the ocean," he told me. "We are nearly there."

I nestled closer into his arms, determined not to move until I had no other choice. The wagon's cargo was destined for the docks, where it would be unloaded and made into canvas for the windship's sails. Our challenge would be to leave the wagon without being seen. Once away, we would just be three more fairies on a dock where strangers were common.

"Are we there yet?" Rolf whispered hoarsely.

"Almost," Hugh called back. "Best wake yourself."

Sighing a little, I took Hugh's advice. "My hair must be a sight," I murmured, straightening away from him. I could do little besides tucking the loose wisps back into place, but thankfully

Megan had arranged it for dinner in a tight braid. It would have been a proper mess otherwise!

I ventured a peek under the canvas while Hugh got things together, but even after hours of riding in the pitch black wagon, I still could see very little by the starlight. There were certainly no buildings nearby.

"We have a few minutes," I called softly.

"Now," Hugh called back. "Less risk of being seen here."

Frowning, I obeyed again. As I reminded myself, this was a far cry from playing 'soldier' with Jeffrey. Considering the circumstances, I trusted Hugh's instincts over my own—especially since my instincts were simply to follow the plan to the letter.

At the back of the wagon, the ends of the canvas cover had been drawn tight with a thin rope. Hugh was busy untying the rope when the wagon bounced unexpectedly to a stop.

I froze, my hand on his arm.

"What…" Rolf started to speak, but I flailed out in the darkness and hit him in the chest. "Oof," he finished and was silent.

I thought the driver was a guardsman, my imp mumbled anxiously.

Suddenly Hugh was moving again. There was the sound of metal whispering on leather and the thin rope parted with almost imperceptible popping sounds.

"Stay here," he ordered and was gone.

Not knowing what else to do, I grabbed the canvas and pulled it closed again. I could hear Rolf breathing. Then I heard something else—fighting?

Hugh's voice called to the horsefly and the wagon lifted off.

"Out, now," his voice hissed from the back of the wagon.

"Go!" I told Rolf, releasing the canvas. I slipped the strap of my crossbow over my shoulder and threw out our bags just before Hugh reached in after me.

"Woman-fairy," he muttered, kicking a bag out of the way so he could set me on the ground. "Luggage over life, eh?" He turned immediately and bent to pick up something very heavy, the muscles in his back straining under the hand I had left on his back.

When he flew away from me, I swallowed hard and squinted after him in the darkness. What was he carrying and why was he putting it in the wagon? I decided to worry about that later.

"Aunt Rebecca?" whispered Rolf from somewhere to my left. He sounded very lost and afraid.

Gathering my wits, I turned in his direction. "Rolf, get your bag," I ordered. It was not just the woman-fairy in me that made me insist on bringing our things. Something had clearly gone wrong and leaving evidence strewn along our escape path was foolhardy. "Out of the open.

Now." I reached for him and found his hand searching for me. Catching hold of it, I led him swiftly to a clump of grass blades.

"What happened?" he asked, his voice low.

"Later," I evaded instead of admitting I had no idea.

Where are the docks? asked my imp. *If we can smell the sea, we should be able to hear the workers.*

I bit my lip to keep it from trembling and set myself a task. At this time of year the moon would be more to the… Quickly, I calculated our position based on time and probable direction of travel.

"There you are," Hugh landed beside us.

"Hugh! We are off course," I announced the obvious, then cringed.

"I know," he agreed unhappily. "No time to waste." Grabbing the bags in one hand, he took off.

"But what.." I followed, trying to ask what we were going to do.

"Sit," he responded, depositing the bags on something.

At first all I could make out was the overall shape of an oak leaf. When I hesitantly went to obey Hugh's command, I tripped on one of the holes in the leaf and felt the brittle condition under my fingers when I fell forward. This was no ordinary leaf. It was a left-over autumn leaf! This far from an oak tree, it had to have logged hours in the air. And this far from fall, it had logged *months* on the ground…

"We are going to ride on this?" Rolf asked incredulously.

"You are sure?" I asked Hugh doubtfully. I wished I could see his face.

"It is our only hope of reaching the port in time," he responded, his tone grim.

"Can we help?" Rolf asked, still sounding understandably nervous.

"When the leaf starts moving, start flapping," Hugh ordered.

Rolf and I flew inwards from the edge of the leaf. "Not too close to me," I cautioned him, setting my bag as far away as the strap allowed.

"Aunt Rebecca, I cannot fly," Rolf managed to say.

I took a deep breath as that sank in. Rolf's wings were not quite matured and he could do permanent damage to them if we were not careful. I knew it before he reminded me; I just had not immediately considered it in the midst of everything else.

"Rolf, it will be alright. Flap up and flap down, but pace yourself. If you get tired, stop for a minute." I gasped when the leaf rocked underneath us.

"I will guide the leaf," Hugh said. He had somehow found a way to rock the leaf back and forth, forcing it from its resting place. "Start flapping!"

It took all three of us, but the leaf slowly moved off the broken grass blades on which it had wintered. When there came a powerful upward surge of motion, I guessed that Hugh was now underneath the leaf. It was a little unnerving to think that with a bit more light, I would have been able to see him through the holes that time and weather had worn in the leaf.

"Hold on tight," I instructed Rolf, my own hands locking in place where they gripped the leaf. We had to get enough altitude to catch a sea-bound breeze!

Our make-shift windship rattled beneath us as the first breath of wind tapped it, tipped it, and spun it about. The moon came out from behind a cloud long enough for me to get a glimpse of Rolf.

"Rolf!" I commanded when I realized he was not moving at all, "flap!"

His face swung in my direction and hesitantly he began flapping again. From his expression it seemed that the one question on his mind was why he should flap when he was about to die.

"Good! Keep it up!" I commanded again. We were rising. I was seconds away from having to rest when the leaf suddenly lifted and surged forward. We wobbled a bit but the spinning was already slowing. I started breathing again when I realized Hugh was working his way back to the stem.

Once in position he called, "Left wings only!" Working as a team, we flapped against the spinning until the windship steadied and flew a straight course. Not content with the breeze, Hugh gripped the stem and flapped as hard as he could for shore.

I signaled for Rolf to stop flapping, but I kept at it. From this height I could see the streetlights from the dock. I could even see the torches gleaming on the deck of a windship, mere specks in the distance. It required a few moments of careful scrutiny before I deduced that I was watching the sails rising. From the size and number of sails it was simple to come to the conclusion that it was our hospital windship. Rolf must have seen it as well, for he resumed flapping. If we did not hurry, the windship would depart without us. Or perhaps he was simply cold. We had no protection from the breeze that was ushering us to shore.

Soon we were near enough to have heard the shouted commands, had the wind not been blowing them away from us. As we drew nearer I began to be able to see more than just torches flitting about the masts, but sailors also, busily securing lines and testing for tears in the sails. One torch moved abruptly toward the stern, an area still cloaked in darkness. It was only when the moon peeked through the cloud that I could see two men-fairies pointing in our direction.

"That is the mainsail they are hoisting!" Rolf shouted.

"Good!" called Hugh, coming to join us. "This breeze is pushing us out to sea. They will need to intercept us." He frowned as the moon left its hiding place altogether, framing us against the sky for any wandering eye to spot.

The sailors' movements picked up speed, locking the sails into position. I was close enough to watch them tying themselves to the masts. By now, the few fairies on the dock had stopped what they were doing to stare and point.

"They are going to try a manual start!" I exclaimed. I had heard of that maneuver once—in a history class.

So much for a discreet takeoff! groaned my imp.

Onboard, the sailors began flapping in unison. They created a tremendous thrust, forcing the windship up until it was straining against its anchor rope. The captain himself, easily identified by the jacket buttons gleaming in the moonlight, wielded the ax that cut that rope. The windship shot forward, catching the same warm breeze that we were on. By now the breeze had pushed us beyond the windship, so there was no danger of collision. Just the matter of catching up to us—before it was too late.

"The captain has ordered a spear," Rolf observed loudly.

The perfect ending to a perfect morning, grumbled my imp, tensing up. Rolf was right though. I could see the gunner lining up the shot.

"Rebecca, Rolf, hold perfectly still." Hugh's words were just in time, for the cannon report came a mere heartbeat later. The spear broke through the leaf, shot a foot or so above it—then the line stopped coming. Hugh lunged forward, grabbing the spear with both hands.

I watched as he deftly maneuvered himself into an extended position so that when he landed back on the leaf his weight was spread across as much of it as possible. The fact that he might be pulled through the enlarged hole in an already brittle leaf was enough to make me feel sick. But there was no time for that.

The breeze had freshened. With the new stress of being restricted to the windship's pace, the leaf was beginning to flutter and it was only a matter of moments before it would shake apart. Removing my belt, I looped it through the handles on mine and Hugh's bag. I was relieved when Rolf wisely mimicked my actions with his belt and bag.

Stretching myself across the leaf, I fastened my belt around the rope then pushed the bags through the hole. They slid down the rope and were received onto the windship without a problem. At my nod, Rolf stretched himself out and did the same thing with his bag.

"Rolf. Slide down the rope," Hugh barked.

Rolf blanched.

"Do it, Rolf," I ordered. A particularly strong bump sent Hugh edging toward the hole. I threw myself at him, holding him down.

Rolf hesitated for another instant. Wrapping both arms around the rope, he curled into a ball.

When he could make himself no smaller, he plunged through the hole. I forced myself to watch as he approached the windship at breakneck speed. At the last minute a sailor, wearing a safety line and protective weathervest, flew up to intercept him.

I dropped my head against Hugh's chest. "Arabella is going to kill me," I said irrelevantly.

"Your turn," Hugh commanded.

"I am lighter," I pointed out stubbornly. When he scowled at me I continued, "It is your turn to be logical. The rope will fall as soon as the leaf is gone, and the leaf will last longer with less weight."

"How do you plan on getting down?" he asked.

"I will put the spear across the hole," I decided suddenly.

He was still frowning, but I had his attention. "We will go at the same time," he compromised.

"Alright," I agreed. "You hold onto the rope. I will hold onto you." When his scowl deepened, I laughed aloud.

Caught! My imp chuckled, pleased with herself. *He would have sent you to safety and remained here at peril of his own life.*

"Hugh Lawson, if you are ever tempted to try to deceive me again, just remember this moment!" I was already holding onto him pretty tightly from when I had tackled him earlier to keep him from sliding through the hole. Now as he allowed himself to slide toward the hole, my grip tightened. My crossbow went through first and dangled there. I swallowed hard.

"Ready?" he asked when his feet were braced against the far edge of the hole. "Here we go!" We took some of the rapidly degrading leaf with us when we forced ourselves through the hole, but I refused to let go of him. At the last moment he turned the spear so that it stuck, spanning the hole.

I was glad my arms were about his waist and not his neck, for I could hold on as tightly as I pleased! I felt it when the spear tore loose—the line gave a sharp jerk and began dropping rapidly. Then Hugh's muscles began moving under my hands. He was flying, using slow powerful flaps to retard our rapid descent. I started to flap as well, keeping as much to his pace as I could. But the sea air was so cool it was draining the heat from me, making it difficult to persist.

"Are they pulling us in?" I gasped, hoping that we actually were moving up and not just hanging there.

"Yes! They have reached a safe distance from the water as well. We need only hold on a little longer." His reassuring tone was laced with concern.

"I could hold onto you forever," I responded as lightly as I could. The fact that I meant it did not hurt.

"Heave lads!" a gruff voice came from above me. "Heave away!"

I was too cold to help myself properly when they began hauling me aboard—I barely felt it when my shin scraped the railing. But oh! How grateful I was for the blanket that they wrapped around me! In a matter of minutes all three of us, looking like clumsily wrapped gifts in our heavy blankets, had been bundled off to the galley.

It was not a large room, but a blind fairy could have identified it as a kitchen of sorts from the smell of a rich stew left simmering on the stove. I held as still as I could on the thin wooden bench beneath me, knowing that I was too cold and stiff to save myself if I lost my balance. Exposure was one of the many dangers of the sea, even when wearing a warm, waterproof weathervest. I pulled the blanket more tightly around me.

We all looked up when the door opened again, admitting a thin young fairy with a cheerful face and what looked like a physician's bag.

"Welcome to the *Nightingale*," he greeted us, plunking the bag on a table parallel to the bench where Hugh and I were sitting. "You look like you could use a little tending," he added.

"I suppose we have ruined everything," Rolf said dejectedly from where he sat.

I was rousing myself to respond when the physician did it for me.

"Not quite," he chuckled as he examined Hugh. Taking a glob of thick salve from one of his many containers he applied it to Hugh's chaffed palms and instructed, "Rub that in. Nice and slow, until the salve is absorbed."

I waited a moment before returning to Rolf's question. "Are you sure we have not?"

"You might have," the surgeon wiped salve from his fingers onto a clean cloth, "if the captain were not a fast thinker." Coming over to me, he adjusted my blanket so that it was wrapped more securely about my shoulders before tilting my head back to examine the scratches I got on my face when we broke through the hole. "Here, use a little of this," he suggested, placing a small vial in my hand. Turning away he went on, "As far as anyone on the dock knows, you three are in violation of air travel security laws. A few of them seemed to think you would be better off if we did *not* rescue you." He chuckled as he gathered his things and exited the galley.

"It is of little consequence," Hugh said seriously. "We were discovered before we left the post."

"The driver," Rolf exclaimed. "What happened?"

I blinked. I was so relieved to be alive that I had forgotten about the driver.

"Yes," said a new voice from the doorway. "What happened?"

I turned to see the captain standing in the doorway. His brass buttons flashed even in the dim light provided by the cook fire. They matched his angrily flashing eyes.

Hugh met the captain's gaze without visibly flinching. "Our driver was not the man-fairy that the senior introduced me to. When I tried to speak to him, he drew a knife." Hugh shrugged. "Naturally, we had a disagreement."

A little of the ire faded from the captain's demeanor. "So you picked the first weather-beaten leaf you could find and turned it into a crude windship?" he asked sharply.

I intercepted that one before Hugh could decide whether or not it was intended as an insult. "We had no choice," I said, rising to go over to the stew pot. Now that the exhilaration of surviving had worn off I automatically returned to my habit of tending to the needs of those about me. I ignored the protests from my leg; it would have to wait until I could apply the medicine. "The wagon was too slow to have taken us to the docks in time, and if we had stayed there," I ladled some stew into a tin mug, "we might have been captured by the driver's cohorts." I deposited a clean spoon in the stew and handed the mug to Hugh. "That would have been far worse than possibly alerting the pirates to a trap that is already being sprung." I turned back to the pot, ladling a mug of stew for myself and one for Rolf.

Rolf accepted his gratefully. He did not even seem to notice when I ruffled his hair affectionately.

I can just imagine the look on Arabella's face when

she reads his history book, my imp sighed wearily.

"I see," the captain responded.

I looked up, my hand still on Rolf's shoulder. Perhaps it was something I had done, or perhaps it was the enthusiastic way that Rolf was digging into the thick stew. Something had changed the captain's demeanor, softened it considerably.

"Welcome aboard the *Nightingale* then, Your Highnesses. And, Historian," he included Rolf. He seemed to dismiss Hugh and me from his mind altogether as he squinted at Rolf. "It means a lot to the lads," he jerked his head in the general direction of up, "having you aboard."

I sat down beside Hugh, watching the captain carefully. I was still learning to stay on my side of Rolf's particular boundaries, but I would never be able to sit by while someone blithely ridiculed him. Lucky for the captain, I came to the conclusion that he was in earnest.

I kept one ear on their conversation even when my attention drifted to the stew. It had a rich flavor as well as plenty of vegetables and meat. As I savored the heat spreading out from my stomach, I was glad to note that Hugh was enjoying his stew as much as I was enjoying mine.

"What has happened here?" bellowed a deep, surly voice from the steps. "I open me galley to you and you help yourselves to the crew's lunch?"

"Stand down Crusty," ordered the captain, standing up to face the cook.

Crusty wiped broad red hands on the towel

tied about his waist and shrugged. "Meant nothin' by the noise, cap'n," he verbally backed down. "Just speakin' me mind."

"I know, Crusty," the captain smiled grimly. "But our guests have had a difficult morning and might not understand."

A man-fairy that would challenge three members of the Royal Family but knows better than to cross his captain, mused my imp. *Makes perfect sense to me!* She added with a laugh.

"The stew is delicious," I smiled, scraping the bottom of the mug a little harder than necessary.

At the sweet sounds of praise and a very empty dish, Crusty mellowed visibly. "Too bad you got it so early," he grumped, trying to maintain a fiction of his previous ire, "flavor ain't half cooked in yet!" With that he flitted over to the sink and began rattling dirty dishes about.

With a wink, Hugh took my empty mug from me. Walking over to where Crusty was muttering to himself, Hugh made a remark about a strange looking tool that Crusty was holding. One thing led to another and soon they were discussing all sorts of rustic cooking methods.

Bewildered by their talk, I turned to check on Rolf. Much to my surprise, I saw that the captain was leading him out of the galley.

"Not many of the lads can read," the captain was saying, "but they all know a belaying pin from a halyard."

Rolf laughed aloud, the sound infused with

genuine amusement.

Well then, smiled my imp. *Looks like my boys are happy.*

I stifled a yawn. There were a few hours yet before we would reach the Mists. It was just as well that Rolf had found something to do before I insisted he take a nap because I was tired. Taking up my crossbow and pack, I went in search of a cabin boy. When I found one, I was a little surprised to find that he was at least Rolf's age.

"Allow me, Miss," he said, holding out a calloused hand for my things. "That is, um, Highness," he corrected himself hastily.

"Thank you," I overlooked the miniscule breach in decorum with a smile, but retained my crossbow. "I hope you know the location of my cabin," I added, still smiling.

"Oh yes, Highness," he grinned and led the way. "Captain near gave up his own cabin when he heard who was coming."

I believe it, admitted my imp. *This is no passenger vessel, with dozens of spare rooms to be traded casually about.* My imp and I were both impressed, in fact, with how functional the windship was, every twig carefully allocated to the preservation of fairy life.

The *Nightingale* was unmistakable in design as a hospital windship, specially built to take a beating rather than give one. She had a wider beam than most windships and carried only light armaments, like the spear gun and a few small "pebble throwers" as they were called, used mostly for scaring away too-curious fowls. The hull was made of oak leaves, layered and sealed with pitch around the railings to keep the weather out. Cranes were lashed to both of the two masts and there were hatches on the deck, closed now, which would later be used to lower the wounded to the surgery.

"Everything alright?" asked the cabin boy anxiously.

I realized then that I had stopped moving and was staring as if I had never seen a windship. "Yes, fine," I paused. "What is your name?" I asked, smiling apologetically.

"Derrick, Highness," he tried to tip his stocking cap but only succeeded in pushing it to one side.

"Derrick," I smiled and looked back out over the deck. "Have you seen a lot of action?" I asked, watching as a group of medics inspected the cranes and other equipment. Something about them, beyond their obvious youth, seemed to scream anxiety. I wondered if any of them had handled a case more serious than a black eye.

"This be my first, Highness, not counting an accidental civilian ramming a few months back," he answered, sounding grim for the first time.

"Do you know why we are going into battle?" I asked him. There had been so much secrecy— too much?

"Captain ain't one for long-windedness," responded the cabin boy seriously. "Said we could fight now, all of us together, or wait while the pirates got stronger and meaner."

"What do you think?" I asked. It was not a fair question as he barely even knew who we would be fighting, but I had to ask.

"Some fights there ain't a way to avoid, Highness. Sounds like we got us one here."

"Indeed," I nodded, feeling simultaneously relieved and awed at the simple wisdom he had exhibited.

"I sailed on the *Kingfisher* before transferring to the *Nightingale*," he scratched his cheek. The light of laughter came into his eyes as he advised, "Best be worryin' about the pirates, Highness. Those lads from the *Kingfisher* enjoy a good scrap!"

My smile blossomed again at his clumsy effort to reassure me. I listened politely as he regaled me with stories of his former 'mates' while he led me the rest of the way to my cabin. Once he had deposited my things inside the door and slid his cap the other direction, he flew away whistling a brave old fighting tune.

Chapter IV

A few hours later I was looking out the porthole, my chin resting comfortably on the lower sill, when a knock sounded at the door. "Enter," I called.

"Are you alright?" asked Hugh's voice from the doorway.

Alright? my imp pondered the implications of the question. *I am neither happy nor sad, just apprehensive. Is that alright?*

"Well enough. Just feeling very short," I answered at last, dropping my chin from the porthole and securing the end of my new braid. I listened to the sound of him shutting the door and then to the soft flutter of his wings as he approached.

"Becca?" he asked, placing one hand lightly on my arm.

I leaned back, resting my head against his shoulder. "Are we there yet?" I asked, echoing Rolf's question from the wagon.

Hugh's arms encircled me and I felt his warm breath on my cheek as he kissed my hair. "Not even close," he told me. "Still almost three weeks to go."

I blushed as I realized he was referring to the wedding. "Tell me," I invited.

"I love you." There was no hesitation in his response.

I ran my hand up and down his arm, sighed, and reluctantly moved to a safe distance before turning to face him. "I love you." I watched him watch me for a moment.

"The battle, however," he turned away slightly, "is almost upon us." With practiced skill, he inspected my crossbow from the new string to the freshly oiled lever.

I blinked back a surprise tear as I waited for his verdict. I was no warrior, but I did take pride in my ability to maintain the weapon I chose to carry.

Of course, the fact that your life may depend on this weapon has no bearing on how sternly he is scrutinizing it. My imp was not playing the fool this morning.

My heart jumped when someone pounded on the door. Something was wrong!

"Aunt Rebecca?" Rolf's voice barely penetrated the heavy door. "Aunt Rebecca, are you awake?"

With a sardonic smile, Hugh put the crossbow down and went to open the door. The smile disappeared into a too-perfect straight face as he stepped back to let Rolf enter.

"Hugh! Perfect," Rolf grinned even as he gasped his way through the door.

"Rolf, what is wrong?" I asked, stepping quickly forward.

"I just had an idea," he answered.

"An idea?" Hugh responded, folding his arms across his chest.

Something about Hugh's tone made my lips twitch but I disciplined the smile.

"What?" Rolf asked, his eyes narrowing as he looked back and forth between us.

"The way you came bursting in just now," I shrugged delicately, "I am just glad the windship is not crashing!"

Rolf kept grinning. "When you hear my idea, you will forgive my abrupt entrance." He opened his hand to reveal a small leaf-bag. "Fairy dust," he announced.

Put it back! shouted my imp at once. The slightest mistake with that could destroy the whole windship!

"Suppose you set that down, gently, on the table?" Hugh pointed as he spoke.

I took my imp by the arm and led her to a mental corner. She was shaking like a leaf as I helped her lie down.

"Sure, Uncle Hugh," Rolf obeyed promptly, "but it is not dangerous like that. It has to actually be in your hand in order for an effectual wish to be made."

Hugh stared at him for a moment, perhaps distracted by the familial reference, then shook his head. "This is **wild** fairy dust," he reminded Rolf, "which is very different from any tame stuff you may have seen at the magic shows. It is **much** more potent."

Rolf turned considerably paler, but his face still had more color than Hugh's. I wondered vaguely what color my own face was.

"We should sit down," I suggested. "And discuss this calmly." As I was nearest the bed, I sank onto it while Rolf and Hugh availed themselves of the chairs at the table.

"Now, Rolf," Hugh took a deep breath, "you were saying something about an idea?"

We had listened to dozens of ideas at the war councils, most of which had proven as dangerous to us as to our enemies. One idea had been to tip the arrows with a dust-water paste and use them to wish that the vessel they struck would turn to metal. While that would certainly have crashed a great many pirate windships, it was pointed out that there would not be two lines of windships opposing each other. The fleets would be in amongst each other, firing at will—in short, chaos. Crashing our own or an ally's windship was far too likely for that plan to be generally adopted.

Some ideas had been unanimously accepted, however. Each of the nearly fifty captains had been given enough dust to make their spyglasses magic, enabling them to see the enemy despite the swirling clouds inherent to the Mists. It was hoped that there would be enough dust to allow the gunners to magically repair cannons damaged during the battle. Above all, it was hoped that the battle would last no more than a day.

"Suppose," he suggested, regaining some of his previous enthusiasm, "there were no Mists?"

Hugh and I frowned at each other. It was an interesting question. No fog banks or clouds to hide in—for either side. Nowhere to flee.

"It is a battle to the end," Hugh said aloud.

Aye, agreed my imp. *No pirate windship will escape this day's work, but at what cost? Sending warships into the Mists after them when they turn tail will increase the fatalities drastically.*

"How, Rolf? The Mists have been a blight on this sea since our earliest histories." I watched him closely, knowing that he was not one to idly propose such a grand scheme.

"I saw the Mists once before, while travelling with Mother to visit the Sky Fairies," he began. "I was fascinated and begged the first mate to lend me his glass. The captain kept his distance, but I have never forgotten that day. There must be a source for the smoke and clouds, not to mention the cliffs!"

Hugh scratched his chin thoughtfully. "And how would we find this source?" he asked canting his head to the right, a sure indication of interest.

"We would need a small transport, something just large enough for the three of us. I am sure the source of the Mists is somewhere in the center. I believe that there may even be the remnant of an island, or at least enough ground to land on."

"I have heard of something like that," Hugh frowned thoughtfully. Running one hand through his hair, leaving it standing on end as usual, he leaned back in his chair. "It is an old tale, almost as old as the Fairy Kingdoms and from a land beyond the reaches of Fairydom."

"You speak of it as though you do not believe it," I interjected when he paused.

"I never did," he shrugged, "but it was a good tale, one that always insured a few more nights in town…" He straightened in his chair and his tone changed from reminiscent to business-like as he went on, "Explorers have travelled beyond our borders. A few have even returned. Most of the stories are lost to time, but one wrote of the strange things he saw…including a hole in the ground. This hole gave forth smoke, dust, and even steam." Hugh paused again. "If it can happen on dry ground, why not in the middle of the sea?"

A hole, in the middle of the sea? my imp was not convinced.

"Once a merchantman tried to map the Mists," Rolf told us. "He lost a great many windships before giving up—but debris from those windships was never found."

I examined Rolf's face carefully, then Hugh's. A few minutes ago we had been trapped aboard this windship as observers, of as much practical use as a crystal goblet in a galley. Now it seemed a new purpose for our presence had appeared.

"Rolf," I rose, "would you excuse us?" I had some things to discuss with Hugh that were best done privately.

Rolf started to protest, but stopped as quickly as he had begun. He did not look happy as he closed the door behind him.

"You do not believe we can do it?" Hugh asked.

I hesitated. The success of the mission was not uppermost in my mind.

"I do not know if it would work or not," I answered at last. "I only know that, for myself, I think it sounds like quite an adventure."

He rose and began pacing slowly. "You are…concerned," he put light emphasis on the word, "that I have not looked at this through the eyes of a king?"

I inhaled slowly, then nodded.

"Perhaps you are right," he acknowledged without heat. "What do you see?" he asked, stopping and leaning back against the table.

"I am overwhelmed by what I see," I answered honestly. "We stand to lose a great deal if we do not try. Or," I bit my lip to steady myself before continuing, "we could lose everything if we do try."

He nodded. "Is this the right time to send the next king of the Silver Fairy Tribe into mortal danger?"

I blushed as I recognized my own words, rephrased though they were. I had spoken them to Edward just weeks ago when he had volunteered to go on the mission to capture a pirate.

Hugh was at my side in an instant, lifting me from where I sat to a standing position. "I want forever with you," he told me earnestly. "I may even learn to live with the weight of a crown on my head, not just exist but live." His tone emphasized the difference between the two circumstances. "But if I have a chance to save lives that might otherwise be lost, is this not the greater duty?"

Right then, sighed my imp. *Pass the weather jackets. We certainly are not going to let them go alone!* Nor did we. When Hugh went on deck to persuade the captain, I went with him. What I saw made my breath catch in my throat.

The Mists—an area of thick, low-lying smoke clouds and unpredictable rocky outcroppings. From the earliest mention of the Mists in fairy history, the wise windship captains have avoided it rather than have their windships fall prey to malicious winds or jagged cliffs. Pirates alone embrace the area, preferring to dare the elements rather than face the fleet captains. As we drew ever nearer, the flash of cannon fire turned the normally gray clouds a vile shade of orange.

Rolf, Hugh, and I stood near the captain on the deck, our gazes alternating between the distant clouds and the silver plate the captain had wished into a magic mirror.

"You expect me to let you go gallivanting into the Mists in a lifeboat?" growled the captain when Hugh had finished explaining. "You, the next king of the Silver Fairy Tribe?" He shook his head. "I cannot!"

"Captain," I stepped forward. "This is a hospital windship, bound for the hottest part of the battle. Can you honestly promise that we will be safer aboard this windship than we would be in that lifeboat?" I watched him wrestle with his conscience for a moment before adding, "We must try."

He stared at the magic mirror for a full minute before shaking his head. "No magic as yet can tell the future," he said aloud. "Bo'sun! I want a lifeboat ready to be lowered in twenty minutes."

"Captain," I forestalled a flurry of motion with a single word.

Hugh, half-bent to retrieve our bags, frowned and straightened. Rolf was caught mid-jubilation. The bo'sun, the first mate, the helmsman…they were all staring at me.

I turned to Hugh, feeling suddenly very shy. "Marry me, Hugh Lawson?" I asked. "I know it is a bit sudden, and Madame Grey will probably faint when we tell her," I laughed at how different our workwear was from the elaborate costumes intended for the occasion, "but I cannot bear the thought of losing you."

His frown cleared like a schoolroom at the end of a day. He held out both hands and I flew into his arms.

"Captain?" I heard Hugh say, "I need to ask

for one more favor."

"Granted," the captain answered promptly. "If I am to let you face your deaths it may as well be as properly married folk!" Just then a wind-whistle on the mast hit a higher pitch, indicating that the wind speed had increased.

"Bo'sun, get that boat ready!" ordered the captain. Straightening his hat, he then addressed Hugh and me. "Face me, please. It is a strange time and place for a wedding, but weddings are strange things themselves. Two individuals join hands," he paused as we complied, "and set sail on a breeze together."

I felt warm all over as the captain made his sailing analogies. My hand was in Hugh's, for now and forever. Oh, there would be a fancy wedding ceremony when we got back to the post, with three brides and wedding cake. But as the sea spray stung my cheeks and the roar of cannon fire grew louder, I knew I would never regret my decision not to wait on pomp to have the ceremony.

"Hugh Lawson, son of Queen Alicia and Guardsman Lawson, future king of the Silver Fairy Tribe, do you take Princess Rebecca Shaw, future queen of the Silver Fairy Tribe to be your lawfully wedded wife?"

"I do," Hugh answered firmly.

I thought I should never hear sweeter words, not if I should live for another thousand years! In a heartbeat, it seemed, it was my turn to declare.

"I do," I answered the captain's challenge.

"By the power and authority vested in me as captain in the Silver Fleet, I pronounce you husband and wife. You best kiss the bride," he added, glancing sharply at the rapidly approaching Mists.

Hugh had barely pressed his lips to mine when the order came to "Board!" Reluctantly I stepped back, telling myself that there would be many more opportunities.

"Come along, Mrs. Lawson," Hugh invited, scooping up our supplies with his free hand. "We have work to do."

Rolf startled me by leading the others in a cheer. Blushing, I followed Hugh into the lifeboat. I was barely seated when Rolf scrambled aboard and we were away. I looked around to see who was steering and had to look twice to be sure of what I saw. Derrick was at the helm!

"Congratulations, Ma'am," he shouted and touched his hat with two fingers.

"Thank you, Derrick," I smiled back, impressed that he had learned the proper salute.

"Rolf," Hugh shouted from the bow of the boat, "whenever you are ready."

Rolf swallowed and took a pinch of fairy dust from the bag the captain had generously provided. Mindful of the wind, he cupped his hand around the silver button we had cut from his bag.

I could barely hear him as he wished, "I wish

this button were a magic mirror to show us the way through the Mists." I exhaled in relief as he recited the agreed upon wish word for word. Wishes are funny things and we had discussed it at length before deciding on the exact phrasing of it.

"That way!" Rolf pointed into the Mists. As the fog engulfed us, Rolf exclaimed softly when the magic mirror lit up with a soft glow. "I guess we were right to state that wish so carefully!"

I swallowed and peeked at the mirror Rolf had cupped in his hands. We were approaching a cliff, but would pass at an acceptable distance. My stomach tied itself in knots as we maneuvered past several potential crash sites.

"We have to get higher!" Rolf shouted to be heard over the cannon fire. "There are only cliffs here!"

"Wait," I put my hand on his wrist, tilting it so I could be sure of what I thought I saw. "There!" I pointed at the mirror. "We could land the boat and scale the cliff on our own."

Rolf looked skeptical but showed Derrick the way. "Aunt Rebecca, look!" Rolf shouted as we drew nearer and the map showed more of the area around the cliff. "It is more than just a cliff!"

Hugh scrambled back to have a look. "Perhaps we have the remnants of an island here," he suggested. He had brought a length of rope with him and now he cut it in half. "Rolf, tie one end about your waist," Hugh instructed, handing him half of the rope. The other half in his own hand, Hugh turned to me. "We could get separated in this," he told me before slipping the rope about my waist.

"Hugh," I asked quietly, putting my hands on his, "one of us has to go with Rolf."

"I knew you were going to say that," he sighed. "And you are right. Neither he nor Derrick can fly. Not only that," he knotted the rope expertly, "we promised Arabella we would bring him back safely. I will take care of him. You will go with Derrick. Alright?"

I kissed him then, glad that Rolf and Derrick were absorbed in watching the mirror. "Thank you," I whispered while I was still close enough for him to hear me.

"Thank me later," he advised grimly.

"I will," I promised sincerely.

With a sigh and a lingering kiss he added, "I love you."

I slipped into the weather jacket he handed me, fastening it with all the strength I could muster.

"Easy, Highness," shouted Derrick as he traded places with Hugh. "You may want to get that off when 'tis all done!"

Lovely, remarked my imp as I smiled faintly, *a sense of humor.*

I sensed Rolf's confusion when Derrick came and tied himself firmly to the other end of the rope about my waist. I hoped he would not ask.

"Aunt Rebecca," he shouted as we approached the tiny outcropping where we would land, "why are you tied to Derrick instead of Uncle Hugh?"

"Neither of you can fly," I pointed out. Then, knowing him better than that I added, "Also, because I love you both," I shouted back, "and I want you to take good care of him for me." I watched his face change subtly as he considered what I said and decided what I meant. I was proud of him when he squared his shoulders.

"It will be alright, Aunt Rebecca. I promise."

Never promise what you cannot control, whispered my imp, echoing the bard who wrote tragedies. Inwardly I made a face at her. Outwardly, I smiled at Rolf.

"Thank you, Rolf. But let us be careful anyway." I gripped the edge of my seat as we bumped onto the small patch of land.

Derrick was ready, thank goodness! He heaved the anchor over the side as soon as we struck the first time. It held fast and the anchor line drew taut while Derrick and Rolf sprang to lower the sails. Fog swirled around us so that we could barely see each other, let alone the cliff we were to climb.

Rising, I slung my crossbow over my shoulder and clipped the second line to my belt to prevent the bow from striking against the rock face. I tested the spring release while waiting for the blob of light that Rolf held to move forward. The cannon fire behind me intensified so that my ears rang with the sound. Even so, I began to notice a hissing, roaring sound that seemed to come from the direction we were facing.

"Do you smell that?" Derrick shouted to me. "Smells like rotten bird eggs!"

"Ready," Hugh shouted before I could reply.

We stayed near each other as we flew over to the cliff, Rolf unconsciously becoming our focal point.

"Close enough," I heard Hugh shout. The light stopped moving forward and began ascending.

It was eerie, following a swirl of light through thickening clouds of smoke and fog—but I was not really afraid until I began having difficulty breathing. When I inhaled and the smoke got in my lungs I felt a determined tickle start at the back of my throat. It *was* a strange smelling smoke, not at all like the pleasant odors of cedar or pine. Despite my best efforts, I soon began coughing like the others.

"Not much farther," Derrick choked. He began flapping then, risking his wings to keep his weight from dragging me down.

At last the light Rolf held stopped moving up and moved forward again. The smoke was thinner on the top of the cliff, but only because the wind was fiercer. I did not feel cooler and wondered why until I landed.

"Ouch!" I exclaimed, jerking my hand back from the rock I had leaned on. "That is hot!"

"Did you hurt yourself, Highness?" Derrick asked, a blur of smoke-shrouded motion as he hastily removed the sash that was wrapped about his waist.

I shook my head then realized he probably could not see it. "It is nothing," I coughed.

"Here," he splashed water from his canteen on a piece of cloth that he had torn from his sash. "Hold this over your nose!"

I did as he told me. I did not stop coughing at once, but the water he had poured on the cloth made it an excellent filter. I stumbled after him as he walked off in Hugh and Rolf's direction, apparently forgetting that we were still tied together.

Chapter V

"Thank you, Derrick," Rolf coughed through a sash piece.

"Never thought to see the day that a silly sash would be of so much use," snorted Derrick, whose breathing had returned more or less to normal.

"I think I shall decree that every military man must wear one," Hugh said jokingly.

We all laughed at Derrick's desperate, "Oh, no sir, please!"

"He was not serious," I reassured him.

"Of course not," agreed Hugh. "Now then, Rolf, where do we go from here?"

"I am not sure," Rolf answered honestly. "I think I should have added something about being led to where we can stop the smoke when I wished," he added thoughtfully.

"Let me see," requested Hugh. The mirror changed hands and the strange light from it illuminated Hugh's face. "Look," he pointed at something. "I think the smoke is coming from these holes. Can you see them?"

"Yes," agreed Rolf. "So many of them. Do you think we will have enough dust?"

"Even if we only get half of them," Hugh answered firmly, "it will be worth the trip."

We flew in silence for several minutes, heading deeper into the smoke and steam. As we went I became uncomfortably warm. I would have rolled up my sleeves were it not for the gritty bits of ash that began clouding the air.

"Here," Hugh beckoned Derrick and me forward. "Take this," he handed Derrick a small leaf bag. "Careful," he warned, "and wish for nothing until you are right by the hole. There are three holes right here," he pointed at the mirror. "Wish them out and come straight back. We will do the same with these three holes," he pointed at the mirror again.

I squinted at him, wondering if my mask was as caked with ash and dust as his. I wanted to insist that we stay together, but I had no way of telling when we left the windship or how many lives had been lost already. I watched Hugh and Rolf go before turning to follow Derrick. I did not even realize I was actually biting my lip until I tasted the blood.

That is going to swell… my imp wailed. *Claudette and Angela and Megan and…oh never mind. We were going to tell the truth when we got back anyway.*

Derrick proved himself a brave man-fairy three times over as he approached each hole and wished away the smoke. Thankfully the winds persisted, whistling away much of the haze that had been stinging our eyes.

"Success!" shouted Derrick as we turned back.

I laughed at how loud his voice sounded now that the three nearest smoke-holes had been silenced. There was still the cannon fire from the windships and several more smoke-holes roaring about us, but we could almost talk without shouting. The wind snatched at us as we worked our way back to the rendezvous point and I was glad that I was securely tied to Derrick. Nothing seemed to bother him.

"Hi," he signaled for my attention. "Look up there!"

I followed his finger and spotted Hugh waving at us. "He wants us to join him," I guessed aloud. We struggled over the considerable distance to where we had seen him, finally drawing close. I sneezed and shivered, the result of being alternately too hot to breathe and chilled to the bone. The steam from the smoke-holes and my own sweat now soaked my clothes so that the erratic winds had the effect of dropping my body temperature drastically; even the weathervest was inadequate protection.

"It is a giant smoke-hole!" Hugh had to shout a few times, for we were once again in the midst of active smoke-holes and could hardly hear him.

"See here," Rolf pointed at the map. Now that much of the smoke had cleared from the six holes we had reached, a large mass of smoke could be discerned even though we stood inside a field of such holes.

"It must be the size of Castlemain!" I shouted back, staggered by the idea. The holes we had encountered thus far had been no larger than small buildings!

"It may take the rest of our dust to wish it away," shouted Derrick.

"I believe it is worth it," answered Hugh, "for it seems to be producing at least as much smoke by itself as all the others put together."

I watched as Derrick and Hugh exchanged knowing glances. I wanted to cry when Hugh began untying himself from Rolf. I selfishly waited until he had finished and handed his end of the rope to Derrick. If he wanted to leave me here while he and Derrick risked their lives… I did cry when he came to me and began unknotting the rope about my waist.

"Hush now, hush," he smoothed my wind-whipped hair out of my face. "You do not think I could risk you, do you?" He wrapped his arms around me as he removed the rope, holding me tight. "Or Rolf?"

I shook my head, more frustrated than anything else. I *knew* he was right. I just could not help searching for another way—just like I could not help hating the fact that I found none. Or could I…

"Wait!" I put my hand on my crossbow. "What about this?"

Hugh smiled and shook his head. "It could never hold enough dust," he told me. "And even if it could, there would be no way to wish. It would be like pouring it into the wind."

I frowned, my mind racing to find the way around his objections. Sensible as his response was, there *had* to be a way around them!

"The rope! If we tie the ends together, it will be long enough to stretch over at least a small portion of the hole," Rolf suggested eagerly.

"And the wish?" Hugh asked, odd-looking wrinkles of ash and flesh appearing on his forehead when he raised his eyebrows.

"Crusty was talking over supper the other night," interjected Derrick thoughtfully. "He heard tell that a body could wish on wild dust so long as it had something of his'n about it."

We all looked at each other.

Derrick's scarf... my imp grinned.

There was just enough left-over scarf, used judiciously, to use to lash two of our last three bags to each other. The rope Hugh spliced back together so skillfully that it seemed never to have been cut. He handed one end to me while Rolf helped Derrick tie the other end to the bags.

"I have one concern," Hugh told me while we waited. "How does Derrick get the bolt safely?"

I looked at Hugh blankly, then at Derrick. "I could use his canteen for a target," I suggested unhappily.

"Yes, that would work. Do you want me to take the shot?" he offered.

I shook my head. "I can do it," I assured him and tied the rope to the bolt. I had hit targets smaller than a canteen before. "But let us not waste the water!"

While it took a few more minutes to rinse out our masks in turn, it was well worth it. I thought we did not look quite as frightening with our masks rinsed out and it was much easier to breathe without the thick layer of ash we had all accumulated.

"I will go with you this time," Hugh told me. "Derrick will go with Rolf. Now that the smoke has been reduced we should be able to see them at all times."

"Thank you," I told him.

"Shall we?" he grinned.

Derrick carried the bags in one hand and carried Rolf with the other as we flew toward the giant smoke-hole. Similarly, Hugh held the bolt end of the rope in one hand and my arm in his other hand. As we had expected, it got hotter as we got closer.

"Wait," I panted, too hot even to lean against Hugh for support. "I just…need to breathe."

"Almost there," Hugh gasped encouragingly.

I nodded. "Alright."

At last we could get no closer. I thought we had failed until I saw Rolf nodding his head over the map. I could not hear him when he began to speak; however, I understood when he pointed emphatically at the smoke. This billowing smoke appeared the same as the rest of what we had forced ourselves through. It certainly smelled the same!   However, if Rolf's map said we had arrived I would believe it.

Derrick rubbed one hand across his forehead, smearing the soot that had collected there and nodded. Hugh nodded back and took the bags from him. Left to carry only the weary Rolf, Derrick stumbled away, skirting the edge of the smoke-hole based on the map that Rolf still carried.

Hugh handed me the crossbow bolt then dragged himself and the bags of fairy dust a few twigs further along. Turning about to face me, he plunged forward a few steps, dropped the rope, and staggered the rest of the way. I pulled in the rest of the slack, ignoring how hot the ground where I stood was.

I forced myself to breathe as regularly as I could while we waited for Derrick to stop. I did not envy him the decision as to where that would be. Wherever it was, I had to hit the canteen. When Derrick stopped I took a pinch of dust from the bag at Hugh's belt. "I wish you were as fine as hair, strong as steel, and long enough to reach the target," I shouted as I rubbed the dust into the rope I held. I could not hear myself over the roar of the smoke-hole but the coil of rope instantly became everything I had wished. Shifting into a kneeling position, I aimed at the canteen Derrick was holding.

In…and out. In…and out, my imp paced my breathing deliberately. Together we closed my left eye. Slowly we squeezed the trigger. The bolt was away!

I watched as Derrick nearly dropped the canteen when the bolt struck it. I exhaled in relief when the canteen strap held. Now it was up to Derrick. Closing my eyes, I settled back. I was too tired to think. Too tired to… My eyes popped open when I heard a hoarse cry.

"Pirates!" It was Derrick's voice and he was screaming the word at the top of his lungs. The smoke from the temporarily corked smoke-hole had dissipated and visibility had improved a thousand-fold.

Turning in the direction he was pointing, I saw it. A pirate windship, nosing its way out of the last of the thick smoke. Suddenly I was angry. We had worked too hard and gone through too much to lose now! Seizing another bolt from my quiver I levered it into place. Pressing the tips of my fingers against the steel tip and hoping there was just a grain or two of dust left in the grit, I wished. Snapping the stock to my shoulder, I fired at the windship. I could not miss such a large target.

"What did you wish?" Hugh asked, his voice as gritty as my fingers.

"For that," I responded as the side of the windship began turning from leaf to steel. We watched in silence as the windship listed to the side. The smoke-hole really was as big as Castlemain—it swallowed the windship whole.

"Look out," Hugh drew his sword and stepped in front of me. But it was too hot...his sword wavered even as he stood ready to defend me against the few pirates who had successfully fled their crashing windship.

Rolf began cheering incoherently when another windship broke through the smoke.

I joined in his cheers when I saw she flew a Sky Fairy blue flag! As she drew closer I was able to read the name the *Falcon* emblazoned on her bow. A party of ash-covered, masked sailors was over the side of the windship in an instant, capturing the escaping pirates with grim efficiency. Our cheers died when the sailors turned their attention to us.

"I left my crown at the West Post," Hugh coughed as he spoke.

I put my hand on his, lowering his sword for him.

"We cannot defeat them," I pointed out. "And we will be safer going with them than fighting them off."

"We do not have to fight them," Rolf stepped forward. "Please," he held something up for the sailors to see, "we must see your captain."

The sailors exchanged uneasy glances.

"Could be they stole it," one of them muttered.

"Steal a history book?" Rolf retorted indignantly. "I would never do such a thing!"

Derrick chuckled. "Ease up, lads," he

addressed the Sky Fairy sailors familiarly, "we may not look like much, but we ain't pirates."

Well done! cried my imp when she saw the sailors relaxing.

Hugh sheathed his sword carefully. "Thank you, Derrick," he said quietly.

The sailors remained cautious of us as they helped us aboard the *Falcon*. The last man-fairy to rejoin the windship called out something I could not hear and the windship lifted off again. Like all Sky Fairy windships, the *Falcon* was built for maneuvering. She had barely begun to gain altitude before she came about to the south, nearly spilling me flat on the deck in the process.

"Baker," barked a woman-fairy's voice from above us. "What is this that you have brought on my windship?" The fairy belonging to the voice landed on the deck near us. Something about the way she was eyeing us reminded me of the bird the windship was named for.

"Respects, Captain," Baker saluted, "they be of the Silver Fairy Tribe. The lad has a history book with that crest on it."

"Show me," she ordered.

"Baker," Rolf spoke as clearly as he could without coughing, "you will have to break me to take this book from me. But if you ask for it, I will let you borrow it."

Baker scratched his head. He was easily head and shoulders taller than Rolf, with muscles hardened by his sailor's life.

I held my breath while Baker sized Rolf up.

"By your leave, sir," Baker stood before Rolf. "Captain says she would like to see that book of yours."

With more dignity than I could have mustered, Rolf stood and held out the book. "My name is Rolf," he added, "Rolf Warren."

Well done, Rolf, my imp congratulated him silently.

Baker touched his cap with two fingers before accepting the book. "Captain," he held the book out to her.

She never touched it. After glancing at the Silver Fairy crest emblazoned on its cover, she stared frankly at Rolf. "Fetch them some water," she ordered.

"Thank you, Captain…" Rolf paused, frowning when he realized he had no idea what her name was.

"Kimberlite," she finished for him. "Pray excuse me, Historian," she looked back at the helm, "the battle goes on." With a faint nod in his direction, she returned to directing her windship.

Nonplussed, I blinked up at Hugh, who shrugged.

"Historians travel the length and breadth of Fairydom," he explained quietly. "Some of them are better known than even the Royal Families."

We rinsed out our mouths with the water the sailors brought. When I could swish without feeling grit between my teeth, I took a tentative swallow. It was a wonderful feeling, the soothing water slipping down my throat, washing it clean of everything I had been choking on. Of course, we still looked more like ghosts than live fairies. I wished I had enough to remove all the itchy ash from my skin, but I knew better than to expect to find that much fresh water on board a windship. Besides, as the captain said, the battle was definitely still going on.

"Captain," called a voice from above. A rather handsome young man-fairy with piercing blue eyes and short-cropped pale blue hair descended slowly from the crow's nest.

"Prince Cambrian!" I did not think to prevent myself from exclaiming until it was too late. It was no surprise that I had not noticed him amid all the confusion. But when he landed right in front of me it was all I could do to keep from hugging him! Of course, that would not have been proper. Even if it were common for members of one Royal Fairy Family to hug a member of another tribe's Royal Family, which it was not, I was still covered with soot. And, recently married.

He turned to me slowly, looking more distinguished than any man-fairy had a right to in his weathervest and seaman's cap. He took a step toward me, an uncertain expression on his face. He held my gaze for several seconds.

I took a deep breath and quietly quoted, "I

listened to the wind tickle the trees, so they laughed 'til they cried and wept their leaves."

His eyebrows rose considerably and he gave me a swift appraising glance. "Princess Rebecca," he half-smiled, "welcome aboard." The smile disappeared and he turned to face Captain Kimberlite, who had rejoined us on the lower deck. "Captain," he bowed slightly. "Forgive me for interfering, but I should like to introduce Princess Rebecca, the next queen of the Silver Fairy Tribe."

I took note of his deft handling of the situation, acknowledging the captain's sovereignty while asserting his own. He had always been a canny one, able to pull a few feathers without ruffling the rest.

"And may I present," I interjected hastily, "Prince Hugh, the next king of my tribe." I noticed a barely perceptible lift of Prince Cambrian's eyebrows and wondered if I should have said anything at all.

"Welcome aboard," Captain Kimberlite greeted us afresh, formally doffing her hat. She made no effort to hide that fact that she was keeping one eye on her magic mirror, as she had been since we came aboard.

"By your leave, Captain, I shall see to our guests myself," offered Prince Cambrian, smiling dimly when she gave a curt nod.

"Wingman," the captain barked, "find me a faster breeze. We have a rendezvous to keep."

When the windship lurched unexpectedly, I stumbled—as did Rolf, Hugh, and even Derrick. I was the only one, however, who had the misfortune of landing in Prince Cambrian's arms.

"Oh, I am so sorry!" I blushed scarlet as I apologized, trying to straighten away.

"Wait," he instructed and held me lightly in place while he watched the sails. The windship banked this time, a manoeuvre that would have dropped me right back in his arms had I successfully pulled free the first time.

"Thank you," I said, relieved when the deck became level again and he released me.

"My pleasure," he bowed from the waist again, apparently unmoved by the amount of soot and grime now on his clothes.

I blushed again, mortified. "I fear I have broken a cardinal rule of the court," I informed him as I tried to knock a lump of it off his sleeve.

He winked at me in his usual friendly fashion. "At least it is not jam this time," he murmured teasingly. "Come along, then," he spoke in his normal voice and gestured broadly to include all four of us. "Perhaps some of that will rinse off!" He offered me his arm solicitously.

I looked over my shoulder as we led off, intending to smile with Hugh at our odd new situation. Instead I found myself frowning with him—though I knew not what we were frowning about.

"We have no guest chambers," Prince

Cambrian advised, assuming a faintly rigid manner as though he felt the need to maintain appearances even in such mixed company, "but I imagine the first mate will not begrudge us the use of his wash basin." To me he politely added, "You may use mine, of course." He nodded to indicate the last door on the right-hand side of the corridor.

Of course, muttered my imp uneasily. *I think I know now what is bothering Hugh. A little communication is definitely in order here!*

"Very kind of you," I murmured, suddenly wanting a moment alone with Hugh much more than I wanted a bath. Then I had an idea. "By your leave, Your Highness," I got his attention once more, "I should very much like to present to you my travelling companions."

He arched an eyebrow but indulged me, no doubt also remembering our time together so many years ago. Many was the time he had indulged my childhood whims, he and others of my sisters' beaus.

"This is Derrick, cabin boy aboard the *Nightingale*, my good friend and protector," I began.

"Any friend of Rebecca's," Prince Cambrian extended his hand gravely to Derrick, "is welcome to my friendship, also."

I would have blushed if I had not understood the brotherly intent of his words. "And this is Rolf Warner," I took care to refer to him by name first, distinguishing him as an individual before continuing, "my nephew."

"Warner," Prince Cambrian looked at Rolf closely, "Jeffrey's son? And a young man-fairy now. I am pleased to meet you again," he smiled.

I shall never forget the last time I saw that smile, sighed my imp, drawing her knees to her chest and wrapping her arms about them. *So very long ago.*

"And this is Hugh Lawson," I put my hand deliberately on Hugh's near arm, a little worried at the tension I felt in his muscles, which eased a bit when I finished, "my husband."

Prince Cambrian's eyes narrowed for a startled instant. Of course, he had not seen me since I was a child and no doubt recalled me as such…I waited for a full heartbeat before he looked from Hugh to me.

"I was not aware the ceremony had taken place," he said, his voice sounding tight.

"Our royal wedding is scheduled for sixteen days from now," I acknowledged, my hand still on Hugh's arm. "We were wed by our captain just this morning." I felt sorry for Rolf and Derrick, both of whom were shifting from one foot to the other while trying to look anywhere but at the three of us.

Prince Cambrian extended his hand to Hugh then placed his other hand on top of their joined hands. "Congratulations," he said sincerely. Releasing Hugh's hand and ignoring the soot, he wrapped me in a hug. "To you both."

"Thank you," I managed to articulate around the storm of emotion gathering in my throat.

With that he stepped back, bowed, and flew away in an almost leisurely manner.

Derrick and Rolf hastily let themselves into the first mate's cabin, shutting the door behind them.

Hugh flew to the door that Prince Cambrian had indicated and opened it to permit me to enter first. When he had shut the door, I turned to speak to him. Unfortunately, I noticed my reflection in a mirror instead.

"Ugh!" I said, and meant it.

Hugh chuckled and stepped forward so that he was in the reflection as well. "Yes, I see what you mean," he winced.

I fell back into his arms when the windship reeled unexpectedly.

"I would complain about the helmsman," Hugh said as he gathered me closer, "but there are upsides to his erratic maneuvers." We tried to kiss, but there was still just too much grit and soot to ignore.

Laughing, I drew back. "We should not linger," I remarked, sobering a little at the idea that we might encounter mortal danger—again— in the next few minutes.

"About Prince Cambrian," Hugh held me by my arms. "You made a point of letting him know you were married just now. Why?"

"Because," I took a deep breath, "he very

nearly became my brother." Perhaps it was the pain in my voice that confused him; or perhaps that was the clue he needed.

"Joanna's beau," he surmised.

I nodded and rubbed at the tears that tried to trickle down my cheeks. "I have not seen him since," I paused to settle on a date, "since Rolf was just a few years old."

Hugh selected a towel that had a few old stains on it. Dipping it in fresh water that he poured from the basin, he began gently cleaning the soot off my face. He was not quite a layer deep when he smiled and said, "I suppose I shall have to become accustomed to the fact that such a beautiful woman-fairy has friends I do not yet know."

"You mean your wife?" I asked, thrilling at the word.

"I do," he replied.

Under any other circumstances I would have melted down to the ground at a look like that from him. Unfortunately, just then we were lurched back into reality.

"You are right," Hugh handed me the towel. "We should hurry!"

We completed the two shortest toilettes in history and raced back to the main deck. I gasped at what I saw. Two pirate windships, badly damaged, were trying to withstand the *Falcon*'s attack! But, like the bird for which she was named, the windship was fast and dangerous. I held onto Hugh as our windship darted between the others, raking them from stem to stern with simultaneous broadsides. With almost unbelievable maneuverability, the *Falcon* changed course and was out of range before the few remaining pirate cannons could even be fired.

"Strike your colors!" demanded Captain Kimberlite's voice from the quarterdeck. When there was no response she called again, "Surrender!"

I felt the windship turning for another pass at the pirates. Both pirate windships were riddled with holes and the way they were circling, ever lower, told me it was just a matter of time before they crashed. I was about to shout to Captain Kimberlite, to protest—the pirates could be pulled from the water and clapped in irons almost as easily as they could be killed—when the windships fired at us!

Hugh grabbed me and ducked, but he need not have feared. The one ball that struck the *Falcon* was undoubtedly the work of chance. No gunner in his right mind would have aimed for the gunwales on an unscathed windship. The ball bounced off.

"Ready!" Captain Kimberlite's voice cut through the hard laughter that came from her crew. "Aim!" The *Falcon* swooped down toward the finished pirate windships. "Fire!"

They disintegrated under the barrage. Singed bits of leaf landed on the *Falcon*'s deck—and then we were away.

Chapter VI

"There!" Hugh pointed. "The *Nightingale!*"

A bit overcooked in spots, grinned my imp, *but a beautiful sight!*

As the *Falcon* soared into view of the rendezvous of the fleets, a strange, chaotic sight met our gazes. The windships were so thick we almost could have walked back to the *Nightingale*, but we decided it would be wiser to stay out of the way of the working sailors. One windship was a total loss—we watched the sailors from that windship scrambling to offload what they could before they abandoned their home. Captain Kimberlite and the *Falcon* were needed in about four different places at the same time, but she generously loaned us a lifeboat and a sailor to manage it.

"It was good to see you again," Prince Cambrian hugged me goodbye and gravely shook Hugh's hand. "Congratulations, Prince Hugh. Someday," he lowered his voice so he would not be overheard, "you may realize what an extraordinary woman-fairy you have married."

I blushed but did not know what to say.

"Prince Cambrian," Hugh put his free arm about my shoulders, "I realize that every day."

May as well hold our ground, my imp hid her blushing face in her hands; *there is nowhere to go anyway.*

A sailor appeared at Prince Cambrian's elbow, saluted, and reported, "The lifeboat is ready, sir."

At Prince Cambrian's nod, we clambered into the lifeboat. I watched him as the boat swung away. My heart twisted painfully when I saw the sadness he was trying to hide.

"He seems lonely," Hugh observed quietly. "Has he never married?"

I shook my head and settled back for the ride. "He is the second son of a young king," I synopsized just as quietly. "He may wed or not as he chooses. They say he has not looked at a woman-fairy since Joanna died."

The *Falcon* became just another set of sails in a confusion of windships as the lifeboat swung out and around the combined fleet. I reached a new level of humility as I watched fairies from the four tribes striving to piece things back together. A heavy Wood Fairy warship was lashed between a Plant Fairy cargo vessel and a Sky Fairy frigate to keep it from crashing. I watched a sideboat full of Silver Fairy medics making its way from a hospital windship to the most recently arrived windships. Meanwhile, a group of able-bodied windfairies from different tribes were coordinating their efforts to set a jury mast.

I know two things, my imp began thoughtfully. *We are going to be late getting back to the post. And I have never seen such a wonderful mess in all my life.*

We had no sooner set foot on the *Nightingale* than Derrick disappeared into the melee with a quick parting salute. I clung to Rolf's arm to keep from losing him, too.

Suddenly two medics jumped aboard the lifeboat.

"Hurry!" one of them instructed the protesting sailor. "Prince Isaac has been badly wounded and is refusing fairy dust treatment!"

"Wait!" I put out a hand to stop them. I had removed enough grime onboard the *Falcon* that they were at least able to recognize me. "I will go with you. Hugh," I turned back to my husband, chagrined to realize that he was a second thought, but he picked me up and bodily placed me in the lifeboat.

"Hurry," he told me.

I blinked away tears and shouted back as the lifeboat swung away, "Take care of Rolf!"

And yourself, whispered my imp. The pirates may have been vanquished, but the sea was a dangerous place. If we all survived exposure to the cooler temperatures, there were still damaged windships to deal with and a long voyage home to endure.

The *Zelkova*, flagship of the Wood Fairy Fleet, was all but deserted when we got there, every able-bodied sailor having been dispatched to assist other windships. The cook, distinguishable by the apron still tied about his waist, answered our hail. Lashing the wheel in place, he limped down to the main deck and threw us a line.

"Faith, it is glad I am to see ya," he grunted as

he tied the line firmly to a belaying pin. "Prince Isaac is in a bad way."

I followed the medics onto the windship, barely even noticing when the Sky Fairy lifeboat swung away, leaving us there. Numbly I turned down the hallway that led to the captain's cabin. The door to a cabin was open and I could hear arguing coming from inside.

"Admiral, I order you to tend to your windship and the other windships in your fleet," rasped Isaac's barely recognizable voice.

I stopped in the doorway, turned back and was sick in the hall. I had attended the requisite survival medical classes and even assisted the doctor with a few minor surgeries, but I had never seen a fairy body that badly broken.

"Easy now, lass," the cook appeared from nowhere, using his apron to gently wipe my mouth. "Shh, the prince will hear."

I let the cook rock me as I sobbed, my face pressed against his chest to muffle the noise. It was an exceptionally loud roar from Prince Isaac that made me sit up and listen. Sniffling, I wiped my face on the rag the cook handed me. That was it. I could only endure so much weighing of one life against another, so much responsibility pressing down on me. Rising, I dropped the dirty rag on the floor and entered the cabin once more. For a moment I just watched, breathing deliberately.

"If you dare waste a grain of fairy dust on me," roared the wounded Isaac, "I shall hunt you down myself and have you banned from the medical profession!"

"A risk I shall take gladly," retorted one of the medics as he opened his kit on the bedside table. "Or do you think I became a medic to stand by while someone suffers and dies?"

"No one is going to die." I paused, aware that I had interrupted. Seeing Isaac's mouth starting to open, I quietly said, "Well, Isaac? Are you going to threaten me as well?" I had the misfortune of glimpsing my reflection out of the corner of my eye as I approached the bed where he lay. My eyes were red and my face was wedding dress white (except for my nose, which was as red as my eyes). My hair looked like a family of rats had built a home in an abandoned fireplace. Compared to Isaac, I looked tiptop.

"You should not be here," Isaac rasped painfully.

Plunging my hand into the bag of almost-forgotten fairy dust at my belt, I took out a palm-full. "Admiral," I held the bag out to him, "tend to your windships. Prince Isaac will live."

The Admiral took the bag with a bow, adjusted his tricorn, and then strode out like a man-fairy with places to be.

"The dust cannot really make you well," I reminded Isaac. "A wish only lasts for a day. But whatever happens during that day, happens." Taking a pinch of fairy dust with my free hand I carefully set the rest of it on a plate on the bedside table. "I wish Prince Isaac's doctor was here to operate on him."

The Wood Fairy physician appeared before us, blinking and sputtering in confusion.

"Forgive me, Doctor," I spoke to give him something to concentrate on, "but Prince Isaac needs your help."

His attention shifted from me to Isaac and instantly he was all business. I watched as he examined Isaac's wounds, lifting aside gauze patches and nodding over the emergency care Isaac's own medics must have provided.

"It is not a surgery I can perform here, without proper equipment," he said at last, his worried brown eyes meeting mine.

"That fairy dust," I nodded at the plate, "is at your disposal. Wish carefully," I advised, "for that is all that could be spared."

Nodding briskly, he took a tiny pinch between his thumb and forefinger. "Everyone step back, please," he gestured toward the door.

We made haste to comply, and were glad we did! The cabin turned into an operating room, complete with trays of gleaming instruments and a nurse. The nurse and the doctor were both in surgical gowns.

"Will you be needing us, Doctor?" asked the medic who had stood up to Isaac.

"You should all go," advised the nurse.

From her calm demeanor I surmised she was either a creation of the Doctor's wish or the single most unflappable fairy I had ever seen.

"Your Highness," the medic took me gently by the arm and led me into the hall, "we must get you back to the *Nightingale*."

I should have protested. I wanted to. But I was just too tired. I could feel my wings drooping as I put one foot after the other. The cool sea breeze perked me up somewhat— enough that I noticed the Admiral stepping into a lifeboat.

"Admiral!" I called. To my surprise, he heard me and stopped. When I saw his face going hard with the expectation of bad news, I forced myself to smile. "Your royal physician is below, operating on Prince Isaac. But the *Zelkova* is far from home and the wish will expire before Isaac is ready to be without a physician's care."

The Admiral, now looking as though the weight of a crown had been lifted from his shoulders, saluted me briskly. "The *Zelkova* will be underway in less than an hour."

Is that a good thing? questioned my imp, our stomachs flipping at the memory of our brief time aboard the *Falcon*. Even the *Nightingale*, a much more sedate vessel, had still pitched a bit under a strong wind.

I looked down at my palm, the one that had held the fairy dust. A few grains of dust winked up at me, giving me an idea. Pressing my palm to the nearest wall I wished that the *Zelkova* would have a smooth, pitch-free voyage home.

"Easy, Highness," said a familiar voice from behind me.

As my vision grew dim, I felt my feet leave the floor. Good, I could rest…for a few minutes.

"Land ho!" cried a distant voice, luring me from my sleep.

"Ahoy there, sleepyhead," murmured Hugh's voice.

Something warm was pressed to my lips and I woke up enough to kiss him back. "Hello," I whispered, blinking. The room was well lit, beyond the luminescence a mere candelabrum could provide. "Where are we? *When* are we?"

"We are in our cabin aboard the *Nightingale*," he gently kissed me again, as if to emphasize his use of the word 'our.' "And it is almost half a day after we were supposed to have returned to the West Post."

I gently pushed him away so I could try to sit up. I ached all over from the work of the day before. Worse, I still *itched!*

"Are you alright?" he asked, his tone betraying his anxiety.

"I will be," I sighed, staring dismally down at my filthy slacks, "once I am finally clean again."

"The *Nightingale* flew us straight to the West Post," he told me as he helped me off the bed. "We only stopped long enough to off-load the wounded at the fleet hospital on the shore."

"How long did I sleep?" I asked, not sure I wanted to know.

"Almost a day," he answered, releasing my hands to slip his arms about my waist.

"Hugh," I stopped him with a word as he bent to kiss me. I surprised us both by laughing. "Do you suppose we could find something to eat? I am starving!"

"You should be," he laughed and stepped back. "Lunch was a very long time ago!"

I was relieved to see my bag waiting for me at the foot of the bed. Once I had washed off a little more soot, I could change into something clean at least. Hoping the water pitcher was full, I struggled out of bed. I nearly dropped it when I tried to lift it, though, and was glad when Hugh caught it.

"Yesterday was a lot more physical exertion than any of us are used to," he reminded me. He even had the good grace to wince as he gently deposited me on the edge of the bed. "It tested us emotionally, too," he added as he poured an ample amount of water into the basin and set the basin on the table beside me where I could reach it. "This will have to do for now," he said regretfully. "But I will try to find some food while you change." With a friendly smile, he turned and left, drawing the door firmly shut behind him.

It was a relief to shed the ruined clothes and rinse off most of the grit. I wanted almost to scratch off my hair because my scalp itched so badly! It was impossible to do a proper job, but I was finally able to stand being in my own skin by the time I was done. I felt so much better, in fact, that I had the energy to care that I had made a mess—but not the strength to do much about it. My clothes I turned inside out and rolled up as tightly as I could, binding them with yesterday's belt before stowing them in the bag. Setting the first towel to dry on the wall rack, I wrapped the second towel about my damp hair.

"Come in," I called when someone knocked.

Hugh entered, smiling triumphantly. "The captain was clever enough to take on some food while we were at the hospital," he told me, setting down a tray with a flourish.

My stomach growled and we both laughed, for it was hardly the first time. Hugh helped me with my chair, then handed me a fork.

"Go ahead," he nodded at the tray. "I at least got some breakfast this morning."

At his encouragement, I broke the crust on the meat pie. It had cooled sufficiently on its trip from the galley to the cabin, and was delicious. Of course, I was probably hungry enough that I could have eaten arugula with just as much gusto.

"Better?" Hugh asked, reaching for an apple.

I nodded and took a long drink of water. "I am almost too tired to eat," I admitted with a yawn.

He chewed and swallowed the bite he had taken before responding, "I checked with the captain while I was gone. The wind has changed, slowing our approach. You have time for a short nap, anyway."

I yawned again. I knew what awaited us at the West Post. First the crowds of curious fairies. Then it could take hours to tell the council what had happened. I stopped mid-thought when Hugh casually pulled a crisp piece of parchment from his jacket. My curiosity rose when a slow, satisfied smile spread across his face as he opened it and began reading.

"What is that?" I asked, setting my napkin on the table.

"Our marriage certificate," he answered nonchalantly. "The captain gave it to me just now."

I stopped yawning. I was instantly at odds with myself—blissfully happy and terribly worried.

"Come here," Hugh invited quietly, rising. He set the certificate carefully on the table and held out his hand invitingly.

I went without hesitation. I nestled close when he wrapped his arms around me. I was full, the itching was almost gone, and I was with Hugh. If only 'now' could last forever.

"You think too much," he whispered, stroking my hair.

"Force of habit," I sighed. "My life has always been a game of Stratagem, trying to stay ahead of the next compliment or insult, anticipating the next question. And now, by my own doing, I have probably offended half the houses in my own tribe."

"I believe we did the right thing," he told me. "I always knew that, in life, one could not tug on a string without affecting all the interlaced strings. Ban a man-fairy from a troupe and his entire family suffers. Add water and the garden grows." He ran his fingers through his hair. "Forgive me, but when I heard you ask me to marry you, my first thought was for the kingdom. I have spent enough hours at fittings and with Edward and Alfred to have come to the conclusion that royal weddings are very serious indeed."

Shh, my imp hushed me when I was about to speak. *Listen while your* king *is speaking.* Lady Charlotte had said those exact words to me when I attended my first state function and Father had risen to address the gathering.

"I came to the conclusion that marrying you then and there was the right thing to do because I loved you. That certificate," he nodded at where it lay on the table, "is first and foremost a written testimony of our love for each other, something I intend to treasure for the rest of my life." Stepping back, he took my hands and dropped to one knee. "I also came to the conclusion that I would be glad to stand for you again. I would be honored if you would consider doing the same."

My lips curved up in a trembling smile. Unable to speak at first, I just nodded. "Yes," I gasped at last, "yes!"

He rose at once and kissed me until I was no longer crying.

"I love you," I told him directly. "I will stand for you. And—I am *proud* that you thought of the kingdom first. At least one of us did."

He raised one eyebrow questioningly. Chuckling, he kissed me again.

Reluctantly, we drew apart. The damp towels and tray we left for the cabin boy. Hugh took my bag in one hand and offered me his other.

Taking up the certificate, I put it securely in my own pocket. Then I placed my hand in his and we went up on deck.

Rolf saw us first. "Aunt Rebecca!" he exclaimed, coming forward to hug me fiercely. "Are you alright?"

He asks after he adds to my bruises? wheezed my imp, smiling affectionately.

I hugged him back. "Yes, fine," I assured him, then drew back, alarmed. "Rolf! Why do you smell of Helen's potion? Are *you* alright?"

"Oh that," he groaned a little. "I was helping in the infirmary after we left the rendezvous. There were lots of smaller injuries and whenever the medics had done cleaning the wounds they sent them to me."

"To you?" I asked, raising my eyebrows but trying not to sound too skeptical.

"I would dress the wounds and the nurses would bandage them," he shrugged, trying to sound grown-up.

I could not help noticing that he went a little pale as he spoke. Deciding that we were both too tired to really care about age differences, I indulged in another hug.

"Sounds like you were a lot of help," I told him, ruffling his hair gently.

"Thanks, Aunt Rebecca." Looking about to make sure no one else could hear, he added sheepishly, "I threw up once. But just once."

I understood perfectly. "Do not worry," I told him firmly. "I probably would have done the same thing."

"Really?" he asked, sounding his age again.

"Without a doubt. Now, what else did I miss?" I changed the subject, for my stomach was starting to twist with the memory of how recently I had done just that.

Rolf told me in great detail about what had happened after I left him with Hugh, so that it was half an hour before I had to think again. (Beyond how to calm Arabella down, that is.) When the West Post came into view, the *Nightingale* dipped as low as she dared go, but it was still too high for us to reach the ground safely with naught but our wings. I was wondering how we would resolve the impasse without stranding another lifeboat when I heard a shout from the lookout.

"Dragonflies approaching off the stern!" he called.

I leaned against the railing, one arm around

Rolf's shoulders, and waved down at the crowd with my other.

"I doubt they can see us," Rolf pointed out as he dutifully waved with me.

"Major Daniels can," I waved harder as the dragonfly squad approached.

"Seems it is time to say goodbye," the captain's voice said from behind me.

He bowed to me and shook hands solemnly with Rolf.

"Let me handle that, sir," the captain forestalled Rolf as he reached for his bag. "It has been something of a wild ride for you, I fear," he added and the two of them walked away from me.

Mismatched in age and size, mused my imp, *and apparently grand friends.*

Since it was just the three of us—and since the need for secrecy was past—we met the dragonflies at the stern. Major Daniels saluted before helping me take my seat behind him. Hugh made a wry face but obediently clambered aboard behind one of the other riders.

When it was Rolf's turn, I held my breath until he was safely settled. He had consented to the safety harness without a blink or blush, knowing it was a simple fact that he could not fly as yet. The captain wished us luck with a salute then turned back to his windship.

I could hear him issuing orders as we flew away.

"Heave to, lads," he roared. "Back to the sea!"

"Back to work," noted Major Daniels, pulling his dragonfly to a hover for a moment once we were clear of the windship.

"Yes," I smiled, still shivering a little inside from the cheer the sailors had given at the captain's command, "and they love it."

"How did you like the sea, Highness?" he asked, banking around to catch an accommodating breeze.

"The sea is lovely," I responded diplomatically, "but I am not sure I would care to go sailing again in the near future."

He laughed and gestured to his squad.

"Where are we going?" I asked, feeling quite sad as I waved goodbye to Hugh.

"Safest place I can think of for you," answered Major Daniels. "Your rooms. Besides, the king and queen will be wanting to see you."

"Of course," I yielded.

And you could use a proper wash, added my imp hopefully.

Chapter VII

Hurrying through a hot bath is like eating imaginary food—wholly unsatisfying. Megan insisted, though, on taking the time to wash my hair out and dry it thoroughly. I pretended to argue, for I did not want to delay the official proceedings, but I think she knew all along that I did not mean it.

"That is better," she said as she added the last pin to my hair. "You looked like a chimney sweep before!"

It was good to laugh. It was even good to be in my quasi-familiar rooms at the West Post. I took a final sip of milk and got to my feet.

"Thank you, Megan," I hugged her.

Blushing, she fluttered over and opened the door to my sitting room.

Ah, if only we could go for a lark with the children, sighed my imp, *or hide away in the library until supper.*

With both hands I reached down to gather my skirts and my strength of will. Mother and Father were waiting for me when I stepped through the door. I was grateful for their self-discipline.

Mother settled for a simple hug and, "We were so worried!"

Father stepped in and hugged us both.

I was not surprised to find that Mother was misty-eyed when we stepped back. My own eyes were moist. We laughed together when Father produced two clean handkerchiefs, one for each of us.

As we had agreed, Hugh joined us in my room before we went to face the council. Father solemnly took our crowns from where Megan had left them on my desk and placed them back on our heads.

Hugh and I both hesitated when my parents turned toward the door.

"Darlings," I began, "we have done something rather irreversible."

"Something," Hugh added, "we had planned on doing anyway."

Father looked at us closely. "Go on, children," he prompted kindly.

Reaching into my pocket, I produced our marriage certificate.

"Things did not go quite as expected," Hugh said, "which we will explain more about for the council's benefit."

"We got married," I interjected breathlessly. As I watched, they exchanged startled glances.

"Married?" Mother repeated incredulously.

"Steady," Father patted her hand, "we knew they were planning on it." His lips quirked up in a smile for almost a full second before his face smoothed back out. "Suppose you tell us how it happened."

"It was a bit sudden," I admitted, blushing.

"We were almost as surprised as you are,"

agreed Hugh bashfully, apparently comfortable enough with my parents to let his discomfort show.

"We had to leave the windship, to do something important…" I began.

"Something dangerous," qualified Hugh, frowning.

"And I just could not go without first being married to him," I let the words rush out as they came to mind. "The captain," I unfolded the certificate and held it out to Father, "performed the ceremony himself."

Father inspected the certificate closely before handing it to Mother.

"We realize the situation will require a certain amount of finesse moving forward," Hugh conceded.

I could not help being reminded a little of Rolf when I saw the way Hugh was standing, shoulders back and chin up. It seemed to me that he was looking not just Father in the eyes, but the whole tribe.

"Yes," Father agreed. "I know a little something about that," he added, looking down at Mother with a tender expression in his eyes.

"We are still planning on a formal ceremony," I said quietly.

"And I am still planning to conduct that ceremony," Father approved.

Still emotionally off-balance, I had to struggle to maintain my composure as Father and Hugh shook hands.

"Congratulations," Mother hugged me again.

Do not laugh or cry, advised my imp sagely. *Breathe instead.*

I obeyed. A small tear squeezed out when Father hugged me next, but I was on guard to keep my emotions at bay after that. Time enough to sort through my feelings after the council had finished questioning us.

"Rebecca?" Hugh offered his arm to me.

I placed my right hand lightly on his left wrist. I followed his lead when he flew after Father and Mother. It was again new and strange to me to not be at the end of the line of adults as my family flew sedately toward the ballroom, which had been rearranged for this meeting.

The council was waiting for us by the tables and chairs that had been set up for them. A smaller table and three chairs were set up opposite, waiting for Hugh, Rolf, and me. Mother and Father moved quietly to their places, but did not seat themselves. Hugh and I also remained standing, as did Rolf when he joined us. Only when the entire Royal Family had entered the room did Father and Hugh exchange nods with Councilor Branwick. We sat. The entire room sat, creating a wave of swishing sounds as fabric settled into place.

Councilor Branwick brought his gavel firmly down on the sound block, the report echoing through the room. The meeting was begun.

I was once again exhausted by the time Hugh and Rolf and I had answered the councilors' questions to their satisfaction. Yes, we made it to the hospital windship in time—barely. The driver was unknown to us. Yes, we agreed that it merited a thorough investigation. The task was promptly assigned to two guardsmen, who saluted and left.

No, none of us had seen the bulk of the battle. Yes, we had left the *Nightingale* voluntarily. Yes, we had seen three pirate windships go down. No, there were no survivors from those crashes. Yes, I had gone alone to the *Zelkova*. Yes, I was confident that Prince Isaac would survive his wounds.

More than once the spectators gasped or cheered as we recounted the events. It was a victory, so they did not seem to mind our previous deception. Councilor Branwick used his gavel a few times to bring them to order again.

"And the pirate Bane," Councilor Branwick asked specifically. "Do we know his fate?"

Hugh waved the question over to Rolf, who rose to the occasion.

"According to the reports from Admiral Trask, Bane was sighted aboard a pirate vessel. The *Hawk* and the *Picea* valiantly pursued that vessel until it was destroyed. Bane was not among the survivors rescued," he reported succinctly.

At one point, perhaps because he sensed I was growing tired, Hugh reached under the table and took one of my hands in his. I performed the same service for Rolf a moment later. We all sat a little taller, taking strength from the knowledge that we were still together.

"If the council has no further questions," Councilor Branwick said at last, looking carefully at each of the councilor's faces.

"If it pleases the council," Hugh rose, still holding my hand in his. "I," he paused as I rose to join him, "*we* have an announcement to make. We did face the mists," he stated. "We risked our lives in the hopes of saving the lives of others. Some here seem to think that was a great deed." He took a deep breath before continuing, "But I had little to fear, because I had Princess Rebecca with me," he drew our marriage certificate from his pocket and gave it to an attentive page to be taken to Councilor Branwick. "Whom I had just married."

Councilor Branwick appeared stunned. He let the spectators go on for several seconds while he examined the paper the page handed to him.

Hugh raised his hand for their attention. Almost immediately the room fell silent. "We were two fairies in love and married each other as such."

I squeezed his hand lightly before adding, "We will soon be married as prince and princess. It is our mutual hope that you will all join us for that solemn occasion—and for the celebration afterwards."

Angela began applauding from her seat near

my family. With a grin, Sean followed her example. Their goodwill was infectious, spreading first to my family and the other engaged couples, then out to the room, even to the council. It was a deafening racket, full of good humor and well wishes for us.

I looked in Councilor Branwick's direction, intending to mouth an apology. To my astonishment, he had risen and joined in the ovation with the others! Remembering what he had told me once about knowing that Hugh loved me, I blushed a little.

"It is incredibly awkward at times," Hugh smiled as he spoke, "to have this many fairies involved in the private details of one's life."

I laughed softly and slipped my arm through his. "You are going to love touring," I told him teasingly.

I had intended to eat in my room but that was no longer an option. Drawing on a different kind of strength, I laughed my way through dinner. I tried to stay near Hugh and Rolf, and found it so abundantly easy that I concluded they were doing the same. In consequence of our close proximity to each other, I overheard when Arabella approached Rolf about an hour after dinner.

"How are you feeling?" she asked, resting one hand lightly on his shoulder.

"Tired," he admitted with simple frankness. "Do you suppose I might be forgiven if I retired early?"

I watched as Arabella searched his face, her surprise at his words disguised quite well except from those who knew her best.

"I am sure it will be alright," she assured him, smiling a little strangely.

"Then with your permission, Mother," he took her hand from his shoulder, kissed it with all the decorum of a man-fairy twice his age, "I shall say goodnight to Grandmother and Grandfather."

That will be me someday, my imp mused, watching Arabella. She sat down suddenly.

I approached Arabella cautiously after he had left, not quite sure if she would prefer to be alone.

"Oh hello, Rebecca," she greeted me, a distant expression on her face. "Did you hear that?" she asked, her eyes still on Rolf's retreating back.

"Yes," I answered honestly. "I just wanted to see if there was anything you needed."

She shook her head and actually smiled at me. "Rolf told me a little about what happened. I think he was trying to make it sound better than it was, for my sake." Her brows knit together as she asked, "Do you think he worries about me?"

"I know he does," I answered promptly, then searched for a way to clarify. "He loves you and is your son. Do we not worry about our parents?" I linked my arm through hers as I asked the question, nodding toward where

Mother and Father stood.

"She looks so lovely in her imported lace," Arabella sighed a little wistfully, "but I think she is growing tired." With an exchange of smiles and girlish giggles, we split up.

I ambushed Ambassador Feren with a small plate of his favorite delicacy, crisp sugar cookies. It required little effort to draw him away, with his apologies of course, from where he had been monopolizing Mother and Father with stories of his estate. I probably could have found my way around his estate blindfolded, for that was all he cared to speak of.

Arabella executed a similar maneuver, complimenting the Duchess Valerie on her shawl, which had exquisite needlework. Mother and Father received more apologies before Arabella led the Duchess to a soft couch where they no doubt began chatting about various, delicate things.

I endured part of the ambassador's endless stories by imagining Arabella describing her twins, which her hand gestures indicated she was doing, and what she planned to buy for them next season.

You might have daughters, thought my imp, *or even sons.* She sat down, slowly.

I nodded dutifully when the ambassador ran out of cookies and excused himself to go find more.

"Melt in your mouth delicious," he praised

them, "and just what I needed. I was getting a little hungry."

"But of course," I pointed him in the general direction of the dessert buffet, "a man-fairy of your energy certainly would."

If only all of us could eat like he does without looking like most of us soon would, sighed my imp.

"You look exhausted," said Hugh's voice from behind me.

I smiled, more amused by his directness than disturbed by the thought that my 'mask' was slipping.

"Why thank you," I bobbed a half curtsy and fluttered my eyelashes at him. The playfulness went out of me when he took me gently by the wrist. In all seriousness, I rested against him as discreetly as I could. "I am still fatigued," I confided in a low voice.

"It is only natural. Less than a day has passed since we were all choking on smoke," he reminded me.

"Are you tired?" I asked, suddenly curious.

"More than I care to admit," he answered unhappily. "Is there no rule of etiquette small enough for us to break so that we may rest as Rolf is doing?"

I glanced up at him, read concern in his eyes and frown that matched what I heard in his voice. "I will be fine," I straightened away with a smile. "But to answer your question," I absent-mindedly tapped him on the arm with my fan, "there is a way out of here."

"An escape?" he asked, his eyes lighting with mischief.

"Precisely." Resisting the urge to wink at him, I quickly surveyed the room.

Gwyneth and Alexander were shielding Mother and Father from further drawn-out conversations by putting themselves in play, conversationally speaking. When Gwyneth caught me watching she used her free hand to twist a curl of hair, a sign from our youth giving me leave to slip away.

"Slowly," I warned Hugh, "back slowly out through the window."

We took the long way around to my chamber window. We even paused in the garden to enjoy the variety of scents, from night-blooming jasmine to honeysuckle.

"For a while I thought the sulfur had burned my nose," Hugh bent over a fragrant blossom, "so that I would never smell anything else."

Reaching out, I ran my fingers through his hair. "I thought I would have to cut my braid off and wait for the rest of the sooty part to grow out," I told him, marveling at how soft his hair was. "Would you have loved me anyway?" It was a silly question, for I felt silly.

"Yes," he answered. Without permission or explanation, he picked me up and flew me to my rooms. "Get some sleep," he instructed me as he set me on the windowsill. He hovered there a moment, wings flashing in the moonlight, the edges emerald green and the finer lines faintly silver. With precise flaps he brought himself near for a goodnight kiss, then disappeared.

I sat for a moment on the windowsill. The nights were warm again and the moon was high. I could easily imagine villagers dancing in that same moonlight, rejoicing in the safe return of the fleets from the pirate battle. Of course, there would be mourning tonight as well. While it was astounding that we had lost so few windships in the battle, there would be too many empty windship slips tonight.

My mind wandered back to dinner. Father had started with a salute to the fallen. The court scribes had scribbled it all down and it would eventually be distributed by official messengers, along with a full year's wages, to each of the deceased sailor's families. It was little enough to do for those who had secured our freedom with their lives.

Better do as Hugh said, advised my imp resignedly. *Tomorrow will have its own challenges and you will need your energy.* She yawned then, which made me yawn. Exhausted as I was, I counted to five hundred before I finally fall asleep.

Chapter VIII

I enjoyed my fittings after that. Madame Grey was her usual cheerful self, unmoved by recent events. Oh, she clucked a bit over the bruises Claudette discovered while helping me change, but she did not pester me for details or ask silly questions.

Helen and Cassandra were likewise ports of calm in a storm of curious fairies. One or the other of them was frequently at my side, ready to sidetrack obstinate fairies that apparently could not wait for Rolf's account to be copied by the scribes and distributed to the village libraries.

Dear Rolf…his formal induction as Historian took place just a few days after our safe return. I had the honor of standing just a few feet away from a beaming Master Collins throughout the ceremony. Except for a slight wrinkling of the chief historian's nose, for Rolf's history book reeked of sulfur, the ceremony was without incident.

And I was able to see Alfred and Edward. Finally! I was disappointed though, that I was not able to hug Edward.

"This scratch?" he shrugged as carelessly as he could with a chest wound. "The guardsman that finished the pirate is receiving a commendation," was all he would say about it.

Now it is we who must wait for the accounts!

groaned my imp. Her quirky sense of humor allowed us both to laugh at how the tables had been turned on us.

Alfred hugged me gingerly, as if he were afraid I would break. "You had us all worried," he told me affectionately. "For future reference, tardiness is only tolerable when appropriate communication accompanies it."

I smiled though I wanted to cry—just a few happy tears. "I shall remember," I promised him, then released him to Cassandra. They made lovely couples, Edward with Helen and Alfred with Cassandra. I could tell from the way Cassandra smiled up at Alfred that their understanding had only deepened. Alfred had grown by leaps and bounds during the gala, not only as a prince but also as a man-fairy. I dare say that Cassandra had always known his potential and loved him for it.

What could be ailing those two? questioned my imp, noticing faint frowns on Helen and Edward's faces.

"Edward," I interrupted as the group began to break up, "might I have a word?"

Alfred pretended to glower at me as Cassandra left him to take Helen's arm.

"We have work to do elsewhere," Cassandra smiled at me.

I wondered at the slightly anxious expression on Helen's face as she allowed herself to be led away.

"I see how things are," Alfred sighed. Then with a wink, he took off in the direction of the council chambers, perhaps to find and detain Hugh.

"What is wrong?" Edward asked.

"I am not sure," I put my hand lightly on his wrist as we began moving aimlessly down the corridor. "I was hoping you would tell me."

His frown deepened. "It is the wedding," he began, then shook his head vehemently, "I mean, it is the *ceremony*."

Puzzled, I said nothing.

"Eric will do for a final chaperone," he went on, "but we have no parents…"

I heard pain in his voice as his voice trailed off, and bit my lip to prevent a rush of sympathetic words. The former Count Bullierd was as close to dead as a live fairy could be.

"Have you considered proxy parents?" I suggested after some time had passed.

"Whom would we ask?" he sighed. "Helen knows no one at the post except Queen Dianna and we could hardly ask her."

"Why not?" I wanted to know.

"Why? Because then *I* would have to ask King Wilson!" he retorted with his old friendly frankness.

"Edward, I am surprised at you! Surely by now he has forgiven the pranks you indulged in at your last visit to Florcena," I teased. As I had expected, his ears went pink with embarrassment.

"It has been over fifty years," I pointed out more seriously, "and I think he would be honored."

"Honored?" Edward was not convinced. "To stand in the place of a rebel and traitor?"

So long as it is not at an execution... my incurable imp muttered indelicately.

"Edward," I stopped flying and landed. Once he had joined me I asked quietly, "Do you have any genuine, heartfelt objections to having King Wilson as your proxy father?"

Slowly he shook his head.

"I do not know him well," I admitted, "but if he is anything at all like Queen Dianna, he will be the first to point out that while an apple does not fall far from the tree, a nut usually travels a great distance."

Edward struggled against it for a moment, then surrendered to his sense of humor and laughed.

"If you would permit me to assist you in this matter," I ventured, smiling with him, "I should be happy to extend the invitation to them myself."

He considered a moment before answering, "Let me ask Helen first. If she agrees, then I would be grateful if you would." Humbly he bowed over my hand before leaving in search of her.

"What was that all about?" asked Hugh, slipping in through a window.

Laughing in delight at his unexpected appearance, I held out my hands to him. "Just giving a young-old friend some much needed advice."

"You must be careful, my darling," he shook a finger at me in mock seriousness, "not to advise folks too much, just because you are a young-old married woman-fairy now."

"Hmm," I smiled up at him as he took my hands and stepped closer, "I shall try very hard to remember that. In the meantime," I fluttered my lashes at him, "I think I shall need your advice."

"My advice?" he feigned horror. "Things have come to a pretty pass when you need the advice of a mere prince!"

"Actually," I turned so that my left shoulder was near his right, and wrapped both of my newly freed hands around his bicep. "It is a job for *Prince* Hugh, specifically."

"Intriguing," he frowned at me thoughtfully as we started flying toward the other end of the corridor. "Tell me more."

"As you know," I began slowly, "Helen is an orphan." With as much discretion as possible, I explained the situation to him. I knew from the way he nodded and frowned that he would also be discreet. I was also glad for an opportunity to discuss it with him so that I might ask how he planned to handle his own situation.

"That is a marvelous idea," he assured me when I had finished explaining about asking Queen Dianna and King Wilson. "I am sure they will agree."

"You do not think that King Wilson will disdain standing as substitute for Edward's real father?" I asked bluntly.

"I think not. I told him the truth of Edward's role in the attempted rebellion," he reminded me.

"That is one friend assisted," I mused.

"You need not concern yourself with Alfred," Hugh squeezed my hands gently. "He and I have already discussed the matter."

"Oh, really?" I asked, trying not to sound too amazed.

"Oh, yes," he grinned. "Alfred and I have become quite good friends."

"No doubt a result of you spending so much time in such a small space," I teased, thinking of the tiny quarters the three groomsmen were sharing.

"That and a slight parallel between our situations," he agreed affably.

Slight? squeaked my imp. *Temporarily in line for the same throne, the same bride, both with deceased fathers, and the list goes on!*

"What resolution did you find for his situation?" I asked curiously.

"I suggested that Alfred ask one of my guests," Hugh smiled mysteriously.

I hesitated, then laughed. When Hugh joined me, I did not have to wonder what he was laughing about, either. Even the *thought* of how the Duchess would react was enough to make anyone laugh—except for her.

Hugh dabbed a tear from his eye and said, "It is a good thing that Edward and Alfred will have such fine men-fairies to serve as their fathers, even temporarily."

"I had thought that you might want to ask King Wilson for yourself," I broached the subject tentatively.

He shook his head. "It is better that King Wilson and Queen Dianna serve Edward and Helen, I think."

Two orphans, sighed my imp. *Certainly they deserve such a small concession.*

"But who will act as your father?" I asked, still concerned that he would have regrets after the ceremony.

"I asked Jeffrey, and he has agreed."

Stunned, I felt my jaw go slack.

"And Rolf will fill Jeffrey's role as final chaperone…if that is agreeable to you," he stopped walking to look down at me.

"I love it!" I answered enthusiastically.

A bell pealed at the post—eleven times.

"I am glad you still like to walk occasionally," Hugh told me as we began walking. "It can be rather enjoyable."

I listened as he prattled on about the council meeting. He kept up a steady stream of it all the way to my rooms, but more than once I caught hints of deep concern or genuine satisfaction as he glossed over a case they had reviewed.

"Then the farmer brought in his star

witness—his best milking goat!" he ended his last story with a laugh.

"I am sure the goat had some very pertinent testimony to give," I parried amusedly, "as the one who had to eat all that inferior hay."

"It was a turning point in the case, to be sure," Hugh paused before my doors and bowed. "If I hurry, I might make it back to the room before Edward and Alfred."

"What happens if you do not?" I asked, my eyebrows rising of their own volition.

"They get the mirror first," he answered matter-of-factly, then disappeared down the corridor.

I tried to tell Megan about Hugh and the mirror, but I was laughing so hard that I gave myself the hiccups. Half a pitcher of water later, I had drowned the hiccups and tried again.

"I can just see the three of 'em," she chuckled as she threaded the lace on my slippers, "grown men-fairies fighting for the mirror!" Her tone made it clear that she did not believe it, either. "You, on the other hand, are a sight to see!"

Methinks 'tis not the dress nor the gloves, but the happy glow that makes you look so different tonight, mused my imp, though she was not displeased with our reflection.

"You are too kind, Megan," I kissed her cheek and accepted the fan.

Now that the Admirals and military officers had returned to their various postings, my biggest challenge at dinner was to keep certain folks apart. Of course, there was also the task of seeing that everybody sat with Hugh and me at least once.

"Remember," I told Hugh when he came to fetch me, "tonight we have Lady Vaniece and Lord Bartlett at our table."

"Yes," he frowned in concentration. "I have been wondering about that. Is it an accidentally-on-purpose matchmaking attempt?"

Oh come now, sighed my imp. *Just because Lady Vaniece has eight daughters and Lord Bartlett is a widower with many unmarried male relatives…*

"Perhaps," I responded airily. "It may be our most interesting evening yet!"

An hour later, I was regretting my brilliant decision. Lord Bartlett might or might not have been an outstanding conversationalist, but Lady Vaniece was a marvel! She managed somehow to talk and eat almost in the same breath, without ever getting caught with food in her mouth. In the end, it was Hugh that saved the evening.

"Lady Vaniece," he leaned forward, "is it true that you like riddles?"

"Oh, indeed," she bubbled, "indeed I do!"

"Ah, then perhaps you would indulge me?" At her eager nod Hugh said, "I am as light as a feather, but even the strongest cannot hold me for much more than a minute. What am I?" Leaning back in his chair, he took a sip of his drink while waiting expectantly.

Lady Vaniece blinked rapidly. Then she consulted her roll, separating it into four perfectly equal parts and buttering them thoroughly.

In the interim, I hazarded a remark to Lord Bartlett. "I hear that spring has brought lush growing conditions on your estate." It was a weak attempt, but I had no guarantee how long it would be before our time was up.

"Yes," he agreed with my remark succinctly. He chewed a bite of meat, watching Lady Vaniece closely. When she began nibbling at a piece of her roll he ventured to say, "It looks like a fine year for pears."

"Oh, I do hope so," I spoke with genuine enthusiasm. "The Bartlett estate has been renowned for its pears since my grandfather's reign!"

To my pleasant surprise, he responded like a flower to sunlight. We were deep in conversation when the dessert course—pear and frangipane pie—arrived.

"This was made," I announced solemnly as I took up my fork, "with the last of the fall pears."

"I shall have to make sure that Castlemain gets our first bushel of new pears," Lord Bartlett smiled and raised his forkful of pie. "Smells delicious!"

"Forgive me, Lady Vaniece," Hugh spoke kindly to the woman-fairy, "I fear I chose my riddle poorly."

"Alas," she sighed and toyed with her pie, "I

have racked my brain to no avail. I must surrender."

Hugh laughed genially. "Very well. What is it that is light as a feather but cannot be held for much more than a minute? One's breath." He delivered the answer in a suitably mysterious tone, which allowed Lady Vaniece to laugh with us all.

"How clever," she acknowledged, "how terribly clever!"

After that, the conversation was more balanced, thankfully. Not that it takes long to eat dessert, even when one savors every bite, but I marked the experiment a success when Lord Bartlett offered to escort Lady Vaniece to the musical event.

"We were planning to come," Hugh explained when asked, "but then we received another invitation we could not refuse."

I smiled. "My twin nieces, Juliette and Jennifer, have asked us to join them this evening."

"Ah," nodded Lady Vaniece, "yes, good. Though they are young now, they grow up all too quickly."

That sparked a remark from Lord Bartlett and resulted in a conversation about family in general. They were so absorbed in what they were talking about that they flew away without bidding us adieu.

"I am impressed," Hugh murmured as we

watched them walk away. "I would never have expected this result."

We remained a few minutes more, speaking with the few who seemed intent on it and wishing them a pleasant evening.

"We should dine with Minister Kolak soon, I think," Hugh thought aloud once we were clear of the press. "He has some very interesting points to make about the trading regulations between our two tribes."

Listen to him! my imp marveled. *It almost sounds like he is enjoying this!*

I held tightly to his arm all the way back to the twins' room, which had three additional couches to accommodate our large group. I knew instantly which suite each couch had been borrowed from, yet somehow they seemed to blend with the room's décor—perhaps because they were occupied by fairies I loved very much. Carefully, Hugh and I flew over the children that were arranged in various spots on the floor. As we took our seats it became apparent that they were having an argument of sorts.

"No more pirates!" wailed Jennifer.

"I want to hear about a party!" declared Juliette, eyeing her male cousins as if daring them to disagree.

"Yes, yes," Jennifer clapped her hands, "a party with fancy dresses and dancing and…"

"May I be excused?" Steven rolled his eyes.

"Suppose," Mother interrupted the mayhem,

"I told you the story of how I met your grandfather. Would you like that, Steven?"

An interesting choice, mused my imp, *especially with Hugh here.*

I almost gasped when I felt the muscles in Hugh's arm go hard as a rock. Though it had been months since he had spoken to me of his mother, my father's first wife, I vividly remembered Hugh's tears on my fingertips. I also remembered how surprised he had been to learn that Queen Alicia had come to love my father.

A few months of knowing the truth after years of believing a lie? My imp shook her head. *Sometimes old wounds take longer to heal than we expect,* she pointed out gently.

Instinctively wanting to comfort Hugh, I bit my lip and threaded the fingers of my hand through his. Nestling closer, I rested my head on his shoulder. Slowly, the lump digging into my back began to feel like an arm again.

Meanwhile, time had not stopped. Steven was frowning. At only forty-five years old, he still thought that parties were boring—but he did not want to be rude to his grandmother.

"We could try to like it," his brother Daniel volunteered bravely.

I managed a faint smile when I saw Daniel's mother, Gwyneth, reward him with a wink. Then I moved my foot to avoid Steven's as he squirmed into a more comfortable sprawl. Hugh's arm tightened about my waist, supporting me and drawing me closer to him at the same time.

"Then I shall try to make it likeable," Mother promised. "Long ago, before most of you were born," Mother's voice was warm as she began, "there was a very sad and lonely prince."

"A sad prince!" Jennifer pouted.

"Jennifer," Jeffrey admonished immediately. "Shhh," he pressed a finger to his lips. "Sometimes happy endings have sad beginnings."

I watched as Jennifer, somewhat mollified at the hint of a happy ending and a bit abashed at the public remonstration, settled back into the plush pink carpet to listen.

"He was very sad," Mother went on almost as if there had been no interruption, "because his wife had just passed away. He missed her a great deal, but, because he was the Crown Prince, he was kept very, very busy."

"Did he have time to cry?" asked Juliette.

"Not really," Father answered.

I felt Hugh's arm go hard again, but was not quite sure how to interpret it.

"After a while," Mother slipped her hand into Father's, "he stayed busy so that no one would have time to tell him that he needed to remarry. Eventually, his friends began having parties just so they could invite him to come," Mother smiled.

"And because he was a prince," Jennifer inserted happily, "he had to say yes!"

"That is right," Mother agreed. "He was smart and it was not long before he knew what his friends were doing, but he kept saying yes because he had to. There were all sorts of parties—dinner parties, costume parties…even dances."

The twins simultaneously shivered in delight at the thought of all those parties!

"There were always women-fairies at those parties, of course. They never thought of it as a duty, though," Mother squeezed Father's hand lightly. "We were so thrilled to be invited! It would happen very unexpectedly. You might be sitting at home, reading a book or doing something perfectly commonplace, when someone would come buzzing up on a dragonfly. All the single women-fairies would run to a window—was it…yes, it was! The rider was wearing palace livery, splendid with its silver vest and leggings!"

Dear little Jennifer sighed and relaxed on the carpet as though all of her bones had gone out of her.

Mother hesitated until Arabella gave her a slight nod that Jennifer was quite alright. "Then came the knock at the door," Mother smiled when Steven rapped his knuckles on a table, creating sound effects. "Oh! The excitement in that household! The ladies buzzed like bees all the days between the arrival of the invitation and the party."

Juliette collapsed next, followed in turn by Daniel and Steven, though the lads swooned with some rather gruesome sound effects, as befitted their pained deaths.

"In fact," Mother ignored them and drew something from her handbag, "I still remember the day that I received my invitation." She held up her invitation, sealed in a watertight pouch, for us all to see.

Instantly there was silence. Daniel and Steven hastily rearranged themselves in attentive positions. Even the girls came back to themselves to stare, open-mouthed, at their grandmother.

It was then that I felt Hugh trying to lean forward. Relieved, I leaned forward with him.

"I thought it would be great fun to see the prince …I even thought I might meet him," Mother smiled with the wry amusement of hindsight.

"I, on the other hand," Father smiled sheepishly, "was expecting it to be just another of many nights where hours seemed to take days. The food always looked delicious—great platters of roast robin or ham," he smiled at his intrigued grandsons, "cakes the size of small chairs, and punchbowls deep enough to bathe Antoinette in."

The children giggled at the thought of bathing a baby in a punchbowl.

"But Grandfather," Daniel asked anxiously, "did you never get to *eat* the food?"

"Not often," Father shook his head solemnly. "I got in the habit of eating a sandwich on my way to the parties, just in case I had to spend the whole night talking or dancing."

Daniel and Steven looked crushed. "Poor grandfather!" their facial expressions seemed to cry out.

"There were some very nice fairies at the parties," Father clarified, "most of whom wanted to speak with me, it seemed."

Ah, the privileged life of a king, my imp groaned sarcastically. Then Hugh sighed softly, and neither my imp nor I felt much like joking anymore.

"I was too shy to try to speak to him, though," Mother took up the storyline again. "What I expected to be a simple party had become a large, complicated affair, full of courtly customs that I had never learned."

"Shy was not how I would have described her," Father grinned. "Every time I looked up, she was dancing with a different man-fairy."

A charming blush crept up Mother's cheeks. "I could not help that," she protested. "Most of the other women-fairies were busy trying to capture a Crown Prince and the poor men-fairies had to ask *someone* to dance."

Arabella, Gwyneth, and I laughed together. We had loved this story as children, especially when Father helped tell it.

"All I knew at the time was that she was the

one woman-fairy I could not recall meeting, beyond an obligatory bow in the receiving line," Father smiled broadly. "And once I had noticed her, I seemed to see her everywhere—dancing with a handsome lieutenant, laughing with the Minister of Finance, letting the fencing master bring her a cool drink…"

"Until," Mother interrupted, "someone came over and invited me to dance with the prince."

"Someone *else* invited you?" Rolf asked, sounding surprised.

Father came as close to squirming as I had ever seen.

"I was engaged in conversation with my host…and his young cousin, Giselle," Father said by way of explanation. "I was fortunate to beg a moment to speak to my aide!"

"A very handsome young man-fairy," Mother teased. "But I was too startled to be insulted; besides, I was curious. I had never been to Castlemain and I wanted to know everything he could tell me about it."

"That was the other thing that intrigued me about her," Father smiled. "I had spent so much time listening to the other women-fairies that I expected her to do all the talking. Instead, we just danced—and she did not seem to mind the silence."

I leaned back when Hugh did, not wanting him to loosen his arm. I was glad that he had relaxed; I could even hope he was enjoying the story.

"I was tongue-tied," Mother admitted, squeezing his hand again. "He was so reserved and serious. I was even reluctant to mention the weather, for fear of making him worry about the farmers and their crops!"

"Finally, the music ended. That is when I panicked," Father stated ironically.

"Panicked?" exclaimed Daniel and Steven in unison.

Father nodded, a deadpan expression on his face. "I had just spent four minutes with a woman-fairy who did not dominate an uninteresting conversation. Faced with the prospect of rejoining a random group of fairies who would quite probably talk over themselves in an effort to speak to me," he shrugged, a gesture he did not commonly indulge in, "I clung to your grandmother's arm, turned, and headed straight for the gardens!"

I smiled at hearing him refer to Mother as 'grandmother.' I had spent enough time in the libraries at Castlemain, where portraits of the Royal Family hung, to have a fair idea of what they had looked like when they were married. Strange as it might seem to Daniel and Steven, Mother and Father had been just like Hugh and I.

I, for one, look forward to becoming just like them, my imp whispered, snuggling deeper into Hugh's one-armed embrace.

"I was a little perplexed by his action," Mother noted, "but I loved gardens. And he was so quiet that I almost forgot he was there!"

"Did he pick you flowers?" Jennifer asked dreamily.

"No," Father answered, "though I wanted to. It would have been in poor taste to take flowers from my host's garden without first requesting his permission."

"Oh," said Jennifer, a funny expression on her face as reality invaded her fairy tale story.

"But what I did do was almost worse," he went on. "I spent the rest of the evening in her company."

"We even started talking!" Mother laughed. "I wanted to smell a rare cultivated silver rose and caught my finger on its thorns. He asked me if I was alright…" Her voice trailed off as Father reached for her right hand.

I blinked back a tear as he paused to examine the tiny white scar on her finger. I had never seen Hugh's scar from when Edward's half-sister, Amber, had tried to kill us both. I remembered visiting him in the surgery, though. I doubted I would ever forget seeing her arrow protruding from the bandages on his torso.

"I think that is when I knew I was falling in love with her," Father said huskily. "Her wound was no more than a tiny prick, yet I felt awaken in me an overwhelming urge to protect her."

I happened to glance at Rolf just then, and saw the most intensely thoughtful expression on his face. I put my right hand on Hugh's left, and nodded in Rolf's direction.

Hugh gently kissed my right temple and murmured, "Like father, like son."

I flicked a glance at Jeffrey, who was gazing at Arabella. The expressions on his and Alexander's faces were that of complete understanding. I risked a glance up at Hugh's face. When I saw the exact same expression on his face, I felt a rush of love for him that warmed my cheeks and put stars in my eyes.

"What happened next?" asked Juliette, when the pause had grown too long for her young attention span.

"We saw quite a bit of each other after that," Mother smiled. "The host of the party where we met quietly arranged to have me invited to the next party."

"And the next, and the next," Father chuckled. "When I found myself looking forward to parties because I hoped she would be there, I knew I had to do something."

"What?" Juliette and Jennifer asked at the same time.

"We began courting," Mother answered. "After a very interesting three months of going riding, having picnics," she paused when Steven spoke up.

"Did you actually *eat* at the picnics?" he asked suspiciously.

"We ate very well," Mother assured him good-naturedly. "We even took time to talk.

Then, he asked me to marry him."

"Like Hugh and Rebecca?" asked Juliette dreamily. She and Jennifer turned to look at us expectantly.

Hugh and I exchanged glances. Sensing that he had an answer that he was struggling to suppress, I nudged him gently. The sooner he began acting like himself around my family, all of the time, the sooner he would feel that he was truly one of us.

"I did not ask Rebecca to marry me," Hugh said slowly. "But I know what Prince…" he hesitated, "your grandfather means. I was very happy, though, when Rebecca asked me to marry her."

Juliette and Jennifer stared at him, looking for all the world like hungry baby birds, with their eyes and mouths wide open.

I was not half so nervous then as I am now, with all of you staring at me, my imp grimaced.

"Did *she* really ask *you?*" Daniel asked Hugh, disbelief evident in his tone.

"Yes," Rolf rescued an embarrassed Hugh. "On the *Nightingale.*" Noting the continued frown on Daniel's face Rolf added, "I was standing less than a twig away at the time."

"I did not have time to be nervous," I intervened, scrambling mentally for a way to return everyone's attention to the story. "But your grandfather did."

"*Were* you nervous?" Rolf asked helpfully.

The children obediently turned back to hear their grandfather's answer.

Father winked at me before resuming, "Indeed I was. It is one thing to ask a woman-fairy to dance with you or spend an afternoon in your company—and quite another to ask that same woman-fairy to face spending the rest of her life with you. I did have one thing in my favor, though. I had *no* imagination."

The children giggled at that. They had been surprised by their grandfather more than once, so they knew better.

"I just made up my mind to ask her and I did," Father smiled triumphantly.

I bit my lip and Gwyneth hid a smile behind her fan.

"It only took him an hour, once he got started," Mother remarked. Having recaptured the full attention of her audience, Mother began painting a verbal picture. "It was a fine spring day, and there were hundreds of suitable places for our picnic. By then I was somewhat accustomed to seeing a lot of Nathaniel and just assumed we would be spending a regular afternoon together. But he hardly spoke to me! I knew that he sometimes found silence preferable to idle conversation, so I did not really worry until he had been silent for almost an hour. Finally, I asked him what was wrong."

"What did he say?" Steven asked, curious despite himself.

"He told me," Mother took a deep breath, "that everything was wrong and would never be right again…unless I would agree to marry him."

Daniel did an admirable job of keeping a straight face, but poor Steven looked dismayed.

"So I married him," Mother smiled. "And we had four beautiful daughters."

I watched Father grip her hand a little more tightly at the word 'four.'

"And they had us!" Juliette shot into an upright position. Her twin, Jennifer, instantly followed her example. In a moment they were dancing giddily about the room.

We all laughed, even Mother and Father.

"Girls," Arabella handed Antoinette to Jeffrey then rose to tend her daughters, "it is possible to be just as happy with only half as much noise." To prove it, she took them by the hands and joined in their dancing—quietly of course.

"Here," I held out my arms for Antoinette and made sure to hold her so that she was able see her family's antics as Jeffrey and a long-suffering Rolf took part in the fun.

"I love your family," Hugh chuckled softly.

"It is yours, also," I reminded him. I watched as he looked around the room.

He paused, his eyes on my smiling parents. "And I am very glad to be part of it."

Chapter IX

The days fell into a routine that I found relaxing partly because of the routine. Instead of secret meetings, I attended fittings. Instead of dividing my days between three suitors, I looked forward to spending my dinners and evenings with Hugh. Instead of puzzling over maps, I worked with Mother in her rooms to finalize the guest list. We had first cut our list by two thirds so that the other couples could send their own invitations, then agreed as to which couple would invite whom among our mutual friends. With barely two weeks to go, it was now or never.

I, for one, would feel slightly more at ease if I knew exactly whom Hugh was inviting. muttered my imp, folding her arms across her chest. *Alas, I shall have to be satisfied with what I do know. Hugh was chosen to be the next king for quite a few reasons; and, he has only asked for three slots.*

"Rebecca, are you quite sure we should invite Prince Cambrian to the wedding?" Mother frowned slightly, her concern for her almost-son-in-law evident in her tone.

"Without a doubt," I spoke decidedly. "It has been far too long since he has visited the Silver Fairy Tribe."

Mother sighed and leaned back a little in her chair. "I still remember watching him with Joanna." A fond smile played across her lips.

"They were both very young, but I always thought I would be happy if they decided to marry."

"I liked him enormously," I set my quill down on Mother's desk and picked up her miniature portrait of my sister. "He used to like to draw her," I told Mother, smiling at my sister's face. "He showed me once, almost an entire sketchbook filled with pictures of her."

Mother patted my free hand. "You are right, I think," she added Prince Cambrian's name to the list, "though I wonder what we shall do to entertain him."

"Nonsense," I laughed, "the libraries are full of books written since he last visited. We even have a few new paintings that might interest him." I was not very sure of that last bit, but Mother seemed satisfied.

"There," she shuffled the papers into a neat stack and handed the list to her maid. "Please copy this and bring me the original. Then take the copy to the stationer and have him prepare invitations for the new names." After her maid had closed the door behind her, Mother turned to face me. "Alright," she gave me an appraising look, "what has you so dreamy-eyed today?"

"I was just thinking," I smiled at her teasing tone. "I was never one for making lists of names for my children and now," I shrugged and tapped the original guest list with the feather end of my quill, "I have a plethora of names to choose from."

Her eyes widened. "Seven hundred children might even exceed Councilor Branwick's expectations!" she exclaimed after a moment.

Father entered a few minutes later and found us crying from laughing so hard.

"What is this?" he asked, surprised.

"Oh, nothing Father," I winked at Mother and glanced at the guest list. "We were just discussing what names I should use for my children. What do you think of Julius Thomas Wilhelm Patrick Ferdinand?"

He blinked. "All those names for one child?" he scoffed, falling into the game with practiced ease. "The poor lad would not know what to think of himself!"

When we had all caught our collective breath, Father explained that he had come to suggest that we begin preparing for dinner, as nobody else could eat until we arrived.

Laughing still, I allowed him to shoo me out the door. I imagined that they would appreciate a few minutes alone, especially Mother. Besides, the shadows were growing long and I *was* getting hungry. As expected, I found Megan in my bedchamber.

"You are early," Megan greeted me from where she was laying out my dinner things.

"Am I?" I parried the unspoken question. While we had agreed that she was free to discuss the guest list with any fairy she chose, we both enjoyed the mental exercise of her trying to tease new information out of me.

"Things comin' together for the wedding?" she came over to unbutton my collar for me.

"Oh yes," I confirmed. Slipping out of my dress, I waited while she added it to the laundry bin. "Periwinkle tonight, I think," I told her when she paused before the row of dinner gowns. "We anticipate that every invitation will be accepted, though I fear Prince Isaac will not yet be up to travelling."

"Hm," she retrieved a set of matching periwinkle slippers for me and knelt to remove the golden calf-height boots I had been wearing. "I 'spect he will be out of circulation for a while at that."

I stifled a small sigh. Isaac was a bold fellow but preferred sports to flirting. Nevertheless, whenever the women-fairies gathered his name always produced a round of girlish giggles.

"May I have my lilac fan, please," I asked when she reached for my periwinkle fan.

She frowned a little but brought it anyway.

"And the lilac sash, please," I requested. To my pleasant surprise I found that I enjoyed the contrast between the two colors.

Not too much, not too little, my imp surmised happily.

Hugh's response was a little more complimentary, perhaps because we had not seen each other all day.

"You look lovely," he told me, shutting the

hallway door just long enough to steal a quick kiss 'hello.'

"Thank you," I answered breathlessly.

Hugh started to open the door, then stopped. "Have you heard about the wagon driver?" he asked, arching an eyebrow.

I shook my head. I had not thought of him since our return, which struck me as rather odd.

"He was a pirate spy," Hugh said, "sent to check on things at the post. Apparently he saw Edward at the village, in his merchant pose, then back here with all of us and put it all together. Had he arrived even a few days earlier, the entire plan might have been ruined."

"You amaze me, Hugh," I folded my arms and looked at him narrowly. "How, exactly, do you know so much about it?"

"No trick at all," he showed me his open right hand, turned it palm down, made a fist, then opened it again to reveal a small rosebud. Holding it out to me he finished, "The Silver Guard apprehended him when he tried to return to the village yesterday."

I took the rosebud from his hand and inhaled deeply before placing it in a water glass. "How are Edward and Alfred doing?" I asked, lingering over the bud a moment.

Hugh chuckled. "I am not quite sure. Anxious for the wedding, I would say—certainly anxious to be in less cramped quarters!"

I sighed. "You have all been such good

sports about sharing that room. I would have suggested you move back to your original quarters…"

"But Queen Dianna and her entourage will be returning in just a few days," he finished for me. "We understand," he smiled.

I turned to embrace him. Closing my eyes, I inhaled the fragrant scents of ginger-blossom and grass that clung to him. "Thank you."

"You are most welcome." He kissed my hair, and then stepped carefully back, offering his arm. "Shall we?"

I managed a smile that no one questioned when we flew into the hallway and maintained it through the first course of fish soup. During the next course I relaxed into a conversation that, strangely enough, was being carried primarily by Ambassador Julene. It was more of a story, to be honest, but she seemed in no hurry to tell it, indulging questions from her fascinated audience as the telling stretched through the main course.

"No, no," she smiled coolly when Madame de Gaulle asked if she had been afraid. "I grew up in the mountains; the birds are not strangers to me. The hawk only needed a quick look to know I was too small to be worth chasing." She went on to describe how she made her way home after the hawk flew off and proudly led the harvesters back to the nest. "There were enough feathers to outfit the entire tribe for the Fall Festival that year." She finished her apple pie while the others exclaimed over the tale.

Madame de Gaulle gushed, "My, what a fascinating story! I never should have done that, never in five thousand years! Going off alone," she shivered, "and then to turn out the hero!"

I dabbed at my mouth with my napkin to remove any telltale remnants of delicious apple pie. It was not my place to correct Madame de Gaulle by pointing out that Ambassador Julene had been accompanied by Prince Cambrian that day. The major points from Julene's version matched Cambrian's perfectly and I wondered how much I could actually deduce from what she had not mentioned.

I wonder, interjected my imp, squinting at Julene, *that she has never married.*

"A very interesting story," agreed Hugh smoothly. "I had not heard it before." With that, he set down his fork and stood.

I waited briefly while the attending servant pulled out my chair, then took Hugh's proffered hand. Tonight was a casual ball, where we all simply moved from the dining hall out to the eastern lawn. The dragonflies had been released and the firepots lit, ensuring protection from marauding mosquitoes. I spent most of the evening safe in Hugh's arms, the more discreet fairies choosing to dance with other partners rather than separate us. We sacrificed a few dances to our guests that were being overlooked, of course. When the musicians began playing the final waltz, Hugh claimed me again.

"Tomorrow," I mused aloud, "we should ask Alfred and Cassandra to begin the ball."

"Good idea," Hugh concurred.

My mind wandered a little as we danced, though it never left the general subject of my partner.

"A gold flake for your thoughts," Hugh teased gently.

Surprised I protested, "You offer too much, sir!"

His brow puckered thoughtfully before he said, "For nothing, then, tell me you were thinking of me."

Something about his tone and proximity made me lose my breath. I dropped my eyes a moment to gather my scattered wits. "Of course I was," I answered honestly.

Even as he smiled his manner became more serious. "What were you thinking?" he asked.

"About the story Mother told the other night." I was nervous about being that blunt, but he already knew something was not quite right.

He glanced across the dance floor. "A most interesting story."

Wait, did he just... My imp's jaw dropped. We had watched with amusement as Hugh had grown more adept at using vague, diplomatic phrases in self-defense during public gatherings. *But with me? With us? I think not!*

"Hugh," I struggled against the urge to shake

him, "we both know it was more than that."

He maintained his cool exterior for a few more heartbeats before his expression changed. It was like watching a crack appear in a wax statue's face.

I instantly regretted bringing it up in public. My own curiosity could wait its turn, certainly for a more appropriate time. My heart sank as the music stopped. Hugh's face closed again—but this time it closed me out, too.

He was a perfect host. He paused to speak with many of the couples on the dance floor; he made his way over to an elderly couple half-asleep on one of the couches, where he politely roused them long enough to say good night.

I hardly spoke a word. I had watched his skill at social playacting develop over the last couple of months, but this frightened me. His performance now seemed more of an overall attitude rather than a mere charade assumed for his public.

Where is the Scamp in this smooth-talking fellow? my imp frowned. Our hope lay in the fact that he never let go of my arm.

"Fly with me," I whispered when the crowd had thinned a little. His arm muscle twitched under my hand but until he actually began easing us toward a window I was not sure he heard me. Once we had exited through the window, we flew for several seconds in silence. I was reluctant to broach the subject again as I had so nearly—and recently—embarrassed us with it.

"The moon is bright tonight," Hugh remarked.

I thought the comment irrelevant until he drew me off the path and into a secluded area of the garden. "You are not angry?" I asked when he bent to kiss me.

He hesitated, straightened away. "I am…upset," he said, choosing his words carefully. "But not angry. I thought my life was finally settling, that I would get married and grow old comfortably with the woman-fairy I loved."

I leaned forward, slipping my arms about his waist. "Have your plans changed?" My head rose and fell with his regular breathing as he pondered the question, his arms cradling my shoulders.

"I still plan to marry you again and grow old with you," he murmured into my hair. "However, I begin to see that it is not likely to be a comfortable experience." He drew back then, looking me in the face as he hastily added, "I mean to say that there are still many things that cause me discomfort. I…"

I laughed and kissed his mouth, before he could verbally dig a deeper hole for himself than the one he thought he was in.

"You mean," I said eventually, "that marriage will not solve all our problems?"

"I could not have said it better myself," he smiled.

"If you do not want to talk about the story," I began to say.

"Perhaps we should," he interrupted. "I am glad your mother told it."

"You are?" I asked, as pleased as I was surprised.

"Yes," he confirmed, leading me back onto the path. We began walking, arm in arm. "It was not until you told me the truth about my mother that I even considered liking your father for himself, instead of just respecting him as my king. As for your mother," he sighed and took several steps before continuing, "I have spent a lifetime resenting her for taking my mother's place."

I had an inkling of how difficult it must be for him to confess such things to me, the daughter of the fairies he was struggling to like. It helped, a little, that I was accustomed to the idea that not everybody automatically adored my parents. Having no words to make the situation easier for him, I said nothing and squeezed his arm instead.

"Now that they are more than just names to me, I like them very much. Yet I find myself confronting echoes of past feelings as I interact with them." He shook his head.

Fanning myself a little, I ventured to speak. "I understand." I did not flinch from his searching gaze when he turned to look at me. "I would no more expect you to be able to dismiss," I decided against mentioning an actual number of years, "a lifetime of such feelings than I would expect you to be able to change your eye color."

We enjoyed a comfortable silence for several seconds before he said, "Thank you." Lifting off he changed the subject. "I suppose Megan waits up for you?"

I had to chuckle at that. "Yes, usually," I nodded, rising with him. "She is most attentive."

"Do you miss Angela very much?" he asked next.

"Yes, I do," I sighed. "It is strange to have her close by and so far away at the same time."

"Have you asked her to join the ceremony?" he prodded gently.

"Not yet," I admitted.

"I must provide Master Collins the final seating instructions for the Royal Family," he coaxed. "Shall I ask him to include a chair for her?"

"Yes," I nodded, determining that I would ask her the very next day.

That is what you said yesterday, and the day before that, frowned my imp. *How fortunate that coming face to face with a time limitation has such a positive impact on your resolve!* I was still frowning in annoyance at what she had said when I realized where we were going. He was taking me to my window—the long way round.

Chapter X

The next morning I leaned out my window and took a deep breath of fresh air. The days were no longer cool, so I relished the few minutes I had before the day officially began. Things were moving so quickly! My royal wedding was just a week away now. Already the jungle-lawns had been cleared and basic wooden foundations were being constructed as areas where our wedding guests would set up their temporary living quarters.

"Good morning, darling," Hugh flew up to my window.

"Good morning," I returned, straightening so he could sit on the sill.

"Did you sleep well?" he asked.

"Oh, yes," I answered amusedly. It had become clear to me on past mornings that these visits were just an elaborate excuse for a morning kiss.

While we lingered at my window, discussing various things, I tried to store it all up in my memory. The morning breeze on my cheeks, the scent of breakfast wafting up on that breeze, the rapidly lightning sky…the *Hugh-ness* of it all. I became fascinated by his left eyebrow, which quirked up at the slightest excuse. I watched his hands as he gestured descriptively and spoke of summers past.

"I have to go," he said at last, reaching up to fiddle with his collar. "The council requires my presence this morning."

"And I am due for a meeting with Mistress Judith and Cook," I sighed. "By the way," I casually changed the subject as I straightened his collar properly, "you never told me who you were inviting to the wedding."

"No," he tried to frown, "that is true." He captured my hands and kissed them.

Oh dear, thought my imp. She saw the laughter in his eyes as well as I did.

"Are you going to?" I prompted, still hoping for nonchalant but sounding more breathless than anything.

"Do you want to know?" he asked, arching his eyebrows.

Of course I want to know! shouted my imp.

I looked down at our joined hands, struggling with the answer. "Part of me does," I answered honestly.

He stood, drawing me up with him. He closed the window behind me and we began flying in the direction of the kitchen.

"Let me guess," he said. "It is the part of you that worries about the etiquette of state functions, about having enough strawberry tarts to satisfy Ambassador Feren, about what would happen if Admiral Trask began debating the Battle of the Boundaries with…"

"In short," I cut him off, a little unnerved by

how quickly the list grew, "the part that worries."

He nodded, smiling wryly. Squeezing my hand he said simply, "I have invited a few fairies that I care a great deal about. I promise they will behave during the ceremonies, and I have alerted Major Daniels that they may require a bit of…tending the rest of the time."

I digested the news slowly. I would not have Hugh apologize for his friends, no matter how rough they might turn out to be. I was impressed, however, that he had chosen such a wise ally in the impending 'clash of cultures.'

"If I can help," I offered, but he shook his head.

"You have enough to worry about," he told me with a friendly wink. He drew up then to collect his kiss, but lingered still. "I am off to the council chambers," he frowned.

I waited, puzzled by his frown.

"I appreciate the willingness of the council to tutor me in the laws and traditions of the Silver Fairy Tribe," he said after a silent minute, "but I feel that some of them have reservations about actually yielding the authority of a king to an…unconventional prince." He smiled wryly at his choice of words.

My imp's stomach clenched with trepidation. *Where other grooms are nervous about the wedding, I fear this one dreads his impending coronation. Nor can I blame him, for the weight of the Queen's Crown rests heavily on me as well.*

"Even now they must consider your opinion. If they do not all accept you from the beginning, we shall win the others over in time." I included myself in his picture of the future as though confident that we need only persist to prevail. Then I swallowed the lump in my throat as we turned away from each other.

Putting the tribe first is going to be a lifelong sacrifice. Best get used to it, my imp observed glumly. Squaring my shoulders, I flew to the kitchen. My life would not be easy, it was true. But I must not forget that I would see Hugh again tonight. And tomorrow, and the next day, and the next…for hundreds of years. We would bear each other up when the difficult times came.

I rerouted my thoughts to focus on my meeting with Mistress Judith. I could not help but wonder what she wanted. I knew her as an organized woman-fairy who seemed almost clairvoyant in her ability to anticipate the domestic needs of the West Post. I hoped this unexpected meeting was something as simple as her needing my approval of the wedding cake's final design.

I paused in the kitchen door, perplexed to see little groups of maids and serving boys standing about whispering. It was my experience that Cook was lenient enough while the work was still getting done, but I had never expected to see this!

"Ah, Highness," Mistress Judith appeared before me, wringing her hands while she bobbed a curtsy. "Come quickly!" Turning, she flew at once out of the kitchen.

Amazed at her completely discombobulated state, besides being half afraid that I would lose her in the maze of hallways and service ways, I zipped after her without solving the mystery of the kitchen staff. I managed to keep pace long enough to enter the stable yard right behind her.

"Oh," I gasped, dodging back as a small thief ant skittered past with a squad of Silver Guardsmen in hot pursuit. "What is that doing here?"

"I do not know!" exclaimed Mistress Judith, indulging in more hand-wringing. "A group of travelers just arrived and brought…that *thing*!"

I stared at her, willing myself not to succumb to the hysteria I heard mounting in her voice. Certainly domesticated ants were rare, but not unheard of.

Of course you shall not have hysterics, snorted my imp. *That would be far too ridiculous. Still,* she ducked as a flying clod of dirt came too close for comfort, *we cannot simply leave it cavorting about!*

Catching Mistress Judith by the shoulders I asked, "Where are its owners?" I looked in the direction she pointed and was only mostly surprised to see a group of colorfully dressed fairies sitting in the center of the stable yard, watching the ant's antics with only mild interest. If I read their expressions correctly, they were even less interested in what the stable master was shouting at them. I felt myself tighten with anger. A tame thief ant was as strong as a wild one and could do considerable damage if left unchecked.

Hot heads do not make calm decisions, my imp quoted the senior at me.

Taking a deep breath, I made sure the ant was on the far side of the yard before beginning to fly toward the group. I tried to time the speed of my flight so that I could reach the group before the ant came around again, but without appearing to be in a hurry. It was a bit closer than I would have liked—but I need not have worried.

An older man-fairy, still broad-shouldered and radiating vitality, rose from where he was squatting with the others. He watched my approach without a flicker on his worn face, hands clasped behind his back. After a moment, the others followed his example and rose also.

Though I did not see the fellow signal, I was confident that it was his doing when the smallest boy-fairy in the group used a stick to drum a rhythm on the ground beside him. From the corner of my eye I saw the ant slow, then stop. Its head and antenna hung low as it shuffled toward the boy-fairy. The Silver Guardsmen uneasily tried to herd it along without getting too close to its powerful legs. I pressed forward, not slowing until I had reached the group. Deliberately I hovered a moment before landing, trying my hardest not to raise even the smallest puff of dust.

"Princess," bowed the older man-fairy, his fading brown hair ruffling a little as he leaned forward. Again the others followed his example, bowing and curtsying with surprising grace.

"Sir," I returned. "Thank you for restraining your ant." I managed a smile, though if Angela had been present she could have told me which number it was in her list of my assumed smiles. Oh, I was no longer angry. Given what I had heard the stable master shouting at them before he saw me, and the fact that no actual damage had been done to life or property, I was actually inclined to be lenient.

"Her efforts served their purpose," he said stoically.

Hold your tongue! My imp hastily slammed a mental door on several biting remarks that tried to get past her. *It did serve to get my attention.*

"Your pardon, Highness," the stable master bowed. When he tried to insert himself between us, neither the older man-fairy nor I would budge. Forced to resume his original position and stance, he hesitated, nonplussed.

"You may leave us, sir," I dismissed him as casually as if we were not standing in his domain.

First Goliath, now this, thought my imp in annoyance. *I shall strongly recommend seeking a new stable master.*

"Highness, I…" the stable master paused and paled as someone landed beside me.

"That will be all, sir," Hugh's voice rang with

authority though he did not raise his voice.

Looking quite shaken, the stable master bowed his retreat without further protest.

"Hugh," said the strange man-fairy, his tone changing subtly, "it is good to see you again."

"And you, Cial Mar," Hugh returned.

I sensed that something was amiss. Perhaps it was the way they both just stood there, looking at each other. "Do not let our audience disturb you," I murmured to Hugh, taking an educated guess.

At that, Hugh's face relaxed. He moved forward and embraced the older man-fairy.

I smiled, intrigued by the scene before me as Hugh greeted each of the fairies in turn. They had some very unusual names: Tumbler, Twister, Laughter, and Jest were among the group. The young boy-fairy was referred to simply as Jorge and I wondered why.

Troupe fairies, marveled my imp. *But of course!*

Hugh held out his hand to me. "Rebecca, I should like to present our guests. This is Cial Mar—Abigail's brother-in-law."

"Oh!" I was mid-nod when Hugh finished the introduction. "I am so pleased to meet you!" I closed the distance between us, my hand extended.

Cial Mar said nothing and did nothing. For several seconds. Then he stepped toward me, taking my hand very gently in both of his huge hands. "We have come not merely to witness a wedding and coronation," he told me mildly. "We have come to welcome you to our family."

I blinked back the tears that stung my eyes at his simple statement.

"Thank you, Cial Mar," Hugh stepped forward as well, putting one arm about me and his free hand on Cial Mar's, which still gripped mine. "It will be our honor to receive your welcome on the morrow, after you have had time to refresh and rest yourselves."

Cial Mar watched me until I nodded, then released my hand, apparently satisfied.

I listened intently when Hugh, smiling broadly, went back through the confusion of names for me. I was determined to match each new face to its name. I was determined to make a good impression. And I was terribly curious!

I was also acutely aware of their distinctive culture and etiquette. I was introduced as Princess Rebecca, Hugh's fiancée—but they were introduced to me in what seemed a peculiar order. Perhaps by an unofficial ranking system of which I was completely ignorant? Or was it merely as we encountered them while we made our way through the small camp? When I had met all nine adults and five youth, I was finally presented to Jorge.

"Hello Jorge," I smiled and tried not to loom over the boy-fairy when it was his turn.

Jorge looked at me with distrusting eyes, his mouth set firmly in a frown.

Hugh squatted next to him, ignoring the smudges a grimy young hand left on his pant leg. "Jorge," he said quietly, "I would like it very much if you could be friends with my wife."

Jorge looked startled. "But she is…"

"Palace-class?" I finished for him, a little worried about what he might have chosen to say otherwise. "Yes, I am." I could not squat comfortably in the frock I was wearing and I knew better than to lean down, remembering all too well how patronizing that had seemed to me when I was a child. "That is not always a bad thing, though."

Jorge's frown deepened, as though he were thinking hard. "Do you think all troupe fairies is trash?" he demanded.

I shook my head, startled.

"Has you ever travelled by your lonesome, without a gaggle of servants to do yer work?" he asked next, squinting at me.

I wondered that none of the adults reprimanded him, but just nodded.

He heaved a sigh. "Does you love Hugh?" he asked, his tone indicating that this was the crucial question.

"Without a doubt," I answered evenly.

"I guess she ain't so bad," Jorge said to no one in particular. Thrusting out a grimy right hand he added, "Pleased to meetcha."

"Thank you, Jorge," I shook his hand solemnly and refused to look at my own once it was released. There would be time enough for that later. "Welcome to the West Post," I addressed this remark to the entire group. "And thank you for coming."

Hugh nodded at Jorge before straightening. "Indeed. You have travelled far, my friends. If you will follow me I shall show you to the guest pavilions."

I spoke to him discreetly while they gathered their things and their ant. "Hugh, according to Master Collins' reports, the east side of the pavilions has the most completed water system. They are working their way in from the well toward the post."

Hugh did not frown, but he did not smile. "They could mistake it for an insult, being placed so far from the post."

"Oh, yes…" I searched my mind for a solution. "We could have water brought to them," I suggested. "While Master Collins' crew is finishing the work, I mean."

Hugh nodded. "Have some lads fill the western reservoir. Cial enjoys watching the sunset. I will try to keep them occupied for a little while."

"And I will make your apologies to the council." Curtsying to Cial Mar, I politely excused myself. Spotting Master Collins standing by Mistress Judith, I beckoned for them both to join me. "Master Collins," I smiled, "I need you to set a team of lads to filling the western reservoir of the guest pavilions as quickly as possible. Then finish the water system, please."

He nodded and flew away, a small storm of lads and equipment swirling after him. Not subtle, perhaps, but highly effective.

"Mistress Judith," I slipped my arm through hers. "Pray accompany me to the council chamber." I was a little concerned at how limply she obeyed, but promised myself I would tend to her as soon as possible. I led her along gently until we were there, then deposited her on a hallway bench near the door. "I will return shortly," I reassured her before entering the council chambers.

Councilor Branwick noticed me first. "Princess Rebecca," he rose, "to what do we owe this honor?"

Have I been so long from a council meeting that my presence is a novelty? my imp fumed playfully.

"I bring a message from Prince Hugh," I answered, suppressing a wry smile. "He regrets that he is unable to join the council at this time. Pressing matters have drawn him elsewhere."

"And what is so important that he cannot fulfill his commitment?" asked Councilor Chadmen arrogantly.

I did not respond at once. I was deeply disappointed by Councilor Chadmen's disrespectful tone, but not surprised, as he had always been a bombastic fellow. Judging by the expressions on the faces of the other councilors, I was not alone in my reaction. "If it is insufficient for you that your future king has made his decision," I arched one eyebrow deliberately, "I can of course bring your complaint to him."

Councilor Chadmen flushed a deep red.

"That will not be necessary, Your Highness," Councilor Branwick intervened, "though we thank you for your generous offer." He paused to assess the schedule book on the table before him. "I move that we postpone the discussion of the new taxes until tomorrow and move on to the matter of the wind stations."

Councilor Shalray, one of three representatives staunchly in favor of expanding the wind station routes, lifted her hand to second the motion.

"The vote has been called. Indicate, please, if you are in favor." Councilor Branwick looked very pleased when the vote was unanimous in favor of his motion.

Councilor Chadmen relaxed a little, though his face remained several shades darker than usual.

"By your leave, councilors," I spoke up before they could get into cost projections and time estimates. "I also have duties elsewhere."

"By all means, Your Highness," Councilor Branwick rose to his feet.

This prompted the other councilors to rise, even Councilor Chadmen, who rose so hastily that his stomach got in the way temporarily. The men-fairies bowed and the women-fairies curtsied until I was safely out of the room.

I heard the chairs sliding back into place as I retrieved Mistress Judith. I tipped my head to the side and asked her, "Now, what was it that you wanted to discuss with me?"

She did not answer until we were well clear of the council chamber. "I have been trying to remember…but all I am sure of is that I wrote it down," she said at last, a worry crease wrinkling her brow.

"Excellent," I smiled brightly. "Let us search it out then, together." I spoke of generalities on our way back to where she had left her notes in the kitchen and she seemed almost her old self by the time we arrived. I was relieved to find that the kitchen was also back to its usual hum of activity.

"Princess," Mistress Judith interrupted, putting her hand on my arm, "I recall now what it was. Cook has her heart set on serving berries with the luncheon on your wedding day, but we just do not have enough for all seven hundred guests. We need to send out a picking crew…" Her voice trailed off halfway through her solution to the problem.

I frowned in understanding—with all the work on the lawn and accommodations, there were precious few hands to spare.

I know where there are lots of idle hands, chuckled my imp, rubbing her own hands together gleefully.

"I may have the answer," I mused aloud. "Have you a patch in mind?"

"Indeed," Cook joined us, her industrious hands at work polishing a cup, "Major Daniels has been keeping an eye out for us this last week while on patrol. Found a nice patch of plump berries he has!"

Leave it to Major Daniels to be where the food is, smiled my imp.

"That sounds like a fine outing," I announced.

"An outing!" Mistress Judith was stunned for the second time in one morning. "For the guests?" she squeaked.

"Never fear," I laughed kindly, "I have not taken leave of my senses. Here, let me tell you what I have in mind." Taking a half step away, I picked up a quill from Mistress Judith's desk and began scribbling down the main points of my idea. "After breakfast tomorrow, we shall repair to the berry patch. The guests will be responsible for their own equipment, as part of the fun. Major Daniels and his men will be responsible for transporting the berries back to the post. And luncheon tomorrow," I finished, "shall be served outdoors by the berry patch, something light and refreshing." I purposefully left the menu to Cook. "There," I set the quill down, "simple, is it not?"

"I have a root cellar near empty," beamed Cook. "It can hold buckets and pails of berries!"

"'Tis agreed, then," Mistress Judith agreed, having recovered her wits and voice. "I shall have the outing added to the notices of events."

"While I shall mention that I plan to attend," I added happily. "But first I should go tell Major Daniels!"

"Tell me what?" he called from where he was entering the kitchen. He had just removed his hat and his short-cropped hair was dull with perspiration.

"About our new outing, of course," I began. "They," I tipped my head briefly toward Mistress Judith and Cook, "tell me you have discovered a berry patch."

"Yes," he nodded, crossing the room in a few flaps. "Cook mentioned she was planning to serve them at your celebration," he gave her a warm smile, wise man-fairy that he was, "and I recalled having seen a group of patches indicated on a map from the West Post's service days. They are overgrown, but not too wild for my lads." Then his smile dimmed slightly as he turned his attention to me. "It might not be quite what you want for an outing," he said dubiously.

"Afraid the guests will get dirty?" I asked, smiling even though I knew there was a valid reason behind his professional concern.

"They will that, Princess," he acknowledged. "Perhaps more." He let that sink in for a moment before adding, "However, if you should decide to pursue the venture, I have a batch of new recruits that could use some practice in…clearing a campsite."

Pity the poor recruits, my imp responded silently to the thoughtful expression on his face.

"How much time will you need?" I asked, still watching his expression carefully.

"A full day, at least, to secure the area. And even then," he sobered, "I would escort the outing myself."

"Very well," I acquiesced to his condition, "that should surely be sufficient protection. Mistress Judith, if you would adjust the notices for the day after tomorrow, please?"

"A pleasure," she agreed, her smile still understandably dubious.

My business there concluded, I bid them adieu and left Cook scolding Major Daniels, who was sampling breakfast. It was not a whim that took me to the gardens. It was a fond memory of mornings spent with Angela. I was a little intimidated, though, to find her there with her lady in waiting.

"Lady Angela," I greeted.

Angela looked up, canted her head to the side, and dismissed her lady with a flick of her fingers.

"Majesty," Angela curtsied low.

I stopped cold. My best friend, however drastically our relationship might have changed, was addressing me by title. By a title I had *not even assumed yet.*

She maintained her position for several seconds before raising her head to look at me.

I gestured stiffly for her to rise.

"Well done," she said quietly.

I blinked. Memories flooded back to me of dozens of times in our past when I had asked her to help me practice for events that worried me. Dropping my guard, I flew forward and wrapped my arms around her.

"I miss you," I told her.

"I miss you, too," she stroked my hair gently. "It is not easy, is it?"

"To which 'it' are you referring?" I asked with a sigh. As we had done so many times, we linked arms and began strolling slowly through the garden.

"Talk to me," she instructed.

So I did. We laughed about having so many guests at the ceremony, while Hugh was only requesting three seats. I told her how hard it was to spend hours at a time doing what I ought even when I wanted to do something else.

"It seems it was good practice," she noted when I paused, "all those years of rescuing your parents."

"Practice," I nodded, "certainly makes it easier."

"And how is your new friend?" she asked.

"Cassandra? Or Helen?" I returned, laughing a little.

"Hugh," she responded seriously.

Sometimes I think she knows me better than I know myself, my imp sighed.

"He is well," I answered diplomatically. "Though sometimes it frightens me when I think of how much I have to learn."

"May I give you a little advice?" she asked hesitantly.

"I would appreciate it," I admitted.

"We both have a great deal to learn about our new roles and new best friends," she smiled a little shyly. "But I recommend not trying to learn everything at once. There are some things that our husbands may or may not be ready for us to know."

I set aside my initial reaction to that statement and hunted through my tiny storeroom of knowledge on the subject. I had still been quite young when Arabella and Gwyneth had married. Deucedly self-absorbed, too. The few other weddings I had since attended had been for fairies of no special acquaintance to me. Nevertheless, my past experiences seemed to indicate an affirmative response to Angela's remark, generally speaking. Somehow, I was not quite so ready to brush it off as typical of *all* marriages.

"Secrets, you mean?" I coaxed, unhappy with the idea.

"No, not really," she shook her head. "One simply does not tell one's entire life-story in a single sitting."

"Ah," I nodded, relieved. "That might be uncomfortable."

She laughed. "And lengthy! Even though Sean and I were friends for years before we married, things are always changing—for both of us. It takes quite a bit of talking just to keep up with what is happening now, let alone what happened fifty years ago."

I let her words settle in my mind. Once we were crowned, finding time to really talk with Hugh would only become more difficult. I could not even seem to keep up with Angela—when had she acquired a lady in waiting?

"Will you join the ceremony?" I asked her quietly. "I know it is only days away, but…"

"Rebecca," she interrupted, "of course I will."

Her use of my name calmed my fears considerably. "You knew I would ask."

"Of course," she smiled serenely.

"Will you also attend me at the royal cobbler's tomorrow?" I asked breathlessly. Mother and sisters were well and good, but I wanted Angela along as someone whose wedding slippers were still brand new.

"With pleasure," she agreed, squeezing my arm lightly.

Chapter XI

Antoinette squealed happily while I bounced her on my knees. I had volunteered to spend a few hours with her while Arabella and Jeffrey travelled to the village with Rolf and the girls. I was still a bit skeptical about how my lace-loving nieces would react to the village, let alone how Arabella would handle having lunch *inside* an ant hill. Thankfully, they had Jeffrey and Rolf with them—plus Eric, who had accidentally instigated the visit when he mentioned that he had to find a wedding gift for his sister.

"Hello, beautiful," Hugh said, grinning as he bent to kiss Antoinette's cheek. He settled himself beside me, then carefully took Antoinette when she reached for him.

"She likes you," I observed as Antoinette patted his face with her hands.

"Ouch," Hugh said, having leaned too close.

Hastily I caught Antoinette's hands before she could tug again on the fistful of hair she had captured. "Sorry, Antoinette," I shook my head at her, making her laugh, "but it is not polite to pull a boy-fairy's hair!"

Hugh laughed aloud. "That lesson is one that every girl-fairy should learn at an early age!" His tone softened as he added, "I look forward to teaching our children."

I felt my peace leave me like heat escaping a

room with an open door. It felt strange to think of having children of my own. I had always *assumed* that I would have children one day, but had never really thought it through.

"Pretty girl," Hugh told Antoinette, lifting her high above his head and laughing with her.

I smiled as he dodged a bit of drool and lowered her to a safe level again. "You will be a superb father," I told him. Leaning in a little, I kissed his cheek. Suddenly ill at ease, I rose and took a few steps away from them.

"Rebecca?" Hugh's voice followed me.

I took a deep breath and fought for control. This was a first. I found the fact that there was something I was reluctant to discuss with Hugh very disturbing. Bound to happen, of course…I tried to distract myself by mentally reciting the kings of my house's history—alphabetically.

"Princess Rebecca," Marilyn, Arabella's private maid, approached me, curtsying. "I just came for Lady Antoinette. It is time for her lunch and nap." She spoke with the polite self-assuredness of a mother of three healthy children.

"There she is, Marilyn," I looked toward where Hugh sat, still holding her.

"Ah, now, darling," Marilyn cooed as she took Antoinette, "say goodbye to Uncle Hugh." She held up Antoinette's baby fist in a mock-wave, then flew off with her.

Hugh came close, took my hand. "Fly with me," he requested.

We went past the walls of the post, past the furthest sentry. At last he stopped when we had reached the edge of the jungle-grasses. It was cool under the tall grass blades and smelled of moist earth.

I could hear grasshoppers travelling through the grasses, but they were a fair distance away. Wrapping my arms about myself against the cold I felt inside, I waited for Hugh to speak.

"Is something wrong?" he asked at last.

"I do not think so, not exactly." I sighed. "I was just thinking about some new things."

"You mean," he walked forward so that we were facing each other, "worrying about some new things?"

"Yes, I am," I searched for the right word, "concerned."

"Why?" he asked.

I smiled, appreciating his directness. It made it all seem less frightening. "I never thought about having children until just recently." I looked him in the eyes as I spoke, willing him to understand.

"I thought every woman-fairy had long lists of names she planned to argue about with her husband," Hugh said after a long, thoughtful pause.

We both laughed then, though not quite as freely as we might have yesterday. Our relationship was on a different level now. We were on the verge of a new set of rules to govern our maturing relationship.

"I suppose Erys has a few names she is fond of," I hazarded, then wished I had not.

"Oh yes," he nodded, apparently missing any hidden questions. "But I do worry about her children," he grinned.

"Why is that?" I asked, surprised.

"When she got her first doll she called it by a different name every day," he laughed.

I smiled. Taking a deep breath I told the truth, as best as I knew it. "I think…" I paused to search for the words, "that I shall always envy Erys her time with you."

Hugh did not respond at once. "Are you jealous of her?" he asked, no doubt remembering a night at a ball not so long ago.

I shook my head, then held out my hand. When my fingers were clasped safely in his I said, "You and I belong to each other, and that is how we want it. But," I lifted my free hand and pressed the palm of it to his cheek, "she was your friend before I even knew you existed. She has known you for years while I have only known you for two seasons. I envy her those years."

Hugh put his free right hand on the small of my back and raised his left hand so that we were in a formal dancing pose. "Do you remember our first dance?" He stepped back with his left foot, drawing me effortlessly with him. For several seconds we danced to the sweet, silent music of memories. He spun me out, but stepped forward before I was quite spun back, capturing me with both arms so that my back was pressed to his chest. "I promise we shall have years of friendship and more," he whispered into my hair.

I blushed warmly. "You have already promised me that," I admitted, "when you married me the first time. Forgive me?"

"For what?" he asked, surprise in his tone.

"I…am out of practice." I folded my arms over his. "It has been a long time since I have made a new best friend." I turned so that I could see his face out of the corner of my eye. When he loosened his hold, I turned further and we shared a knee-weakening kiss.

"Would you tell me," he hesitated, "if you needed to cry?"

"Are you sure you would want to know?" I asked with genuine curiosity.

He kissed my face. "I hope in time to know you so well that I will know you are going to cry before you do."

I rested my head against his chest. "Thank you for being willing to let me cry," I said at last.

With a sigh he released me. "We should go," he told me. "Cial Mar will be ready for the interview."

I gave in to the urge to make a face. "Jorge interviewed me pretty thoroughly, I thought."

Hugh grinned. "This will be a very different kind of interview," he assured me.

"And if I pass it?" I asked, curiously. I had heard of similar traditions during my cultures class, but had no doubt that the troupe fairies would have their very own way of going about it.

"Laughter and the other women-fairies will present you with gifts to welcome you to the family," he said, lifting off.

I bit my tongue to keep from wondering aloud what they could give me that I did not already have. Instead I followed him for a moment before asking, "And the men-fairies?"

"They will present me with an instrument, probably a dulcimer, to be used on special occasions."

"Do you play a dulcimer?" I asked, surprised to realize we had never really discussed music.

"It has been a few years," he answered, shrugging.

"I love the sound of a dulcimer," I thought aloud.

"In that case," Hugh put an arm about my waist, "I shall have to practice." We smiled the rest of the way to the west side of the guest pavilions.

When I saw the group assembled, waiting for us, I instantly felt out of place. My comfortable brown outfit—made of unbleached bark cloth—seemed inherently dignified when compared with the variety of colors and fabrics they were wearing. However, their somber air more than compensated for the giddiness of their clothing.

"Cial Mar," Hugh greeted him with a formal bow.

"Prince Hugh," Cial returned the bow with equal formality.

I somehow managed a curtsy despite the mind-numbing apprehension that was flooding through me.

"Princess Rebecca," Cial smiled and offered his arm to me.

I took it automatically, relieved to have at least one useful reflex under the circumstances. I sent my imp to slam the door on my growing anxiety, oddly grateful for her company as Cial led me away from the others. When the tent flap closed behind us, I jumped at the sound of someone striking a drum.

"It is alright," Cial soothed me as he indicated a chair. "Merely the beginning of our celebration."

"You begin your celebration before the interview is concluded?" I asked once I was seated.

Cial Mar shrugged eloquently. "Your marriage is in place," he pointed out. "This interview, like your royal wedding, is no more than a formality."

Then why does my stomach feel like jelly and my limbs like wood? muttered my imp unhappily.

"Are you surprised," he began, "to find that Hugh's wedding guests are troupe fairies?"

Slightly more subtle than Jorge, but have I not already been asked this question? my imp asked in surprise.

"Pleasantly so," I acknowledged. "I was

surprised that I had not anticipated it."

"So you admit that you do not know Hugh as well as you should?" he jabbed again.

I blinked. "I do not know him as well as I shall," I corrected carefully.

He tapped his mouth with the first finger of his right hand before asking, "Do you expect Hugh to change from the man-fairy that he is into a die-cut courtier?"

"Perish the thought!" I answered without thinking. Blushing hotly, I added, "I have never wished for Hugh to be less than he is."

Steady, my imp advised.

"Then you actually think he is fit to be king of the entire Silver Fairy Tribe? Hugh Lawson, a half-breed?" There was disbelief in Cial's tone.

I suddenly relaxed. Had I not seen the senior himself use this tactic with a young guardsman once?

"I love Hugh Lawson," I stated composedly. "His decision to act in the capacity of king may have been influenced by his feelings for me—but rather than detracting from his qualifications, I expect his lineage and upbringing to be strong points in his favor." Finally at ease, I inhaled deeply, enjoying the scent of cedar that permeated the tent.

Cial held perfectly still for several seconds, watching me closely. "You are wise for your years," he said at last.

'Tis best to neither accept—nor reject—a dubious

compliment, my imp quoted Miss Patricia.

"I had wise teachers," I answered demurely.

He smiled. "There will be many tests in your future," he predicted.

"More so as queen than as princess," I agreed. I waited patiently for his next move— and it took me completely by surprise.

"I have something for you." Rising, he retrieved a small, polished box from the carved chest at the foot of his bed.

I noted that he carried it with both hands though it seemed unlikely that it could tax the vast physical strength I sensed in him. I treated it with equal care when he handed it to me.

"Open it," he said, handing me the key he had taken from around his neck.

The tent, the box, and Cial Mar himself all smelled of cedar. Carefully I used the antique key to open the box. I lifted the lid. Stunned, I just stared at the amulet inside.

"When the Princess Alicia handed her infant son to her Lady Abigail for safe keeping," Cial Mar said quietly, "she also gave her this box. In it were her favorite pieces of jewelry, all hand-picked to accompany her to the Silver Fairy kingdom."

I forced myself to look away from the amulet, to look up at Cial Mar.

"Abigail gave it to me, in turn, when she married my brother and joined this troupe. Over the years most of the pieces were sold, discreetly, when we needed food more than gold. Somehow," he sighed, "I could never bring myself to sell that amulet. When I heard that Hugh was to wed, I knew that I had been saving it—for his bride."

"I have never seen a more exquisite piece of jewelry in my life," I said sincerely. Then an idea struck me. "Does Hugh know you have this?"

Cial shook his head. "The lad never asked."

"I am sure he would be pleased to know that you have done so much good for so long with it," I stated confidently.

He blinked, a little water in his old brown eyes. "I shall send him to you." With that, Cial ducked under the flap.

Left alone in the tent, I closed the box and looked around. Most of the things in the one-room dwelling were like Cial, old but beautifully maintained. A tiny closet area contained a few changes of clothing and a mended leather bag occupied the center of a small walnut table.

"Rebecca?" Hugh entered the tent, the flap brushing his hair and standing it on end.

I smiled. "I think I passed," I told him.

"I knew you would," he smiled back.

"I want to show you something," I said, beckoning for him to come closer. When he was standing beside me, I opened the box once more. "This belonged to your mother." I gladly handed him the box when he reached for it. I also gave him several seconds of complete silence—inside the tent anyway. The celebration outside continued as though the guests of honor (which is what I imagined Hugh and I were intended to be) were out there enjoying it.

"It is lovely," he said, sounding understandably emotional.

"Put it on me?" I requested. I was pleased when his face lit up. I held my braid out of the way as he carefully fastened his mother's amulet about my neck. "What do you think?" I asked, feeling suddenly shy as I turned back to face him.

"It suits you," was all he could say.

"Someday I shall tell you its story," I promised him.

"Past or future?" he teased, leaning closer.

"We should join the others," I reminded him sensibly. I kissed him back anyway.

I was glad Hugh was there for the celebration, for it all seemed quite unusual to me. Of course, that was probably because none of my previous acquaintances could do a double backflip or bend themselves into unusual shapes. Jorge proved himself to be quite a talented juggler for one so young. I even learned from Laughter, his mother, why he did not have a verb for a name.

"He has not yet chosen his talent," she told me seriously. "Never have I seen such a gifted trouper! One day, when he is grown and has chosen his talent, he will be given a trouper name like the rest of us."

The food was simple and good. Meat with

herbs, wrapped in succulent leaves then roasted in the cook fire. Bread rolls the sizes of hummingbird eggs were then cut open and stuffed with the hot meat. Fragrant cheeses were added before the rolls were passed around. The music died down as the troupers seated themselves on the ground and began enjoying their repast.

I watched Hugh bite into his with gusto before I took a timid bite of my own. To my great relief, the cheese tasted much better than it smelled. It was certainly unfamiliar to me, but quite good.

"Hugh," I asked quietly, "we were planning to have robin dumplings for dinner. Do you think they will mind having such a similar dish?"

Hugh chuckled. "Not at all," he grinned. "And I gave Cook a recipe for the dessert tonight, so you are in for a surprise."

"Another surprise?" I responded, my eyebrows raised questioningly. When he just winked mischievously I took another bite of my lunch and ignored him. Besides not wanting to give him the satisfaction of a pointed question, I was uncomfortably aware of how closely Jorge was watching us. It was hard to think over the enthusiastic music, but I did decide that Jorge was probably not watching to see if I wiped my mouth on my sleeves. In fact, the only thing that made sense was that he was watching to see if I was really eating—or just pretending to. I somehow doubted that anything less than asking for seconds would satisfy him.

"More?" Twister asked cheerfully, appearing before me with a tray loaded with food.

Holding up my nearly-finished roll I shook my head, "I am not sure I can finish all of this, even!" I inhaled deeply, regretfully. There were so many tantalizing new smells on that one tray! "I wish I could," I told her sincerely.

Twister smiled and winked at me. "Better to do one job well than half a dozen poorly," she assured me before fluttering away.

Surprised, I smiled in relief. Giving offense to Hugh's family was the last thing I wanted to do! "Hugh," I asked tentatively, "do you think they would enjoy going berry picking?"

"Possibly. But they would make a day of it." He lowered his voice as though imparting a confidence. "There might even be a berry fight."

"Sounds like marvelous fun," I smiled. I had to stifle a yawn next, even though it was barely lunchtime. "Sorry," I apologized to him. "After a lunch like this, I could happily curl up for a nap."

"And miss your appointment with the royal cobbler?" he asked, pretending to be shocked.

I understood him at once and blushed. Slippers were the final (and some argued the most important) detail of my wedding garb. I smiled as Hugh kissed my hand. "On second thought, I can stay awake a little longer. Alas, I must go or I shall be late."

"It must be hard to get an appointment with him right now, when he is so busy making slippers for the weddings," Hugh teased.

"I made this appointment over a week ago," I agreed before I realized that he was joking. We laughed together, then I slipped Hugh the last few bites of my roll.

"Only a moment more," he pressed my hand to keep me in my seat. At his gesture, the women-fairies left the fire and came to where we sat.

"Come," Twister held out her hand to me.

My stomach flipped and twisted like a troupe fairy as I put my hand in hers. Lunch protested violently but I forced it to stay down. Following them to the women-fairies' tent, I ducked under a tent flap and took the seat that was indicated. I was both surprised and happy to find Abigail waiting inside the tent.

"Welcome," she greeted, holding out both of her hands to me. With gentle graciousness she guided me to a chair and seated herself beside me, retaining her hold on one of my hands.

Laughter waited in the center of the small space until all of the women-fairies were seated. From somewhere—the inside of a sleeve, perhaps?—she drew out a pure white kerchief. Expertly she held it up by two corners, tossed it in the air, caught it and swirled it about, creating a mesmerizing show with naught but a bit of white spider-silk. She moved as she swirled it, her graceful gestures carrying her around the circle of women-fairies. At each chair she paused an instant, holding out the kerchief as though to receive something from that fairy.

I watched closely, but even with my years of attending festivals and Hugh's attempts at teaching me simple sleight of hand, I never saw anything leave the hands that were waved over the whirling kerchief. When Laughter stopped before me, I gasped in surprise. The ostensibly empty kerchief held several delicate fabric swatches! Each swatch had writing on it.

"One fairy can only have so many things," Laughter observed quietly, still holding the kerchief. "And we tried for days to think of a gift for our new sister and queen. We have few material possessions, but we realized that one can never have too many friends." Folding the kerchief carefully, she presented it to me, her hand settling lightly on top of mine as I accepted it. "As a gesture of friendship, we have each written down a secret for you. Guard them well and you have our friendship forever."

Humbled by the thoughtful gift, I stared at the kerchief then at Laughter. What response could I possibly make to their overwhelming trust?

If being queen involves always knowing the right thing to say, my imp commented, *it surely also entails not saying things one does not mean.*

"I have seen sleight of hand before," I said

slowly. "Hugh has even been trying to teach me a little…" I paused and took a deep breath before finishing, "But I have never seen any magician make such delicate material so weighty." I was relieved to see some of the faces relaxing. "Thank you. In token of our new friendship, I shall carry this kerchief in the royal ceremony."

"A fitting use," Abigail spoke, quietly but with authority, "for the kerchief used by Hugh's mother at her first wedding ceremony."

I thought I detected tears in her eyes when they met mine. I rose with her and we embraced. I felt quite shy when I realized that the others had risen as well. I felt their strength as they each hugged me in turn, Laughter being the last to whisper her well-wishing before it was time to go.

"Abigail," I paused at the tent flap. "Will you attend me at the cobbler's?" I thought the other ladies looked pleased at my request.

Abigail came forward, slipping her arm through mine. "A pleasure, Rebecca," she said.

I blinked a little against the sunlight as we exited the tent. It was the perfect way to hide my overflowing emotions. I shook my head at Hugh when he pretended that he was going to get up and come along—but I smiled, too.

"I am glad you are here, Abigail," I said honestly. It seemed a little strange to me that I could be so happy to have so many different fairies involved in my life (certainly it was a great change from my quiet life of less than a year ago).

Yet how could I not be happy to have their kind interest? I listened as Abigail spoke of our first meeting, months ago, in a tiny cell.

"The first time I met you, I thought you were either very foolish or very brave," she said frankly.

"I was both," I laughed, determined not to take offense. "I was beginning to think I would never be rescued. Then you came."

"Scamp sent me," she confessed. "He knew that Bullierd suspected him and would never have let him near you."

The hairs on the back of my neck rose at the mere mention of Bullierd's name. He had never questioned me himself, but just the idea that he might have still terrified me. A stranger asking harsh questions, making threats even, was a small thing compared to having a 'friend of the family' looming over you...

"If not for your father, Scamp probably would have tried to rescue you single-handed," she added soberly.

That is a far cry from what you told me that day, my imp thought sulkily.

"I am glad we are friends now," I said, summing up the dozen or more thoughts vying for expression.

Using an old barb on a new friend is worse than foolish, my imp admitted grudgingly.

I changed the subject after that. Just to be safe. "We are going berry-picking tomorrow," I told her. "I hope you will come."

"We?" she asked, raising her eyebrows quizzically.

"Several of the guests and I," I answered smoothly, "to supply berries for the wedding ceremony's dessert."

"What a charming idea," she said with the dry tone of one who has picked berries in earnest.

I had to laugh. "I grant that there will be some idling and messing about, but surely with a large enough group we will reach the goal."

"Rebecca," Abigail hesitated. "You are expecting seven *hundred* guests. That is a lot of berries. Have you a good patch in mind?"

I nodded. "Major Daniels located the original patches that served the post in my great-grandfather's day," I told her.

"I see," she frowned. "A vast undertaking." She would say no more, though she wore a thoughtful expression the rest of the way to the cobbler's. We found him hunched over his makeshift workbench when we arrived.

The cobbler had travelled from Castlemain for the occasion, but occupied his apartment as comfortably as though he had always been there. Pieces of tanned leather fell off his apron as he rose to greet us, hastily setting aside what he had been working on.

"Highness," he bowed awkwardly. "Madam," he added a bow to Abigail for good measure. His genial smile faded a little when the rest of the group—Mother, my sisters, and Angela—arrived. Gulping visibly, he bowed once more.

Mother, the queen of his youth, calmed him with a dazzling smile. "Aaron," she addressed him with the sweet tone of a woman-fairy who actually remembers the last time she saw you, "thank you so much for agreeing to make the slippers for all three brides."

"To be sure, Majesty," he said, fiddling with a tool on his belt, "'tis an honor." The tool in his hand seemed to remind him why we were all there, for he got down to business. "Highness," he held out his hand to me, guided me over to the one mostly clean chair in the room. Kneeling, he accepted my feet one at a time and carefully removed the boots he had made for me two years ago. Rising, he inspected them critically. "How are they wearing, Highness?"

I anticipated most of his questions, having been a patron of his since my childhood. As always, his creations were practically perfect. They never pinched, and he knew to use thicker leather under the ball of my foot so that the whole sole would wear more or less evenly. Even with the familiarity of the scene, though, I found myself filled with apprehension to the point that I hid my hands under the kerchief.

At last, apparently satisfied that I was satisfied, he set my boots aside. "Of course," he reached for the cloth that he had draped over his project when we entered, "wedding slippers are completely different from riding boots.”

I blushed then forgot my discomfort when he revealed what was under the cloth. “Oh,” I breathed.

“I have only made a few of these,” he warned as he brought them over and knelt again.

And never for me, sighed my imp, recognizing the quality of the workmanship in the delicate slippers. We shivered as the cool eggshell slid onto our foot.

“How does it feel?” Aaron asked anxiously. He held them firmly in place while I flexed my feet and moved my toes.

Cold…stiff…breakable! my imp was horrified. *Why must it be eggshell? White leather is very beautiful, especially when worked by a master craftsman like Aaron.*

I frantically searched for something concrete and not too objectionable to say.

“How do you like the lining, Highness?” Abigail asked before the silence grew to monstrous proportions.

“I…do not detect a lining,” I said, clenching hidden fingers to keep from clenching my teeth.

Aaron’s brow furrowed comically and he removed one of the slippers. “Ah, forgive me, Highness,” he flitted across the room with the slipper in his hands. He muttered as he rummaged through a bag that hung from a wooden peg.

I watched hopefully as he turned away from the bag, holding the slipper in one hand and two pure white objects in his other hand. I gave him my stockinged right foot again, with very different results. Knowing that Aaron and the others were watching me in anticipation, I let my relief show in the form of a smile.

"It feels like a cloud," I said happily. It would still be nearly impossible to walk without breaking them, but thankfully tradition dictated that the bride and groom fly to the ceremony. The slippers' import lay almost entirely in their role between the bride and groom.

Aaron sighed in relief. "There is some polishing to do still," he said as he removed them, "but they will be ready the day before the ceremony." He was still beaming when he smoothed the hem of my gown back down over the tops of my boots.

"Thank you," I kept smiling as he helped me rise. "For my slippers, as well as the others." I left then, with the others in tow. My last glimpse of Aaron, bustling happily about his workroom, revitalized my smile.

Other women-fairies, mostly single, drifted in to join the group after we had put some distance between us and the cobbler's shop.

"Well done," murmured Abigail.

"Thanks for the rescue," I murmured back, linking my arm through hers. "Those linings are amazing!" I added in a tone loud enough for most of them to hear.

Everyone from the original party immediately

began discussing their experiences with wedding slippers. Mother just smiled serenely and took my other arm.

Angela winked at me surreptitiously and we just let their words flow around us. Eventually Angela asked me about the wedding meal, causing the others to still themselves so they could hear my answer.

"Oh, I cannot divulge the exact menu, but I am very excited about the dessert. Cook is planning a simply delectable berry tart. Best of all," I leaned closer to her and pretended to lower my voice, "I look forward to participating in tomorrow's berry picking outing."

There was a subdued flurry of energetic responses to my hint. It seemed that they all wanted to come, too.

"What time will you leave?" Angela asked curiously, as though she had not already read the notices.

"Immediately after an early breakfast," I announced cheerfully. "Though I am sure the picking will go on all day," I added to soothe the chorus of surprised and disappointed exclamations.

We stopped then under an awning on the south lawn, where we could watch Master Collins' crew putting the final touches on the foundations. The wedding guests would begin flooding in tonight and tomorrow.

"Mother," I asked, nodding and waving

goodbye to the women-fairies who were leaving now that they had some news, "do you suppose we shall have enough for so many guests?"

She squeezed my hand gently. "We have additional help coming from Castlemain," she reminded me, "as well as the servants that the guests themselves will bring."

"Hm, plenty of hands," I agreed, "and hundreds of new mouths to feed."

"You have done very well as the hostess this year," Mother complimented me. "But I think you should let me take over now." She smoothed a strand of loose hair back behind my ear, cupped my cheek in her hand. "You have other, more pressing, worries."

I decided I could speak openly before Angela and Abigail, the other women-fairies having dispersed. "I have had a great deal of help to date," I began. "And I thank you for your offer. But if I am left with no duties, I shall not know what to do with myself."

"Then let us share the duties," Mother compromised easily. "Permit me to worry about feeding everyone and entertaining them," she put one arm around my shoulder in a motherly hug, "and I shall be very glad to let you worry about how to divide the pavilions."

I made a face. I could not help it! We all laughed together, even Abigail, who had spent enough time in royal courts to know that tensions run high at times like this.

"It is decided, then!" Mother said, still laughing. Kissing my cheek, she continued, "Now, I had best go have a talk with Cook and Mistress Judith."

I reached up to remove a stray tear from her cheek. "There," I felt a tear of my own starting, "now you are presentable."

Chapter XII

"Lovely day for picking," Laughter sighed and dabbed at her forehead.

I smiled. That was the closest she had come to complaining all morning. It was almost lunchtime now and we had been picking for hours.

"We will stop to rest soon," I promised, setting my basket in the cart. "I may have a nap after lunch!" I laughed.

"Oh," Angela protested, rubbing her arms wearily, "you would not dare! We have better than half of the wedding guests still to place before this evening."

I groaned. I had been looking forward to the berry picking partly because I had not expected to spend it playing mind games. Some of the planning was simple—we had invited the Rourke's and the Cavannas. They did not get along, so placing them far away from each other was an obvious solution. Problem solved—now do it again, about a hundred times. Most of the three hundred additional guests coming to attend the wedding were amiable fairy folk who got along well with others, but the exceptions were outstanding.

"The Riley's," Angela prompted, holding out an empty berry basket.

"The Riley's," I sighed and headed for the

nearest bush. "And the Watson's. If we put the Thompson's between them…"

"Bird!" shouted Laughter.

Dropping my empty basket, I caught Angela's arm and pulled her deep into the bushes.

Ow! my imp whimpered as the thorns jabbed us. I focused on listening to the others. There were at least four dozen fairies at the patch right now. Was I hearing enough noise to account for all of them?

"Bring up the pebble-thrower!" Major Daniels' voice cut through the commotion.

"Primed and ready, sir!" came another shout from a guardsman I could not see.

"Take your shot, Grafton," Daniels barked.

From the sound of the report the small cannon must have been very close. A loud squawk followed it almost immediately and a flash of gorgeous blue streaked past the bushes.

"A tree swallow," I murmured, recognizing the blue and black color combination. "She must have been attracted by all the horsefly and dragonfly traffic."

Not that she would be averse to eating a fairy for dessert, my imp grimly recalled a tragedy involving a merchant windship a few years ago.

"Reload! Hurry!" Daniels' order rang through the now-silent patch.

"Major, permission to use our crossbows!" called another voice.

"She would never even notice," Daniels

responded sharply.

"Primed and ready, Major!" shouted a voice I identified as Grafton's.

"At your pleasure," Daniels called back. "Drive it away!"

"Rebecca," Angela murmured, her voice trembling.

"Hush," I put my hands over her shaking ones. "Even the birds do not dare the inner thorns," I reminded her. The pebble-thrower roared again, and again.

"Fine shooting, Grafton," Major Daniels voice sang out. "Prime it and stand steady. She has gone. Guardsmen, to the bushes."

I kept holding Angela while we waited for someone to open the bushes for us.

"Rebecca, your face!" she whispered.

When I shrugged carelessly, the sharp thorns made a lasting impression on me. Gritting my teeth, I regretted not listening to Miss Patricia's advice against such casual gestures.

"I still have some of Helen's potion," I assured Angela as cheerfully as I could. It had worked wonders on my lower lip, healing it almost overnight.

"You need a lifetime supply of that," Angela sighed.

I laughed aloud at that.

"Highness," Major Daniels' gloved hands parted the bushes. "You are alright," he said in relief.

"Of course, thanks to Laughter's warning," I smiled, amused at how silly it sounded, and gently pushed Angela out through the opening. I followed as soon as she was free.

"A little worse for the wear though, eh?" Major Daniels removed his gloves and used his clean kerchief to staunch the trickle of blood from my cheek. "You should have this tended to at once," he informed me quietly.

"Back at the post, you mean," I took over holding the kerchief in place and shook my head. "Send a messenger to the post, to fetch the doctor."

"May as well bring a wagon load of full pails out here," Laughter said from behind me.

I watched in confusion as she handed Major Daniels her pail and came closer.

"By your leave?" she reached up and lifted my hand away from the cut so she could inspect it. "Not too bad, that." Casually she reached into a pouch on her belt and withdrew a pinch of powder.

"Indeed." I winced as she dabbed it on, but the sting only lasted a moment. When I noticed that Angela's mouth was hanging open I wondered if my cheek had healed already.

Laughter caught my hand as I reached up. "No touching," she warned. "Come to my tent after dinner tonight and I will put a sleeping powder on it. You can sleep in it without it getting all over your bedclothes." She kept a straight face as she handed me her canteen, "And drink plenty of water. It will help."

Obediently I took a sip. "I am glad you were here," I smiled at her. I meant it, too, even if her humor was a bit odd. Bringing berries to a berry patch *was* rather like sending for a doctor when a healer was already present, I supposed.

"As am I," Major Daniels flitted forward. "I have never seen such results," he admitted after studying my face for a moment. "May I ask what that powder is made of?"

"If you two are going to discuss medicine," I handed the canteen back to Laughter with a smile, "I am going to resume picking berries. We still have a lot of guests to arrange."

Angela zipped down after the buckets we had dropped.

"But your back," Laughter protested mildly. "I saw it when I came out of the bushes…" Her voice trailed off uncertainly.

I could neither smile nor shrug comfortably so I just hesitated. All around me my guests were being attended by guardsmen, by each other, just generally being patched up—physically. I could hear one or two of the younger ones whimpering as the soldier-strength medication was clumsily applied to their thorn pricks.

"It is not just about picking a sufficient number of berries," I explained slowly. "I must demonstrate that there is no longer reason to be afraid."

Laughter canted her head to one side, studying my face intently. "You believe in leading by example, then."

"Where possible," I nodded.

"Stay near the others," Major Daniels cautioned unhappily.

"Of course," I agreed without reluctance. I felt a little self-conscious as I left Major Daniels and Laughter to join Angela. I was torn between smiling confidently and trying not to look arrogant. Finally I settled on just being calm.

"Ready?" Angela asked, pretending to ignore her mussed hair and ripped sleeve.

"Not quite," I answered, surprising her. "Let me fix that for you." With practiced fingers I smoothed her hair and replaced the loose pins. It took a lot of effort to ignore the stinging sensations rippling along my back, but it was for a good cause. Then I held still while she completed the same service for me.

"You have a fair number of thorn pricks on your back," she advised me quietly.

"I know," I smiled as though we were having a normal conversation. "Perhaps after lunch we can make a brief retreat to the post?"

"You should have told Laughter," Angela admonished me. "If these are not tended promptly…"

"They shall take longer to heal than if they were," I interrupted. "I must first pick a pail of berries. We both know the others are watching us."

Resignedly she took up her pail and handed me mine. "At least these berries are larger than the domestic variety," she consoled herself aloud.

I stubbornly selected a place that had been skimmed over by inexperienced pickers. Delving carefully into the thornier reaches, I began filling my pail with the berries they had missed. I was only half finished when I heard a rustle on my left. Turning to look, I smiled at Laughter. I was quite relieved when the others, seeing that we were proceeding unharmed, took up their pails and their courage. We were a subdued bunch, to be sure, but that was only a matter of time.

"I think I know how to resolve the other conflicts," I told Angela. "I was thinking about it while we were hiding and it all suddenly became very clear." I smiled when she laughed aloud. Angela's laugh is one of the more infectious adult-fairy laughs I have ever heard.

"We were in a thorn bush, hiding from a bird, and you were thinking about wedding arrangements?" she gasped between laughs.

Laughter joined in, though I privately thought her laugh sounded a bit too professional to be real.

As I had hoped, the others began whispering. I even heard a few incredulous laughs. Slowly but surely, the noise level began to rise as they resumed talking. Once my own voice would be reasonably covered by the general conversing, I resumed discussing the guest arrangements in detail. By the time lunch arrived, we had it all mapped out. I even used some berry juice to scratch out the more critical points on the hem of my underskirt. I did not look forward to explaining *that* to Megan!

"Hello," Hugh's voice said from my elbow.

"Oh!" I jumped, rattling the berries in my pail. "That is not funny!"

"Neither is your back," he said firmly. "Let me have that," he took my pail, "and I want you to go sit in the shade for a few minutes, alright?"

"Hugh, there is so much work to be done," I protested. I stopped protesting when he frowned at me. "Very well," I added breathlessly.

Sean appeared by Angela then, relieving her of her pail without a word.

"Make sure she holds *still*," Hugh issued his order to me via an instruction to Angela.

"Yes, Majesty," Angela curtsied mid-air, then took me firmly by my good arm. "Quietly," she admonished me when I opened my mouth, "or the others will hear you."

Defeated, I did as I was told. The shade did feel good after hours of working in steadily increasing heat. Also, my puncture wounds were itching and burning.

"Have you not done enough?" Angela asked me seriously as she situated me on the legless picnic chair so that I could lean back without putting too much pressure on my injuries. "You worked the entire morning, while other fairies have come and gone."

"I know," I agreed, watching Hugh and Sean rapidly filling our pails. The newest cartload of pickers also included Helen, Cassandra, Edward, and Alfred. "I guess the reinforcements have arrived," I allowed, stretching my legs out on the cool grass.

"There are many other things you could be doing," she pointed out.

When she tried to use her fan to cool me, I responded by fanning her with mine. We laughed together and I relented. "Very well. I shall enjoy sitting after a morning of hovering and standing."

"Well done," Hugh interrupted our conversation and smiled at Angela, then offered her his hand. Helping her up, he looked in the direction of another blanket. "I believe Sean is waiting for you."

I watched in amazement as Angela demurely curtsied and left. Once she was out of hearing I remarked, "I would have thought it would take a team of horseflies to make her leave me like this."

"Like what?" Hugh asked, dropping to his knees beside the chair. "Are your injuries so very bad?" He lifted aside a piece of my torn sleeve, frowning darkly at what he saw.

"No of course not," I put my hand on his chin, forcing him to look me in the eyes. "It is nothing a little salve will not cure."

He kissed the palm that I had pressed to his chin. "You must take care of yourself," he told me firmly. "I am only one fairy, being asked to assume responsibility for the life and well-being of thousands." His jaw tightened and he went on, "I cannot seem to think of anything but you right now."

I felt a shock of understanding. I was not accustomed to having *that* kind of worry expended on me. Even my dear parents had eventually learned that scrapes heal.

"Alright," I agreed meekly. "When the lunch is over and the carts leave, I will be on one with Angela." I saw a spark of emotion in his eyes before his mask dropped at the sound of someone approaching.

"Highnesses," said a young boy-fairy, approaching with a tray of food. "Shall I serve your lunch now?"

"I will serve it," Hugh took it from him. "Go on," he added with a friendly smile when the lad hesitated, "plenty of others to tend to."

"You are rather wonderful," I told Hugh after the lad had zipped away. As usual, he gave me more than I could have possibly eaten and I laughed when he handed me the plate. "You must think I am too thin," I teased and took a bite of the boiled thip salad. "I shall have to compliment Helen. She is making a marvelous contribution to Cook's store of recipes."

"I will tell her for you," Hugh promised, lying on his stomach with the plate on the blanket before him.

"How can you eat like that?" I asked without thinking. The curiosity in my tone saved the remark from being mistaken as criticism, but I blushed when I heard what I had said.

"Simple." Leaning on both of his elbows and moving just his forearm, he loaded his fork with the salad and put it in his mouth.

"Very funny," I took another bite of the salad myself. "Promise me you will never do that on carpet," I added, half-seriously. It did not take much imagination to picture dressing smeared into lush fibers.

"I promise," Hugh grinned up at me, "if you will promise to let me eat in bed. Occasionally."

Startled, I blinked. *Is he serious?* my imp was not sure.

"Sometimes I have trouble sleeping," he explained, the mischief fading out of his eyes and leaving an uncertain expression in its place.

"Oh," I took a bite of the cold roast robin. It took no imagination at all to picture food stains on silk sheets. I had first-hand experience with that. I began to squirm a little under his unflinching gaze. Finally, I set my fork down and leaned closer. "Under one circumstance," I said softly. "You must not tell anyone that I eat in bed, too."

"Your secrets are safe with me," he promised. He munched happily on a carrot stick then asked, "I wonder how many more secrets we have in common?"

Reaching out, I smoothed his hair, enjoying the feel of it tickling my fingers. I wondered, too. It was certainly easier when we agreed.

We did not say much after that. We ate slowly, almost lingering over our food in an effort to prolong our time together. At the sound of Hugh's fork scraping the plate, I sighed. It was time to go.

"It is not wise to work on a full stomach," I reminded him as he took my plate. I gasped in surprise when he bent and picked me up like a child, setting me on my feet. Despite his best efforts to avoid my injuries, my back began smarting again so that it was a few heartbeats before I lifted my face from where I had hidden it against his chest. "Thank you," I whispered. I had been worried about how I was going to stand up.

"Laughter is going with you," he told me, leaving our dishes to escort me to the wagon. "I know you have a physician," he began trying to explain.

"Thank you," I said again. "It is obvious that she has a great deal of experience with this sort of thing."

"Every troupe has an unofficial doctor," he nodded. "Laughter has patched up more fairies than a sailor has canvas."

I let him seat me carefully on the end of a wagon that was mostly filled with berry pails. Angela and Laughter flew up to join me, but we had the wagon to ourselves. Most of the other fairies that had decided to return to the post were arranging themselves in one of the empty wagons that had brought lunch. Sean saluted me, then flew toward the front of the wagon. I assumed he meant to have a word with the driver, probably to warn him to be mindful of the ladies he carried as passengers. Smiling as though I did not feel full and tired, I waved goodbye to Hugh.

"Laughter," I turned to her, "thank you for coming back with me. I appreciate your help."

"Of course," she nodded graciously.

"Would you mind very much tending me in my chambers?" I asked hopefully. "Angela and I have so much to do before dinner…" I paused when she began to frown.

"You should not overexert yourself," she admonished me. "I do not suppose you often spend a morning out in the heat."

"It has been a while," I agreed, thinking wistfully of past camping trips and survival classes, "but do not worry. Most of what we need to do can be done while sitting down."

"I will even do the writing," Angela promised.

Laughter looked back and forth between us, her expression making me think that she was pondering something. "I suppose sitting will not be too exhausting for you," she said tartly.

My imp sighed. *I have no energy for a rebuttal,* she told me, *but I can tell you do not want one anyway.*

At the end of the short, silent ride we parted ways. Laughter went to her tent to pick up her medical things. I shooed Angela off to her chambers, then hurried to mine and bravely faced Megan.

"What happened to you?" she exclaimed. "You look like a flock of birds got their hooks into you!"

"Oh no," I answered cheerfully. "It was only one bird, and Major Daniels' squad drove it off without too much trouble." My ruined dress and underskirt instantly faded into insignificance. I described it for her while she soaked the back of my dress bodice off me. It helped me hang onto my self-control. Then there came simultaneously knocks on my sitting room window and the main door to my chambers.

"Oh," Megan looked up in consternation. "Now what?" Wisely she chose to open the window first, as that fairy would have to be hovering. "Angela," I heard her say happily, "come in! She is in her room."

Angela came in and took up the job where Megan had left off. "There now," she said when she had peeled off the last of my blood-stained bodice, "does that feel better?"

"May I come in?" Laughter asked from the doorway.

Feeling idiotic in my thankfully modest slip, I beckoned to her. "I must look a sight," I apologized.

"How do you feel?" she returned, clutching a soft leather bag and looking uncomfortable.

"Foolish," I answered immediately. As I had hoped, her gaze turned from the vanity table with its assortment of dainty-looking hair ornaments to me.

"I have no tonic for foolishness," she said in a business-like tone, "but surely I can do something for those pricks." Setting her bag on the bed beside where I was sitting, she opened it to reveal an impressive array of instruments and bottles. "The first thing I must do is make sure that you have no thorn tips inside you."

I understood. I hated the idea, but I definitely understood. "Go ahead," I consented. I focused on Angela, who was focusing on the wedding arrangements. I went through every motion with her as she spread my worksheet-underskirt on the vanity and sent Megan for writing materials. She started at the top of the skirt. That would be—I winced as Laughter's instrument probed the first prick—Admiral Ryland. In my mind's eye, I reviewed the placing of the guests in the pavilion area. It struck me (at about the same time that Laughter reached for a pair of tiny, long-nosed pliers) that we could use the exact same placements for the seating arrangements at the wedding ceremony.

Laughter found another tip, then set her probe aside. When she asked for water, Megan was quick to provide it. "The pricks on your arms are not deep enough to hide a thorn tip," she informed me. She silently mixed one of her powders into a paste. "There will be a slight sting," she advised me. She used a piece of soft cloth, liberally coated with some of the paste, as an applicator, setting it on a prick then removing it.

I counted. Thirteen pricks and only two thorn tips. It could have been much worse. When she set a larger piece of cloth on my back, I suggested, "I would appreciate it if you would tend to Angela's arms, also. Megan can fasten that cloth down."

Laughter did not hesitate to take up a clean square of cloth and move over to where a rather pale Angela was sitting. "You do not look like you are feeling well," Laughter observed.

"I always look this way when Rebecca is being treated," Angela jested.

I was pleased to see Laughter's face soften. I had given just enough medical aid in my lifetime to know that it could be equally as taxing for the physician as the patient.

"Do your cuffs unbutton?" Laughter asked, setting her jar of paste and clean cloth on the table. Gently she undid the cuffs so that she could roll the sleeves out of the way. "I am glad you wore a loose-sleeved shirt."

I frowned when I saw that Angela had not bothered to do more than rinse the blood off her arms and change before coming to my chambers.

That explained how she had gotten here almost before Laughter did.

"Hmm, you were lucky. This will only take a moment," Laughter said reassuringly.

"Rebecca went in first," Angela said, her eyes fixed on Laughter's deft fingers. "She is always doing things like that."

I shifted uncomfortably, then apologized to a worried Megan, "No, you are doing fine."

"You often find yourselves hiding in berry bushes?" teased Laughter as she smeared paste on the new cloth.

"Not usually, no," Angela smiled wryly. She caught her breath with the first sting of the antiseptic but relaxed as the anesthetic properties of the medicine numbed her skin. "Though we have been in a fair number of prickly situations."

"Angela is far better with fairies than I am," I responded, concerned that Laughter might misinterpret my relationship with Angela as being less than mutual friendship. "I have relied on her many times to extricate me from difficult situations."

Laughter seemed to be waiting for Angela's rejoinder, but it never came. Not that her fingers stopped their ministrations. "A thin cloth should do for a covering tonight," she told Angela, going to retrieve said cloth from her bag. The cloths were a little too long for Angela's arms and Laughter had to trim them to size before they could be secured. "Better sleep in them," she advised. "Tomorrow if your pricks are light-colored and smaller, you will not need another treatment."

"I suppose I will need a few more treatments," I sighed from where Megan had finished wrapping me.

"Yes, at least two more. I will administer the first when you visit me this evening." Laughter gathered her dirty instruments onto a single cloth before turning back to me. "I suggest you wear a long-sleeved gown tonight, too."

"Perhaps your peach-skin," suggested Megan helpfully, hurrying to the closet to get it.

"Perfect," I agreed, smiling for Megan's benefit. "Though I fear I have worn a hole in the matching slippers." I only mentioned it to give Megan something to do. If I knew her at all, she was exhibiting signs of a considerable amount of nervous energy.

"By your leave, Highness," she left the closet and went instead to my shoe rack. "I can repair it for you. I am terrible canny with this sort of thing."

"Would you Megan?" I beamed at her. "That would be wonderful."

Laughter was silent until Megan left. "Too tight?" she asked when she was binding the cloth about my arms.

I shook my head. "Thank you, I feel much better."

Nodding briskly, she tied up her things in the cloth. "If there is nothing else," she said.

Concerned by her brittle tone, I watched her for a moment before rising. "Thank you very much," I told her, holding out my hands in a friendly gesture. Perhaps it was my reaching out to her. Or perhaps I just looked too ridiculous to be angry with, wrapped up in my slip and bandages. However it happened, I was glad to have her take my hands in hers.

"You are welcome, Highness." She had a strange expression on her face when she spoke. She seemed sincere in her response, but her use of my title confused us both. Abruptly she left the room, letting herself out the sitting room window.

"I cannot decide," Angela thought aloud, "whether or not she likes you."

"I believe she likes *me*. She may simply not be accustomed to dealing with royalty face to face." With that, I dismissed the incident and we got to work.

"I was thinking," Angela said, rolling her sleeves back down, "that we could use this same plan for the seating at the ceremony."

"Exactly what I was thinking," I agreed. Taking up the papers, I moved us into the drawing room. The larger desk in there could accommodate two without the risk of us bumping into each other. "Now, where were we?"

We worked steadily, smoothing out the rough edges on the plan. We were occasionally distracted by the buzzing of horsefly teams, bringing wagons back from the patch. Better yet were the times when the sounds of laughter and singing drifted up from the lawn below. Finally, Angela was so interested that she got up to look.

"I do not believe what I am seeing!" she declared firmly.

"What is it?" I asked, hardly daring to look up. Was my idea a disaster after all?

"It is Lady Vaniece! She looks like she was in a berry fight or something."

"A berry fight?" I frowned. "Is she angry?"

"Not at all," Angela denied. "Perhaps she was on the winning team?"

"Angela, be serious!" I admonished her.

"I *am*," she protested. "The entire wagonload of fairies looks like they were picked up and dunked in berry juice. None too carefully, either."

Too curious not to risk it, I set aside the papers and rose gingerly. At best I expected an instant, unrelenting prickle and itch all over my back, but incredibly there was minimal discomfort.

"Laughter's medicine is very effective," Angela took me by my good arm. "I can barely tell I am injured."

"Indeed," I accepted her assistance and made my way to the window. "I…see." Turning wide eyes to Angela's face I promised, "I shall never doubt you again!"

"I have heard that before," she stuck her tongue out at me briefly then pointed. "Oh, look!"

I looked. Coming from the direction of the berry patch was a train of horsefly wagons. "Are they through already?" I asked, surprised.

Angela chuckled. "*Already*? We have been working for hours. It is almost time to dress for dinner!"

I looked more closely at the near wagons. "They are filled to bursting!" I exclaimed, astonished. More singing and laughing floated up from the furthest wagons.

"It would seem that your outing was a grand success," Angela said quietly.

"Do you suppose they may have picked *more* berries than Cook can use?" I pondered aloud.

Angela raised an eyebrow. "Probably not." Grinning, she took up a set of papers from the desk. "I will see that Master Collins and Mistress Judith each get their own copy of this."

"Thank you," I stifled a yawn. "It is a good day's work done. I am not looking forward to trying to sleep tonight, though."

"Oh, yes," Angela frowned thoughtfully. "Perhaps if you sleep on your stomach?" She added more briskly, "Your cheek looks very well, though."

"That is a relief," I smiled then shook my

head. "I should very much like to make it to the altar with no visible scars!"

Angela laughed. "It is well you had your visit with Aaron today. Tomorrow the work starts in earnest!"

Tomorrow…the sunlight will spill over the fields and the guests will spill into the post, my imp groaned.

Chapter XIII

"We are not under attack, Major," I protested, astonished, while guardsmen piled out of their barracks.

"Can we review that statement at a later time, Highness?" Daniels responded. "We must set up the landing zones."

"Go," I answered simply. The horizon was dark with approaching carriages, the sound of the buzzing horseflies already assaulting my ears. "Angela," I put out my hand and she took it instantly. "Please help me not to make a fool of myself," I pleaded.

"Breathe," she admonished me. "Now, let us stand over here." She guided me to a spot overlooking the guest quarters. "This way, the guests can form a line over to here from where their carriages deposit them. Mistress Judith and Master Collins both have the papers and will be directing the luggage."

Glancing to one side, I caught the eye of a young page. Despite my own nervousness, I smiled at him. When he smiled back, apparently more excited than concerned, I decided that he had the right idea. Idly I stroked the organdy top-layer of my skirt, which was still crisp from the morning pressing Megan had given it.

I watched as the men-fairies assisted their women-folk out of the first few carriages. Lord

Bascomb, possibly the oldest Silver fairy I had ever met, waited patiently while his wife was settled into her mobile chair. Other, younger, couples waited respectfully for them to lead the way.

Aloud I greeted the Bascomb's in a voice approaching a shout. "I am so glad you could come!" We exchanged the appropriate salutations before I signaled for a page. Smiling down at the page I had drawn courage from, I announced that he would be showing them to their quarters.

He knows his job, my imp chuckled, *and now so does the whole line!*

It was a simple matter after that for me to greet my guests, accept their well wishes, and assign them to a page. What I found dismaying was that Major Daniels had to push the landing zones back even further to make room for the ever expanding line.

Why did we invite so many guests? my imp asked when my throat began to ache.

I kept smiling. I shook hands. I asked about travelling conditions. I laughed at single sentence whimsies that the older gentlemen shared. I even began tentatively employing state affair tactics of derailing long-winded conversation attempts. My head began to hurt. Generally, I felt as flat as the top layer of my organdy skirt.

"You must be sure to remember me to them, Lady Crenshaw," I beamed before the dear woman-fairy could tell me about the rest of her extended family. I smiled gratefully at Angela when she neatly inserted a page between Lady Crenshaw and any next words that she might have been tempted to speak. I noticed, too, when Angela gave a surreptitious nod, but had no idea to whom she was nodding.

"Highness," Helen called to me from behind.

Turning to face her, I was elated to see that she was carrying a tray with what looked like a cool glass of something. I was puzzled, though, when she curtsied like an ordinary maid.

"Your opinion, Highness, of this beverage?" she asked demurely.

As I flitted forward to take the glass, a crew of four men-fairies dropped onto the spot where I had been. In a matter of seconds, an awning had been erected to shield me from the sun. Surprised, I managed to reel my jaw in enough to swallow my first sip of the drink.

A potion! my imp gagged. *A vile, vile potion!*

"You must drink it all, Highness," Helen caught my hand as I tried to set the glass politely back on the tray, "to get its true flavor."

I wondered if my face had turned green. I felt green, after just a sip of that…beverage.

I trust her, my imp said weakly.

Inhaling a lungful of air, I held my breath and downed the rest of the drink. I felt someone take the empty glass from my unresisting grip. I recognized Angela's hand putting the glass back on the tray.

"I do not think," I swallowed hard, "that I can recommend this beverage for general distribution at this time."

Helen's mouth quirked up in a wry smile. "Very well, Highness." With that she turned and disappeared into the throng of servants and spectators.

"Is it working?" Angela whispered to me.

"My head feels a little better," I admitted grudgingly.

Does your head feel better? Or does your stomach feel worse? my imp moaned.

Turning back to the stalled reception line, I ignored my imp. What made me feel better all over was seeing Hugh waiting for me under the awning. I had been expecting to face the crowds alone all day because I knew how busy his schedule was.

"Sir Riley," I smiled at the next man-fairy in line, "allow me to introduce Prince Hugh." It was wonderful having Hugh there beside me. The potion aftertaste was a lasting reminder of the medication I had just consumed, but I liked to think that my head and throat felt better because I had someone to share the talking and thinking with. He even adjusted the awning as the sun moved through the sky.

"I am getting hungry," he whispered after he had been there for a few hours.

"We are almost done," I promised. And we were. For the first time since morning, the line was getting shorter rather than longer.

"A pleasure to meet you," Hugh bowed over a dowager's hand. To me he whispered, "You missed lunch."

I smiled at a Baroness then passed her graciously to Hugh. "Prince Cambrian!" I found myself holding out both my hands to the next guest.

Just like him to join the line instead of expecting 'royal' treatment, my imp grinned.

"Princess Rebecca," he took my hands, using them as a way to hold me out for a brotherly 'once-over.' "You are looking very well today," he teased.

I laughed at the contrast between this and our last meeting. "Thank you, sir," I curtsied, even while wishing that I could hug him as I had while I was still a child. "Will you sit with us for dinner?" I asked, suddenly hopeful. Dinner tonight would be outdoors, not unlike the relaxed meal we had enjoyed after the tourney.

"I should be glad to," Prince Cambrian smiled. With a polite wink to me and a nod for Hugh, he beckoned for a page.

To me, the last few guests felt a lot like the first few, except that by now my heart was holding my body up. Hugh's arm slipped about my waist.

"That was the last one," he advised me cheerfully. "Come on."

I paused long enough to wave to anyone who

might have been looking. Then I surrendered. After standing for close to six hours, it was nice to be in a different position.

"Could you hold me a little tighter?" I asked without looking at him. "Ah," I gasped when he obliged and my back popped.

Hugh grimaced. "Better?" he asked, easing his grip.

"Much," I nodded. "I got a kink about three hours ago, but I could do nothing about it."

He sighed. "You have to be a lot stronger than I thought to be a princess."

"Mmm," I agreed, not really wanting to talk about it. "Where are we going?"

"Your parent's chambers," he told me. "They promised to leave the latch up on the window and some food on the table."

"You are always thinking with your stomach," I laughed.

"Well, if you are not hungry," he began to slow his flight.

"Wait," I blushed a little when I realized how I had let him trap me. "I am famished." I rested my head against his shoulder after that, satisfied to just be along for the ride. The wind tickled my bare arms and cheeks as we rounded the post to slip in my parent's window.

"Will we always eat with large groups of fairies?" Hugh asked as he deposited me on the settee.

"No," I rubbed a twinge in my neck. "Lunch

is the meal we will most often miss. Dinner is probably the meal we shall share the most often." I looked up as he brought over some apples and cheese.

"And breakfast?" he asked, frowning unhappily.

"Best to eat something in our rooms before our days begin," I told him before taking a bite of the apple he handed me.

"Days?" he echoed, arching his eyebrows as he settled himself beside me.

"Our duties will not permit us to spend a great deal of time together," I said reluctantly.

"And we will live at Castlemain," he said.

I took another bite of apple. I could not—did not—blame him for the lack of enthusiasm in his voice. But I thought it wiser to not 'help' him think it through. I was glad when he put his arm about my shoulders, gently rubbing the tenseness out of my neck.

He took a bite of his apple, offered me some cheese. "What will your duties be?" he asked curiously.

I swallowed the cheese. "They will not be very different from my duties here. I will meet with Madam Rouchard and Master Collins to review requests and reports, arrange entertainment for guests, sit in on council meetings, attend state affairs that I have orchestrated, worry about the king and queen…" I stopped there, smiling as I put a hand lightly on his arm.

"Tend children?" he suggested, leaning closer.

"With a lot of help," I nodded after a moment of surprise.

"I know you do not think of it often," he said quietly, "but I do not want it to be the surprise to you then that it was just now."

Seeing the frown on his face, I wondered what *my* face had revealed to merit such concern. Surprise, certainly. Dismay?

"I have my doubts as to my ability to raise children." I forced the words out, admitting it to myself as much as to him.

"Oh?" he asked. His tone was gentle, seeming to indicate confidence in me without elaborating as to why. That tone, and the look in his eyes, drew the answer from me as no sharp-tongued interrogator could have.

"It is partly my nature," I took a deep breath. I did not want to make our life together a guessing game, yet this was something that I found difficult to put into words. "I have a lifetime of training in so many things. Dancing, cultures, etiquette, riding, woodcraft, sewing, weaponry, wood skills..." I frowned and paused, struggling still to express the root of my fear. "Even as a child, I was always frightened the first time I put my hand to something. Afraid of the needle, afraid of the sword," I looked up to meet his gaze, thinking I would find the truth of his reaction in his eyes. What I saw almost made me cry in relief, although I knew better than to yield to tears when such powerful, diverging emotions were that close to the surface.

"I love you," he said, taking my face in his hands. "You are aware of your fear, yet possess the courage to set it aside. Now be aware of this—you are not alone. We will learn these lessons together."

Have I ever heard a fairer promise? my imp managed to wonder before he leaned even closer. I cannot be sure who kissed whom, only that the promise was sealed.

"Hugh?" I murmured between kisses.

"Yes?" he kissed me again.

"Hugh," I pulled back gently, smiling. "We have to go. Mother's maid will have a lot to do before she helps Mother dress for dinner."

Sighing, he straightened away. "We are not going anywhere," he told me sternly, "until you finish your apple."

Obediently I ate the last few bites of it, shaking my head and pretending to be exasperated with him.

"What are your plans for entertaining our guests tonight?" he asked, scooping up three apples and juggling them expertly.

"Do you never read the notices?" I laughed. I outlined the evening's activities—dinner, dancing, and a short music recital—in as few words as possible. "Then we shall all retire early."

"Because tomorrow is the wedding?" he asked, feigning nonchalance. There was no break in his apple juggling, but a corner of his mouth quirked up in a pleased smile.

"Yes, because tomorrow is the wedding," I agreed. Tossing the apple core into a lined wastebasket, I rose. "I must check with Cook and Mistress Judith, to see if there is anything they need."

Hugh caught the undamaged apples and set them carefully back in the bowl. "I suppose I should check on Cial Mar and the others."

"Oh," I paused. "Do they have suitable clothes for this evening? I would not want them to feel out of place."

"Every troupe fairy has at least one dark outfit," he assured me, frowning slightly. "For funerals."

I frowned back. "Would they take it amiss if we offered to arrange other clothes for them? I know they consider it bad luck to wear funeral attire at anything *but* a funeral."

"And how do you know that?" he asked, raising both eyebrows.

"I told you I was trained in cultures," I reminded him amusedly.

"You were trained well," he bowed slightly. "It is a good point, too. I will make the suggestion. Alfred alone will have enough outfits for the men-fairies."

"Angela, Abigail, and I surely have enough compatible pieces to make outfits for the ladies," I volunteered my friends easily.

"Compatible pieces?" he echoed, looking confused.

"For a woman-fairy, it would be almost as bad to arrive in someone else's outfit as it would be to arrive in funeral clothes. But if we pool our wardrobes, combining similar pieces to make a completely new outfit," I shrugged. "Well, that is completely different."

"Oh," he nodded as though he understood, then shook his head in obvious bewilderment.

"Go," I pushed him toward the window, "the ladies will understand and we will need the time we have to prepare."

Laughing, he let me push him right out the window! He even fell a little ways before spreading his wings and taking off.

Scamp, my imp grinned. *Now—back to work.*

My visit to the kitchen did not take long. Cook had the robin cordon bleu roasting, the bread baking, and the soup simmering. I gave her my compliments and made my way out to the lawn where we would be eating. As I had expected, Mother and Mistress Judith had it well in hand.

"Rebecca," Mother looked surprised, "you should be resting." She slipped an arm about my shoulders and kissed my forehead.

"I should," I agreed, surprised that I had not thought of it. "But I feel fine. Perhaps it was the potion Helen gave me?"

"Ah," Mother nodded. "Thank goodness for

those whose skills include medicine! Nevertheless," she took my arm and turned me to face the post, "this morning was just the beginning. There is still dinner to get through tonight, and tomorrow you have *three* weddings and a coronation to attend. Go lie down."

I should have. It was the wise thing to do. Instead, I went to see Laughter. It was easy to slip through the chaos of servants in the guest quarter area and reach the troupe fairy ring. My back was not hurting, so my only excuse was discussing tonight's wardrobe, which I was not even sure Laughter would be interested in.

"Highness," Twister spotted me on the edge of the ring. "You should be resting!"

I blinked, startled. "That is exactly what my mother said!" I laughed.

Twister brushed back an errant streak of pale brown hair self-consciously, a frown flitting across her face.

"Wisdom knows no age, I suppose," I sighed, scrambling to remove any unintended sting from my words.

Age would be a concern to a troupe fairy, my imp realized. *Especially one named Twister. But surely she is no more than five hundred years old?*

"And if you admit it would be wisdom to rest," Helen's voice interrupted, "what are you doing here?"

"Helen," I greeted her happily. I gave her a friendly hug before saying, "Thank you for the potion. It relieved my headache and my hunger."

That is a polite way of saying it drove our appetite away, my imp sniffed.

Helen laughed. "Yes, I am sure it did. Come," linking her arm through mine, she led me over to where Laughter and the other women-fairies were sitting in the shade. "Hugh was just here."

"Oh?" I hesitated. "Did he mention me?"

"He mentioned you, and your kind offer to lend us clothing customarily worn at state affairs," Laughter's smile lent sincerity to what might have been just words. "We have been discussing it," she nodded at the circle of chairs.

I looked around at the serious faces and noticed an extra chair. "You were expecting me," I hazarded.

"Of course," Laughter gestured for me to sit. "How is your back?" she asked.

I settled into the legless, stiff-backed chair. "It is difficult to tell that I was ever injured." I smiled at the soft ripple of pleasant responses.

"Good," Laughter approved. "Now. As to our costumes for tonight. We had anticipated that events here would require dressing in ways to which we are unaccustomed. We had not planned for assistance, however. May we ask why you offer it?"

I considered the question as well as the fairy doing the asking. Laughter was clearly a leader in the troupe's loosely defined hierarchy. I felt sure that she was inclined to accept the offer, but also understood that she led by virtue of the respect the others had for her. I was also curious as to her mode of speech, which sounded almost courtly. Was it possible that she had a formal education as well as her troupe training?

"I am your hostess," I said quietly. "It would be inexcusable for me to not offer that which might make my guests more comfortable—within reason."

Laughter nodded. "We are well aware of the importance your culture places on costumes. We thank you for your offer." She paused to visually survey the gathered women-folk. "We accept."

I knew that 'we' literally meant all of them. Impressed, I held Laughter's gaze a moment before nodding back. "If you would accompany me to my chambers, you may have your pick of several costumes." I used her word in place of 'outfit,' and thought privately that it was really quite appropriate. I had riding costumes, eating costumes, dancing costumes… It was my own opinion, of course, but in that light it seemed clear that there was a danger of allowing a preoccupation with 'costuming' to overshadow individual worth as a manner of gauging one's interest in another.

Exiting the guest area was not quite as simple as entering it, for such a large group disrupted the flow of the scrambling servants. Realizing suddenly that we were leaving the troupe fairy ring unattended, I signaled to a guardsman.

"Please wait here until Prince Hugh returns," I instructed him, "and tell him that Princess Rebecca sent you." It was a strange order, one that would undoubtedly end with Hugh smiling as he dismissed the guardsman, but with so much chaos I could hardly leave the area open to more than curious eyes.

Helen nodded her approval of my action and we were on our way again. I sent pages for Lady Angela and Lady Abigail, who met us at my chambers.

"Well," Abigail rose from the settee as we came in the sitting room window. "What is this?"

Angela must have had an idea already, for she rose also. "A marvelous opportunity," she smoothly covered Abigail's confusion. "I have always wanted to see my crème-coloured rose petal gown with Rebecca's lavender accessories. I hope one of you will choose that combination," she smiled at the entire group.

Abigail must have put it all together from Angela's words, for she began smiling also. "Yes," she agreed, "a marvelous opportunity."

Rather than trying to fit all three of our extensive wardrobes in the same set of rooms, we divided the group by size and shape. Those that most closely matched Abigail's slightly stouter figure and darker colouring went with her, while those closer to Angela went with her. That left me with Twister and Jester. It was great fun, playing 'dress-up' with them, though I was on the alert to not insult them. Once they relaxed, I thought they began to enjoy it as much as I was.

"You dress like this *every day*?" Twister asked incredulously as she smoothed down a peach-skin skirt.

"Almost," I sighed, fingering the bark-cloth riding suit that I had left in the closet.

"She would rather wear boots and britches," chuckled Megan, straightening the bow on Jester's gown.

I blushed but we all laughed. It was a pleasant change to associate with women-fairies who did not count buttons or compare tailors.

"You both look lovely," I assessed them honestly.

"Might we not do somethin' with your hair?" Megan suggested, taking up a comb. "Ladies hereabouts does fancy things with lace and ribbons!"

"I usually wear a braid, myself," I added hastily.

Twister declined with a simple shake of her head.

"'Tis no trick at all to do our hair up," Jester said confidently. "An elegant hairdo fancies up the plainest clothes."

"Agreed," Megan and I said at the same time. Again we all laughed.

It took a few more minutes to be sure appropriate accessories had been secured for all of the ladies, but eventually a quiet settled over my chambers again.

"How long until dinner, Megan?" I asked.

"Enough time to get you dressed," she answered.

"Oh dear," I yawned. "However am I going to stay awake?"

While she had no answer, she did her best to make dressing easy for me. I even nodded off while she redid my hair.

"Time to wake up," I heard Hugh's voice say.

"Already?" I mumbled. "I feel like I just fell asleep."

"You probably did," he lifted me carefully to a standing position.

Yawning, I rested my head against his shoulder. "I should have listened to Mother," I told him. When he did not respond, I forced my eyes open. "Is it time to go?"

"I am not planning to move anytime soon," he answered seriously.

"You darling," I laughed. "As much as I would love to stay here, the sooner we go, the sooner tomorrow will come."

He did not release me. "Thank you, for posting a guardsman out there today." He kissed me lightly.

"Where is Megan?" I asked breathlessly.

"Somewhere else," he answered vaguely. He winced as a knock sounded on the outer door of my chambers. "Someone else who thinks with their stomach." He stole another quick kiss then stepped back. "Are you awake enough to stand?"

"I am now," I teased. "But promise you will keep me awake during dinner?"

"I promise," he grinned mischievously.

Chapter XIV

"Perhaps I should have declined your invitation," Prince Cambrian said quietly as he reached for his fork.

I put my hand lightly on his arm. "You are my brother in my heart, if not by law. I am glad you joined us." I met his eyes for a brief moment to be sure he knew I was in earnest, then reached for my own fork.

It was customary for the wedding group to eat dinner together the night before the wedding—the bride and her parents with the groom and his parents. Under the circumstances, it had *seemed* like a good idea to have all three wedding parties at one table. I had tried to arrange our unusual group so that the seating was not too disagreeable.

Scanning the table briefly, I decided I had not done too badly on that score. Across the table from me I saw Queen Dianna smiling at Helen and Edward, who were seated to her right. Cassandra was answering King Wilson's polite questions politely, as I had known she would. That had been easy. Looking to my right—Cassandra's left—I watched Alfred introducing his mother to Abigail then Cial Mar. Of course, Hugh was at Cial's left, which I hoped would help things run smoothly. That brought my thoughts back around to me, and to Prince Cambrian, who was seated between Mother and me.

I wondered now if we were not all intruding on each other. Did Helen really want me (and others) to hear when she shyly whispered her thanks to Queen Dianna for acting as her proxy mother? And did I really want everyone at that table to witness, without necessarily understanding, my friendly conversation with Prince Cambrian? It was odd enough for me to have seated him on my right, between Mother and me. Even as tired as I was, I could not have slept through those questions.

"The slippers are such an interesting custom," Queen Dianna remarked as the server placed a plate before her. "I believe the groom is meant to put them on the bride?"

"Before leading her out to the ceremony," Helen nodded. Her face somehow softened at the same time that her expression became even more serious. She had just learned of the custom herself, not having been raised as a Silver Fairy.

"It is quite an elaborate tradition," Alfred stated carefully. He was well aware of the complications inherent with mixing tribes and traditions. Besides the different upbringings of Helen and Hugh there were troupe fairy traditions, Sky Fairy traditions, and Plant Fairy traditions all seated around a Silver Fairy table. A short, friendly explanation tonight might save all sorts of misunderstandings later. "But it is believed to be bad luck for anyone but the groom to be the first to see the bride in her full wedding outfit."

"Which," King Wilson raised a regal eyebrow, "is where the final chaperones play a role?"

"Yes, sir," Alfred smiled. "One or more male relatives of the bride accompany the groom to where she, with the help of her women friends and family, has been dressing for the ceremony. When she is completely ready, except for her slippers of course, the women-folk leave and the chaperones turn their backs, leaving only the groom facing the door through which his bride will enter the room."

I smiled as I noticed that while Alfred was gesturing idly with one hand, his free hand had moved to cover Cassandra's near hand.

"The bride comes in." Alfred's voice dropped to a hushed, theatrical tone. Our table was silent, with several of his listeners holding their breath. "She is perfect, down to the last curl caressing her neck. Only one thing is lacking. The groom flies forward and kneels before her. From the box he has been anxiously protecting he produces slippers for his bride. Slippers made of the purest white Tree Swallow eggshells. They complete the bride's ensemble. Now they are ready to attend their wedding."

"Why eggshell?" frowned Cial Mar. "If they are so important to her wedding outfit, surely a more durable material should be chosen."

"It is considered symbolic," Duchess Beatrice

answered stiffly from where she sat, under protest, beside him. "If the slippers break while the groom is putting them on his bride, he will break her heart. If they break during the ceremony, the bride will break the groom's heart." She finished with a sniff that seemed to indicate a disapproval of all three of the weddings about to take place.

I ducked my head to hide a smile.

"And if they break between the ceremony and the reception?" Cial Mar asked, his frown deepening.

"Tradition dictates that theirs will be a short but happy marriage," Hugh answered. "The reception is held immediately after the wedding, primarily because of that tradition."

I looked up from the roll I was buttering, surprised. He had answered correctly, but so darkly. What was wrong? Surely he did not believe such a silly tradition.

"Then why do they smash the slippers after the reception?" Abigail asked. Her tone indicated that she had wondered that for quite some time; probably ever since her lady, Princess Alicia, had married Hugh's father, Guardsman Lawson.

"Deliberately?" Cial Mar asked, sounding thoroughly confused.

"Yes," I smiled at him. "It is only thought to be bad luck if they are broken before the wedding. After the wedding, the couple is assured a happy marriage and they smash the slippers as thoroughly as possible, in the hopes that they will have as many happy years together as there are fragments of slipper."

Cial Mar shook his head. "And they say troupe fairies are superstitious!"

"What are the troupe fairy wedding traditions?" I asked impetuously.

Cial Mar touched his napkin to his lips, then settled it on his lap again. "Though it has been a long time since my wedding," he began his answer with a smile, "I remember it well. A troupe will commonly have a single wedding gown that all the brides share. The last bride tends it until the next bride needs it. And, it is believed that folks should do more than *wish* a couple well. Every fairy in the troupe will supply some part of the couple's future. The men-folk build them a wagon and the women-folk donate a bit of something to make it a home for them." He seemed to be seeing distant campfires as he stared at the candelabra that lit the table where he sat. "We do have one tradition, though, about the wedding night. The groom will assist the bride into their new wagon, her having never seen it, and her first reaction is a shadow of their days to come."

I reached under the table and took Hugh's hand. Was that what was bothering him? We had neither wagon nor 'home' to offer for decoration. Castlemain had been decorated thousands of years ago!

"What of the Plant Fairies?" Helen asked in innocent curiousity.

Most of us could have answered that question, thanks to our cultures training, but we all waited while King Wilson exchanged a smile with Queen Dianna.

"Our tradition begins with the proposal," Queen Dianna explained. "The young man-fairy must start a plant from seed and bring it to the woman-fairy he wishes to wed. If she accepts him, she becomes responsible for the care of the plant. If the plant is not in good health on their wedding day, it is said that their marriage will be an unhappy one."

"What sorts of plants are most commonly used for that process?" Mother asked.

"Flowers are fairly common," King Wilson answered, "though in many of the smaller villages a groom who gave his bride an orchid plant, for example, would be considered impractical and promptly rejected."

"What about roses?" Cassandra asked. "Parts of them can be used for medicine as well as food."

Queen Dianna shook her head. "Any plant with a thorn, barb, or other potentially injuring part is considered an insult if given as a betrothal gift."

"I suppose that includes poison ivy?" Cial Mar asked roguishly.

Our entire table laughed at that, then broke

into separate conversations. I listened, any desire for sleep having fled from me. Cial Mar and Abigail were still chuckling over the idea of telling the other troupe fairies about the eggshells. King Wilson was further explaining Plant Fairy traditions to Alfred, who was pretending to listen intently. Mother drew Prince Cambrian out by asking how his parents were doing. When I noticed that Father was aimlessly pushing food around on his plate with a fork, I found myself wondering what plant he had given to Princess Rachel.

"Are you well?" Hugh asked me quietly.

"Yes," I answered as quietly. "Are you?" While it was hard to be sure, even with the light of dozens of candelabras, I thought he looked strangely weary.

"Well enough," he assured me, taking my hand.

"Should I be insulted," I asked, fluttering my lashes, "that you have been bringing me roses all this time?"

"Take it rather as a statement of confidence," he advised me with a wink. "I knew you could hold your own with them, and with any other prickly situations that will come our way." He kissed my hand lightly.

The next two courses passed without serious conversation, but when dessert came, Prince Cambrian refused his and requested instead that his glass be refilled.

"This, my friends, is a Sky Fairy tradition," he announced, rising. "A toast, from Prince Cambrian to each of the three happy couples here tonight." He put one hand self-consciously behind his back to keep from gesturing with it as he had been known to do, then said, "Two hearts can meet while the land lies under snow, and 'ere spring winds with summer storms do blow, those two hearts beat as one. A mere thought has here begun a new life for them both." Pausing, he raised his glass. "As crops in summer grow from storm as well as sun, may you count not just the petals which fall, but also the fruit born of smiles hard-won."

He wrote that, my imp recognized at once. *For us? Or for himself and Joanna?*

As Prince Cambrian drank to his own toast, enough of us knew their tradition to join him. The others knew enough to join us.

"Thank you," Hugh rose, reaching over me to extend a hand to Prince Cambrian, "for your well-wishing."

After dinner, when I was not dancing with one of them, I watched Cambrian and Hugh very carefully. They seemed to have some mutual fascination with the fire pots. If that had not been enough to catch my attention, there was the fervor with which they were discussing them. I waited through three sets. Then I begged off from further dancing and approached them.

"Perhaps," Cambrian said as I came into earshot, "but if you will countenance the advice of a younger man-fairy," a sly grin played across his face, "you will not hesitate to take the chance for happiness that is being given you."

What are they talking about? my imp wondered. *The wedding? Is Hugh considering…* I slowly closed the lid on the rest of that thought.

"Gentlemen," I greeted them as though I had not heard and was not the least bit frightened. "Forgive me for neglecting you." Stepping between them, I put one hand through each of their arms. It was no trouble at all to turn them toward the garden and take them a few flits toward it.

"Forgive me," Cambrian paused at the garden's edge. "I have not yet danced with your mother, Rebecca." Flicking a glance at Hugh, he then kissed me gently on the forehead, turned and left.

Confused, I looked up at Hugh. "What have you been saying to Prince Cambrian?" I did not mean it in the nature of an accusation, but there it was. Perhaps next time I would try to say what I meant, something more along the lines of, *Is something wrong?*

Smiling faintly, Hugh led me further into the garden. When the music and laughter had faded to the point that we could hear each other plainly, he drew up. "Please," he indicated a bench. Once we were seated, he reached for my hands. "You are trembling," he said, concern in his voice. "Are you cold?"

I shook my head.

"Then you are upset," he deduced. "So am I."

"About what?" I asked. "Have I…"

"No," he interrupted me firmly. "You have done nothing." He smoothed my hair, and looked away. "Nothing but fall in love with a man-fairy several times your own age," he said at last.

I caught his hand as he tried to withdraw it, pressing it against my cheek. "Your age. My age. This is what has upset you?" I did not wait for him to respond. I needed to know something else. "Why now? We have known each other for nearly six months."

He focused on my last question first. "Rolf. I…we were talking, and," he shrugged as if to dismiss the meat of their discussion.

"Rolf," I repeated dazedly.

Uncle Hugh, my imp mimicked Rolf's voice, *someone was telling me you were over eight hundred years old. Do you think it will be strange, marrying a woman-fairy less than a hundred years old?* I discarded that thought along with the next half-dozen answers to the question of what they had been discussing.

"Where was Rolf tonight? I did not see him with his family." I was not sure why I asked that question. What possible relevance could it have? Then Hugh shifted and I knew that it was, somehow, important.

"He asked me if his seating assignment could be changed," Hugh said casually. "I did not want to bother you."

I was already mentally reviewing the dinner arrangements. If Rolf had not been at his parents' table, who had been? The Duchess of Windsong, very good. Where was she supposed to…oh!

"Hugh!" I cried. "Rolf and Barbara Weatherly?"

"Is that so surprising?" he asked, eyes widening.

"Well, no, not if one remembers Rolf's age as more than a numerical figure," I rose and took a step away. I would have gone further, but Hugh caught hold of the hand that I had been holding his hand with.

"Are they so wrong for each other?" he asked, bewilderment in his voice.

I took a deep breath, noting that even in his private distress he was concerned that he might have done some ill toward Rolf. "I would not say that," I answered honestly. Turning back, I looked down at him. "She is a very pleasant young woman-fairy," I admitted, "probably quite suited to Rolf, and a long-time friend of his." Raising my eyebrows I added, "She is also only a handful of years younger than he. Is that what made you start thinking about this?"

I took my seat again, turning so that my knees were touching his and leaning forward, putting both of my hands in his. "This is not a conversation I would like to have again, so please listen carefully. The difference in our ages is of no consequence to me. Father is nearly two hundred years older than Mother, and my grandfather…" I stopped talking. It did not seem to me that Hugh was the least bit consoled by what I was saying.

Instead of telling him how you feel, you should try to understand how he feels, suggested my imp.

"Why does it bother you that we are not the same age?" I asked.

His eyes played across my face, pausing on my lips before lifting to meet my gaze. "I had gone decades without seriously thinking of marriage before meeting you. When I did think about it, I never thought it might break the heart of the woman-fairy I loved."

I could have kissed him for saying that he loved me, but I needed to hear the rest of what he had to say. Since I had no idea what words he wanted, all I could do was wait while he fumbled for them.

"Have you given any thought to your old age?" he asked, raising his eyebrows. "Of course not," he answered for me. "You are too young. Do you realize that by the time we have been married seven hundred and fifty years, like your parents, I will be middle aged?" He spoke more rapidly as he continued, "Your parents are planning a trip for after their yielding. What could we plan? A permanent trip to the West Post?"

I waited to be sure he was finished. "For the record," I murmured, "my parents are not just planning a vacation. They are planning a second wedding trip." I laughed softly at the surprised expression on his face. "It is hard work, being king and queen. They have had little time for each other, even in their seven hundred and fifty years." I laughed again as another thought occurred to me. "Now that you have brought it up, there is a point of law I should like to clarify."

"A point of law?" he repeated, frowning as though he wondered if he had heard me correctly.

I nodded and leaned forward so that my cheek was against his. "The selection of my father's successor was not entirely without precedent. A few great-grandfather's ago, there was a king who had no children at all. That was how my ancestor came to be king, as the nearest male relative. After he had been crowned, the former king and queen finally had a child, and called him John." I paused to breathe, enjoying being this close to Hugh, hoping it would help him forget to worry. "John Finch claimed a right to the throne, but the tribe was happy with how my ancestor was ruling and refused to acknowledge him."

"When did it become part of the law?" Hugh asked, kissing my cheek.

Smiling I answered, "Right then. That is when the Council of Citizen's came to be, also, or my ancestor might have stepped down."

Hugh leaned back to look at me. "They insisted he remain king?" he asked.

I nodded fractionally, not wanting to bump noses with him. "And forever after, any progeny born to a king that has already yielded the throne were not considered members of the Royal Family, but rather ordinary citizens with no claim to the throne."

"Fascinating," Hugh remarked and kissed me.

I blushed as I teased, "On second thought, if you ever feel old again…"

"Come," he interrupted, rising, "we should get back to our guests."

It was the proper thing to do—we were host and hostess after all—but I was nonetheless reluctant. "A moment," I rose with him, putting my hand on his arm. "Shhh," I warned him, "no talking." Slipping my right hand into his left, I brought his right hand up to rest on my waist. It was hardly the most subtle dance invitation I have ever issued, but I was grateful when he accepted it.

As always, being in his arms was magic. With the gentlest of cues he guided me through the steps of the waltz, then lifted us into the air. We soared through the moonlight, keeping time with the music and ignoring the dozen or more wall sentries who saluted as we passed.

"I never knew you could hear the dance music all the way around the post," I whispered when my feet were safely on the garden path again.

"There you are!" Jeffrey appeared on the path, apparently heading back toward the dancing. "I have been looking for you two for ten minutes!"

I smiled at his feigned annoyance and doubted he had been looking too hard. "They are waiting for us?" I guessed.

"Well," he came forward and began herding us back toward the group, "it is a little difficult to have the final waltz without someone to start it!"

Laughing, we yielded. As we took our place in the middle of an empty, grassy floor, I was reminded of our first dance together, back before I was sure he *could* dance. He looked just as handsome tonight, wearing his crown on his head and his heart in his eyes.

"I started this," Hugh said softly as he took me in his arms, "and I will finish it."

Chapter XV

"Only you could oversleep on a day like today," Arabella said in an exasperated tone.

Here we are again, thought my imp, *getting ready for another 'it.' Usually there are only a handful of 'this is it' moments sprinkled through a lifetime. In our case, that 'sprinkling' is more like a downpour.*

I yawned and ignored her. "Is anybody helping Helen and Cassandra?" I asked nobody in particular. I could understand sharing my wedding morning with those women-fairies that I loved best, but I was experiencing the first symptoms of claustrophobia!

Mother laughed. "Arabella," she summoned her eldest, "come sit beside me."

"Sorry," Arabella whispered to me as she relinquished my train to Claudette and moved to obey Mother. "I am just so nervous!"

Claudette expertly attached the train and began lacing up the bodice back, pulling it all together so that it looked like one piece.

"I should be afraid to put this on, I think, if it were not part of marrying Hugh," I admitted to her in a low voice.

It is a lot of lace and ribbon for someone who has always been more comfortable in bark-cloth, my imp concurred uneasily.

Claudette's reflection smiled at me over my shoulder. "Nonsense," she admonished pleasantly. "Madame Grey does not make mistakes in her designs."

"Thank you for being willing to assist me today," I blurted what had been on my mind since dinner. "Megan is so anxious she is not certain she will be able to arrange my hair even."

Claudette chuckled softly. "Listen," she instructed me.

Puzzled, I did as I was told. Arabella was telling Mother about Antoinette, who had a bad night because she was getting two new teeth in. Gwyneth was laughing at some funny story that Angela was telling, about me if I was not mistaken. Laughter was, oddly enough, the only solemn one in the group. Her full attention seemed to be focused on Megan, who was alternately elated and stiff with apprehension as she described how she might arrange my hair. In short, life was moving around me at its normal pace.

"No time to fret when you have so much to smile about," Claudette told me as she checked the seams and ties scrupulously for the slightest flaw. "There," folding her hands, she fluttered back enough to see all of the dress at once.

I smiled at her simple wisdom. I could not avoid my duties or planning for the future, but generally speaking worrying would not help. I inhaled slowly, deeply, feeling the rose petal fabric stretch with me and congratulating myself on my decision to *not* be sewn into my wedding gown.

"Gracious," Megan squeaked from her corner, "is it time already?" She stood, bumping the table in the process.

Laughter put out a steadying hand to keep the table, along with an assortment of brushes, combs, and so forth, from toppling over. "Princess Rebecca is certainly fortunate to have such a skilled hair dresser," she smiled at Megan.

With Claudette's help, I knelt on a low bench. While she arranged my skirts around it so that they would not rumple or wrinkle, Megan timidly began taking out my hairpins.

"Nothing fancy," I warned her teasingly. "I am already in danger of being mistaken for the wedding cake." As I had hoped, my levity injected enough normality into an otherwise tense situation that she visibly relaxed.

"Nothing fancy," she promised. "Reminds me," she reached for a brush, "of the day my Archibald got married. His Traci had to have her hair done by me," a note of pride entered her voice as she began deftly separating my hair into parts. "Said there was no woman-fairy in the village that had my touch when it came to hairdressing."

"I can well believe that," I smiled, holding Claudette's hands to keep from tumbling over backwards, victim of Megan's newly found enthusiasm for her task. In a matter of minutes, my hair went from a simple ponytail to a low-hanging bun. It ran from ear to ear just below the hairline on the back of my neck, a lovely combination of braids, curls, and fresh white roses.

"Did Hugh bring you those?" Angela asked, nodding at the bowl Megan was drawing flowers from.

I started to nod, then changed my mind. "Yes, just this morning. He removed all the thorns," I added with a smile. I had been too tired to sleep last night, and Angela had kept me company, arriving without my bidding her and remaining until sometime after I finally dozed off.

"There," Megan pinned a final rosebud in place and stepped back.

"You look lovely, dear," Mother rose and faced me.

I nodded wordlessly—breathlessly. I had the eerie feeling that I was looking at a stranger's reflection. The gown was familiar and the hairdo not unlike several that I had worn throughout my life. It was I who was different.

"Oh Rebecca," Angela squeezed my hand gently, "it is almost time."

At last, we are going to be married—again. My imp clapped her hands in delight.

Megan and Claudette curtsied before leaving, their exit the first indication to the waiting men-folk that the bride was almost ready. Looking about the room, I sensed that all normality had gone with them. Arabella in particular looked like she was going to cry. With two measured flaps I lifted myself off the bench and stood before them.

"Thank you again," I told Madame Grey, "for everything." I kissed her soft, worn cheek lightly, prevented her from curtsying with a short shake of my head, and escorted her to the door myself.

My emotions ran high when I saw that Angela was next in line. I could not even hug her, for fear of crushing my gown. There would certainly be no time to spend repressing it. Thankfully I was not wearing my gloves yet and we gripped each other's hands as though they were lifelines.

"Just keep breathing," she advised me. "In and out, all the way through the ceremony."

I laughed, with just a hint of tears in my voice as I agreed, "Yes, it would be awful if I fainted like Cousin Georgina." With all we had said last night, there was still too much left to put into words. We acknowledged that with an exchange of smiles, then she left to join Sean.

Gwyneth approached next. "You do look lovely," she echoed Mother's words. Smoothing my ever-errant hair she added, "Just because you are about to be crowned queen it does not mean you will stop being my little sister. If you need anything, from a quiet moment to an impromptu revel, you may count on me."

I nodded, accepted her kiss to my cheek and the kerchief she tucked into my sash.

Arabella came next, though she waited a moment for me to take a steadying breath. "'Where does the time go?" she asked, tenderly straightening my collar. "One minute I am helping you find your shoes and the next you are waiting for your bridegroom to bring you slippers." She shook her head and leaned closer. "I never wanted to be queen," she whispered, "but you will wear that crown well." Kissing my cheek, she helped me carefully into my gloves, whispered, "I love you," and left to take her place on the platform.

For a crazy moment I found myself trying to picture the other brides. If Helen was already dressed, she might be flitting about her room, waiting for her maid to signal and wondering what was taking me so long. If Cassandra were taking as much time with her family as I was, she might be wishing that I *not* hurry.

"Shh," Mother whispered, coming near and wiping away my tears with her fingers. "There now," she brought my forehead to rest against her cheek. "What is the matter, darling, did you have a bad dream?"

I smiled at childhood memories of being comforted in her arms, though never for bad dreams. Those had not started until after I had been kidnapped.

"No," I tried to blink back the tears. "A beautiful one."

"I see," she straightened and led me over to the basin. "Will you tell me about it?" she asked as she set aside her own gloves.

I watched her delicate hands lift the heavy

pitcher and pour water into the basin. She dampened a cloth, wrung it out, then pressed it lightly to my eyes. With my eyes closed, I tried to tell her about my dream.

"I dreamed I was going to grow up to be you," I told her at last. I heard a sharp intake of breath and pushed aside the cloth to find that she was crying! "Shh," I smiled at her, my own tears done. Taking the cloth from her, I tenderly blotted her cheeks and eyes. "Time to make my dream come true." I kissed her cheek and she kissed mine. Then I held perfectly still as she fluttered just high enough to set my crown carefully on my head. It was the last time I would wear it, until after my own Day of Yielding.

We left the dressing room arm in arm. Mother stationed me beside the couch in my sitting room and made her way down the row of chaperones. I kept my eyes lowered but I could tell as she spoke to and turned each of them to face the wall. First Rolf, then Alexander, Jeffrey, and finally Father. At last I heard the door close behind her. I raised my eyes shyly to look into Hugh's.

He flew toward me, holding a small box in both of his hands. "I brought you something," he told me, and set the box aside.

To my delight, he drew his mother's amulet from his waistcoat pocket. I laughed softly when his fingers tickled my neck as he clasped it in place. Then, without a word, he dropped to his knees before me and reached for the box. I was glad to see that Aaron had fastened the linings in place somehow, for the tiny slippers would be trouble enough on their own. I held my breath and the back of the couch, willing my whole self to stay perfectly still. Others might blame the groom if the slipper cracked right then, but I would not.

"One," he whispered, setting my foot on the ground carefully. Taking my other stockinged foot in his hands, Hugh painstakingly removed the second slipper from the box and set it in place. "Two," he exhaled.

It had all been done very carefully, so as not to leave even the faintest bruise on my rose petal gown. Rising triumphantly, Hugh offered me his arm.

"Gentlemen," he addressed our chaperones, "may I present my bride?"

Father was the last to turn to face us. I watched him closely, worried that he was still worried.

"How do I look?" I asked him, feeling as though I was fifty again and showing him my first ball gown. His response took my breath away.

"Like a queen," he said simply.

The sound of trumpets greeting my mother and sisters' arrival at their places forced us to action. Father kissed my forehead, shook Hugh's hand, then left to take his place at the altar.

Jeffrey and Alexander exchanged glances.

"Fair warning, Lawson. If you do not take care of her…"

Hugh interrupted, clearly at ease with his soon-to-be brothers-by-law, "Then you will take care of me."

"King or no king," Jeffrey nodded.

"Frankly," Alexander added, "if we did not think you were already planning on it, things would never have gotten this far."

"Now boys," I admonished. "Be nice." Even as I spoke, I had the funny feeling that they *were* being nice.

"It is alright darling," Hugh took my hand without thinking, "just an old custom common among all the tribes."

"Welcome to the family," Jeffrey extended his hand.

Alexander murmured something similar, then stepped back to allow Rolf his turn.

"Do not worry, Aunt Rebecca," he assured me as he shook Hugh's hand, "they both like Uncle Hugh fine."

I relaxed then, as Jeffrey dropped a wink in my direction and Alexander pretended that he had heard nothing.

Jeffrey smiled at Rolf. "Ready?" he asked his son.

Rolf seemed to grow taller on the spot. "Ready," he assured his father. Once again he was voluntarily exposing himself to the close, potentially critical, scrutiny of complete strangers.

Standing for his father, my oldest sister's husband, he stood at the head of the line.

"Thanks again, Jeffrey, for standing as my proxy parent," Hugh said quietly.

Jeffrey signaled to Rolf that we were ready. "My pleasure," he said, winking at me again.

Wrapping my arm about his, Hugh smiled at me. "Shall we?" he invited.

We left through the window, following Rolf's lead. I looked down into a staggering number of upturned faces and was glad when we dropped to shoulder height. I could see less faces that way. I could still see Cassandra and Helen, though. Helen's innate good taste had resulted in a fitted waistline and slim skirt, with clusters of white baby's breath strategically arranged. Cassandra had selected a slightly more ornate design, with fluted sleeves and hand-stitched embroidery, which she balanced by carrying a simple bouquet of white tulips. All of the grooms looked exceptionally handsome, which I decided was only proper as they were with such lovely women-fairies.

Hugh landed first, then held me by the arms, lowering me carefully to the altar. Whether or not he, himself, believed in the tradition of eggshell slippers, he was willing to play the game for our guests.

I smiled when I noticed Alfred and Edward following his example. The guests, who had been whispering softly about one thing or another, fell silent when Father stepped forward. I thought he looked even more regal than usual, standing there with one hand on the Silver Fairy law book.

"Welcome," he greeted us solemnly. "If you will each take your intended by both hands, please." He waited while we complied, then opened the law book. "The first law our tribe made when establishing itself as a monarchy is as follows: The king, duly appointed and accepted by the Silver Fairy Tribe, shall have the authority to perform marriages." Smiling, he paused, his finger still holding his place. "In that rather dry statement lays a powerful, most delightful magic. For with marriage, two lives become as one—or in this case, six become as three." The guests responded with a small ripple of polite laughter. "I cannot see your futures," he went on when it was quiet again, "nobody can. But I can tell you that today's choices will build the foundation for your tomorrows. As your tomorrows become your yesterdays, your futures will take shape. So choose wisely, my young friends, as you have today." He paused, his shoulders slumping for a fraction of a second. "Now, let us begin."

I let his words wash over me as he performed the first two marriages. I felt an amazing peace as he turned to Hugh and me.

"Hugh Lawson," Father's voice boomed across the assembled fairies. "Do you hereby swear and covenant that you, of your own free will and choice, take this woman-fairy as your wife?"

"I do," Hugh's voice rang clearly.

"Do you swear and covenant that you will defend her to the best of your ability, keeping yourself for her alone, and grant her voice in your joined lives?" Father asked.

"I so swear and covenant," Hugh answered firmly. He looked Father straight in the eyes and accepted the ring Father held out to him.

"Rebecca Shaw," my father addressed me directly. "Do you hereby swear and covenant that you, of your own free will and choice, take this man-fairy as your husband?"

"I do," I answered without hesitation. Oh, I knew marriage was not for the faint of heart. I knew it took daily effort to keep those two joined lives from drifting back apart. I just happened to believe that Hugh and I were both going to apply the necessary effort.

"Do you swear and covenant that you will care for him to the best of your ability, keeping yourself for him alone, and grant him voice in your joined lives?" Father asked me.

"I so swear and covenant," I answered firmly. I blinked back a tear as Father handed me Hugh's ring.

"Let these rings serve to remind you," Father stated solemnly, "that you willingly bound yourselves to each other this day, before these witnesses," he made a sweeping gesture to include all seven hundred guests.

Hugh took my hand in his and gently slipped

the ring, already warm from his hands, onto my right index finger. I marveled for a moment at the exquisite carving on the gold circlet, then gladly placed his ring on his finger.

"Presenting," Father stepped back, opening his hands and arms to include all three couples, "for the first time anywhere, the new Duke and Duchess of Dieford!" The guests cheered. "The new King's Champion Edward Bullierd and his wife, Lady Helen Bullierd," Father announced. The cheers, which had not quite stopped from the first announcement grew louder. "And for the second time anywhere," he smiled at us genially, "Prince Hugh Lawson and his bride, Princess Rebecca Lawson!"

I held Hugh's arm as our guests roared. It was not that any one of them was making a great deal of noise by themselves. It was simply that their combined well wishes were almost deafening.

"Have they forgotten that I must still be crowned?" Hugh asked, a frown in his voice that he did not permit to touch his face.

"In a moment, darling," I shouted and waved to the crowd.

Chapter XVI

For the coronation a company of Silver Guardsmen, including two wings of Sean's Silver Dragonfly Battalion, surrounded the platform that had been hastily stripped of all indications of a wedding. Except for Hugh and me, that is.

I took a deep breath and stopped worrying about my wedding dress. It had served its purpose and was far too delicate to have done more than survive the day anyway. With Hugh's assistance, I knelt before the stand that held the King and Queen's Crowns. A king, I had learned in school, took three oaths. The first was administered by the senior council member, in our case Councilor Branwick.

"Hugh Lawson, prince of the royal house of the Plant Fairy Tribe, I stand before you today to receive your oath to protect the citizens of the Silver Fairy Tribe, both by obeying the laws presently set to paper and by enjoining new laws as occasion demands," Councilor Branwick seemed to shed hundreds of years as he declared the oath.

Now for the answer…'twould be simpler if that were in the law word for word, too, my imp thought anxiously.

"I give you an oath, Councilor," Hugh answered humbly, "so long as I have the power to effect change for good, I will do so."

I swallowed hard, contrasting his sweeping statement with my own weakness of character. But I did not shrink from adding my words to his when the time came.

"Rebecca Lawson, princess of the royal house of the Silver Fairy Tribe, will you stand beside Prince Hugh, aiding him and supporting him to the best of your ability?"

"I will," I stated firmly. I saw Councilor Branwick blink a few times before he nodded.

"The council accepts you, Prince Hugh, and you, Princess Rebecca, as our next king and queen." His work done, Councilor Branwick flew back to stand by Father.

The second oath, my imp swallowed hard and blinked back a few tears of her own, *is to be administered by the senior military officer. My, he looks splendid in his dress uniform, with all of his medals.*

The senior landed before us. It was a moment before he administered the oath, but whether it was due to fine, dramatic timing or a lump in his throat could not have been determined from his expression.

"Hugh Lawson, prince of the royal house of the Plant Fairy Tribe, I stand before you today to receive your oath to protect and defend the Silver Fairy Tribe from all her enemies, be they nature, animal, or fairy in origin."

"I give you my oath, Senior," Hugh answered boldly, "that I will protect the Silver Fairy Tribe as any man-fairy would his own family."

"Rebecca Lawson, princess of the royal house of the Silver Fairy Tribe, will you stand beside Prince Hugh, aiding him and supporting him to the best of your ability?"

Hugh will probably never let me fight beside him again, husbands are like that, my imp retorted.

"I will," I agreed loudly enough to be heard. I met the senior's gaze directly, certain that he was aware of the slight pause between his question and my answer. I was neither afraid nor loath to perform my duty in defending my tribe. I was just deeply disturbed by the recognition that this oath might result in my losing Hugh.

"The military accepts you, Prince Hugh, and you, Princess Rebecca, as our next king and queen," the senior announced in his best parade-ground voice. There was no immediate fanfare or round of cannon fire, though. That would come later.

Once the senior had resumed his place at my father's left, only one oath remained. One further challenge to be presented. Father stood before us again, both hands clasped behind his back. He studied Hugh, then me, then Hugh again. Mother stood beside him, smiling faintly.

"Hugh Lawson, prince of the royal house of the Plant Fairy Tribe," Father delivered the oath clearly, deliberately, as though the words were coming from the depth of his own soul, "I stand before you today to receive your oath to wear this crown," he lifted his own crown from the stand, "with dignity and honor, doing nothing to bring shame to your tribe." There was a profound silence after he finished speaking, the sort that drew one's heart from the chest and made it a lump in the throat.

"I give you my oath, sir," Hugh spoke plainly, "that I will."

Father waited for what felt like forever. "We, the Silver Fairy Tribe, accept you, Hugh Lawson, as our next king."

There was a moment of silence as Hugh reverently removed the prince's crown from his own head.

"I, Prince Nathaniel Shaw, of the Silver Fairy Tribe," Father's voice seemed to fill the world, "do officially, formally, and forever, relinquish and yield my rights, authority, and responsibilities as king of the Silver Fairy Tribe and bestow them upon Prince Hugh Lawson." He placed the King's Crown on Hugh's bowed head. Then he received the prince's crown from Hugh's hand and set it on the stand, there to remain until Hugh's own Day of Yielding.

While the tribe watched Father, I watched Hugh. I noticed tiny wet spots beginning to form on his shirtfront and realized he was crying. I had to look away then, even if it was just down at my own hands. I began blinking furiously in an attempt to keep from crying with him, for my tears were approaching flood levels, and tried to focus on what Mother was saying to me.

"Rebecca Lawson, princess of the royal house of the Silver Fairy Tribe, I stand before you today to receive your oath to wear this crown," she lifted her crown from the stand, "with dignity and honor, doing nothing to bring shame to your tribe."

I looked up at her, words colliding in my head. What I wanted to say (I was not really sure), what I knew I was supposed to say (which seemed suddenly to be terribly inadequate)... I felt that I was emotionally somewhere between a live, raw nerve and a numb one.

Come now, my imp patted me reassuringly on the shoulder, *this is no different than you knew it would be—the crowds, the oaths, even your mother's crown. Take a deep breath, then, and give them your answer.*

"I will," I murmured. Then, taking a lungful of air, I repeated more loudly, "I will."

"We, the Silver Fairy Tribe, accept you, Rebecca Lawson, as our next queen," she announced, her own voice quieter than it perhaps should have been.

I removed the princess' crown and held it my hands, rubbing my thumb over the dent an arrow had left. I was glad I had never gotten around to having that fixed.

"I, Princess Rachel Shaw, of the Silver Fairy Tribe," Mother's voice seemed to fill the world, "do officially, formally, and forever, relinquish and yield my rights, authority, and responsibilities as queen of the Silver Fairy Tribe and bestow them upon Princess Rebecca Lawson."

I gasped softly as the weight of Mother's crown pressed down upon my head. It took a great deal of effort to lift my head and look her in the eyes. I did not immediately hand her the princess' crown. First I had to mentally pry my fingers loose from it. I saw only understanding in her eyes, though, when she received it from my hands and placed it carefully on the stand. Her fingers lingered on the stand a moment, as though promising me that my crown would be safe there.

I looked at Hugh, who was looking at me. I accepted his proffered hand and we rose to face our guests. The first cannon sounded, followed in rapid succession by thirty-nine others. I was impressed to see the first gun crew, which was visible from the platform where we stood, reload the cannon with powder *and ball!* before they stopped to cheer. Not that I could hear them. I could not even hear Hugh over the congratulatory cheers the guests were making, but I smiled up at him as though I could.

We stood there for several minutes as ranking officers of the military branches—the Air Corp, the fleet, and the infantry—approached to salute Hugh, offering their swords to him in token of their fealty. He accepted each sword in turn, shook hands with the officer, and returned the sword to them.

I stood quietly by, my tears temporarily avoided. I was still bursting with emotion, but there were other things to think of. The reception, for example. As the odor of gunpowder cleared, I could smell the light lunch Cook had prepared. I hoped that none of the dishes had been broken by the dry cannon fire.

"Ready?" Hugh shouted to me.

I could not help grinning. It was, after all, not completely unlike our first wedding. My ears rang from all the commotion, I had gotten a lungful of gunpowder haze, and we were about to enter uncharted waters.

I put my hand in his. "Ready!" I shouted back.

Exhausted or not, it is considered bad form for a princ…um, *queen*, to yawn in her guests' faces, so I kept a smile on my face as Hugh led me out the way we had come. I knew I had no duties to perform at the reception, beyond being agreeable, but I could not help mentally comparing what had been planned with what I found upon arriving in the ballroom. Six servers waited with glasses of Helen's vile concoction.

"Better hold your breath," I murmured to Hugh as he handed me mine. We hastily drank them down, followed by a tumbler of water, then formed a line with the other brides and grooms.

At Hugh's nod, a door opened and the guests began trickling in. The first thing they saw, by design, was a row of buffet tables that literally sagged with mouthwatering goodies. I was delighted to find that Hugh's theory was correct!

The men-fairies were gracious and complimentary, but brief. With varying levels of expertise, they managed to coax their wives away from the line and toward the food. From the buffet tables, they were directed to an area outside where large umbrellas and smallish tables awaited them.

"You are a genius," I told Hugh after giving a final smile and nod. "Twice the guests and half the time as my receiving line the other day."

"Are you in pain?" he asked, frowning.

"I…a little," I confessed, reaching up to rub my neck. "This crown is heavier than what I am used to."

He smiled wryly, "I know what you mean."

I had thought I was out of pleasantries until I remembered we were not alone.

"Helen, Cassandra," I left Hugh's side to hug them. "Thank you both for being so patient with all of this."

"Thank you," Helen interjected, winking slyly, "for not marrying Edward."

"Or Alfred," Cassandra agreed.

I laughed with them, and did not bother to blink back my tears this time. As I had hoped, the laughter acted as a thickener of sorts, allowing just a few surface tears to seep through.

"I wish you happiness, Your Majesty," Helen curtsied.

"May your slippers shatter into several thousand pieces," Cassandra added the old saying with her curtsy.

"And yours," I included them both in the wish. I had a funny feeling, as I watched them fly over to Hugh, that closely resembled regret. After some weeks of their company, I was going to miss them.

"Alfred," I greeted, smiling as another tear trickled out. "Congratulations."

"Thank you," he acknowledged my words with a deliberate bow. "May you always find the right wind," he said seriously.

I wiped at a tear and shook my head. "I am not familiar with that saying."

"Cial Mar taught it to me," he smiled.

I put my hand in his when he offered it.

"Goodbye for now, Your Majesty," he kissed my hand, smiled, and flew off to claim Cassandra.

Edward was waiting, an odd expression on his face. Was he remembering our first (and last) kiss? Or the time he dunked me in the pond for being a brat about getting beaten at archery? He had told me very plainly that it was 'unbecoming a princess—or a lady' to behave as I was doing. I might have been born one, but clearly he was going to have to help me become the other. And like a true friend, he had never stopped encouraging me to become the very best I could be.

Wordlessly I held out my hands to him. "Congratulations, my dear," I caught back his name and substituted, "friend."

"And to you, Your Majesty," he bowed slightly, without releasing my hands.

My smile slipped. "We will never be the same, will we?" I asked without needing an answer. "I have gained a husband and lost a friend."

He squeezed my hands gently. "I have lost a friend and gained a queen. No matter how this worked out, it meant change for us."

"At least we shall still see each other at court," I tried to sound happy, though I was not convinced I was looking forward to the taxing process of redrawing our boundary lines. We would never intentionally violate our spouse's trust, but our relationship was such that we might not think it inappropriate to be alone together until it was too late. Or I might hug him without first greeting Helen. Or…

Edward brought me back from the uncertain future by clearing his throat. "You are over-thinking again," he informed me with a smile. "You should not."

"You are right, as usual," I sighed. My neck was too sore to nod, but I did smile back at him.

"Shall we?" he dropped one of my hands to gesture toward where Helen and Hugh were talking quietly.

I watched Helen's face light up as we approached and felt better. Then I tucked my arm through Hugh's and everything was right with my world.

"I think it is safe to say," Hugh began flying us toward the hallway that led to my room, "that we are finally free."

"Mm," I agreed, "tradition alone waits upon us now."

"Ah, yes," he nodded, "your slippers. I suppose now is a good time to ask where we smash them?"

I smiled. "I am told it is a very messy process," I concurred with his unspoken sentiment, "but Megan promised to leave things ready for us." I permitted myself a discreet yawn. One good thing about being so tired was that I was able to mostly ignore the guards snapping to attention as we made our way down the hall.

Hugh waved the servants away when we arrived, preferring to open the door for me himself. "Well," he eyed the contraption in the center of the floor with interest. "It looks very effective." He shut the door behind him.

"Indeed," I agreed, leaning on his arm while I removed my slippers just inside the doorway. "You first," I encouraged, handing him one.

"Here goes." Crouching, he set the slipper inside the box, closed it and slammed down on the lever.

"I have never heard a prediction of what happens if the slippers are reduced to dust!" I exclaimed, wide-eyed at the resulting sound.

"Simple," he grinned as he opened the box to reveal what was left of the slipper, "we live happily ever after."

"Hmm," I reached past him and set the

second slipper inside, "my turn." Gripping the lever with both hands, I tried to slam it down as forcefully as he had. Not that I quite managed it.

"Well done!" he congratulated me anyway.

I wrinkled my nose at him and opened the box. "Oh!" The second slipper, though my efforts had fallen far short of Hugh's, had also been reduced to dust.

"There, see?" he asked.

I let him lift me into a standing position, leaned back against him. "Hugh?" I interrupted when he tried to kiss me. "I have a surprise for you." I smiled at his arched eyebrows. "The bride's gift to the groom." I laughed when he looked around the room as though expecting to find it hidden under a table. "It is not in here," I told him.

"I have had enough gifts for one day," he laughingly protested, wrapping his arms about my waist. "Can it not wait until tonight, after we have started our wedding trip?"

"I have been thinking about that, too," I told him, tipping my head back against his shoulder. After an afternoon of nodding, it felt wonderful to relax my neck. "Do you really want to go on that trip?" I asked.

He shrugged, careful not to jar me. "I have done enough travelling for two lifetimes. But I thought you had your heart set on it?"

"So did I. Then I realized that by tonight, this entire building would be empty." I waited before continuing, "It does seem a little silly to travel to a strange place so we can be alone when we could have the post to ourselves."

"You *are* tired," he chuckled and kissed my hair.

I put my hands over his and closed my eyes. "True." I smiled when his breath tickled my neck. "But not too tired to want to give you your gift. It will not take long," I promised him. "Shut your eyes?" I was relieved when he complied. Lifting his arms from about my waist, I opened the door to my bedchamber. Clumsily I positioned him a few steps inside then flew a little further in myself, turning so I could see his face. "Open your eyes."

He opened his beautiful green eyes and looked. Then his mouth opened in shock. "Rebecca," he looked all about the room, "what…?"

"I invited Laughter and the others to decorate my room for us," I explained, feeling suddenly shy. "Do you like it?" I watched him closely, mindful of the troupe fairy tradition that his reaction was a glimpse of our future.

"Do I," he started to repeat the question, then reversed it to ask, "do *you* like it?"

"I love it," I told him honestly. "The women-folk all had a hand in making this," I touched the crazy quilt that graced my bed, "and the men-folk each made a wind-whistle for our window," I pointed. I inhaled sharply when he took a step closer to me. "And Abigail gave us that rocking chair. I…she said she used to rock you in it," I told him, suddenly out of words. She had also given me some advice about tending babies, but I could tell him that later. I had to look up to see his face, he had come so near.

"Thank you," he murmured, "very much." He kissed my forehead gently. Then he smiled. "And…hello, Mrs. Lawson."

Troubled Skies (Bk 4) Excerpt

Chapter I

Not tonight, he groaned. Not again! His faint hope that he was wrong dwindled as the approaching first lieutenant did indeed land before him, saluting smartly. After a moment's hesitation, he remembered he had to acknowledge the salute before the poor fellow could relax.

"Prince Cambrian," the officer addressed him, "Major Layton's compliments, sir. He requests the pleasure of your company at dinner."

Cambrian kept a straight face as he mentally reviewed and discarded responses that were appealing but unseemly. No, thank you. I no longer eat.

"Very good," he surrendered to his duty after a brief struggle. "I will arrive at the usual time." Nodding in acknowledgment of the second salute, he looked back out over the windship yard.

As the second son of a young king, Cambrian served a special purpose in the kingdom of the Sky Fairies. He could go where his father and elder brother, Oliver, could not. He heard things they did not. Occasionally, he even reported what he had heard, such as the illegal smuggling of rare tanzanite stones, and the cruel falcon and snake baiting ring. Right now, he was supposedly on vacation. At that exact moment, he was supposed to be writing.

From his carefully selected vantage point, Cambrian could see all of Fort Bakarti stretched out before him. Half a dozen windships lined the edges of the harbor, and half a dozen more were at the yard undergoing maintenance or repairs. He watched the docks for a moment, trying to think of something poetic to say about loading supplies onto a windship's sideboat or the cords of seasoned timber being transferred off the squarely-built transport. When nothing came to mind, he stared hard at the sheer drop-off that served as Bakarti's exit point. At this altitude, tree harbors were impractical, if not impossible. Instead, they built harbors inside pockets in the rocky mountainside, and assigned pilots, experts in the local terrain, to outgoing windships.

Pilots… In Cambrian's private opinion, they were all insane. He felt the hairs on his arms rising as he remembered trying to look impassive while the Falcon departed a similar harbor on its way to the pirate offensive. Plummeting down between jagged outcroppings of mineral deposits was almost enough to cause heart failure. How grateful Cambrian had been when her sails had filled with wind and she had leveled off! Having seen them safely out, the pilot had cheerfully saluted Captain Kimberlite, stepped onto his one-passenger sailboard, and hopped off the stern, where he easily caught an updraft and returned to lend his skilled guidance to the other, waiting windships.

Blinking against the sun, Cambrian frowned down at where his pencil lay inert on a page of blank paper. In the distant past, he had been able to write anytime—anywhere! Yet this morning he had spent close to two uninterrupted hours staring at one of the loveliest vistas in the Sky Fairy kingdom without having a single creative thought.

Or was it without thinking at all? Sighing, he closed his notebook and fastened the leather tie. If this was the best he could do, he might as well pack up and go home. At least there he had some say regarding his dining partners.

"Robert," Cambrian nudged his aide, "wake up."

"Hmm? Oh." Robert snapped into a sitting position. "Sorry, Highness, I only meant to close my eyes." Spotting the closed notebook, he held out his hand for it.

Cambrian smiled despite himself. He had chosen to employ Robert more or less because the man-fairy had exhibited no interest in royal affairs. If that included sleeping through a fruitless writing session, so be it. Nevertheless, Robert's carelessness with his duties as a valet was beginning to be annoying.

"I will carry it," he transferred the notebook to his right hand, out of Robert's reach. Then he surprised himself by saying, "I feel like doing some fencing."

Robert's eyes lit up and he was in the air with a single flap. "Race you," he suggested with all the enthusiasm of a lad half his age.

"Agreed," Cambrian said after an instant's hesitation. "But no cheating!"

"Highness," Robert gave an exaggerated sigh. "I never cheat. I simply take the most direct route." With a flash of his well-known, mischievous grin, Robert was gone.

"Yes, of course," Cambrian muttered to himself as he lifted off, "silly of me not to realize." He had his own plan, though. The fencing area was on the far side of the enlisted men-fairy's barracks. Where Robert was heading up and over the building, Cambrian flew right through. Due to the warm weather, there were plenty of open windows!

Landing gracefully at the practice grounds, he dropped his notebook on an empty bench and stripped off his waistcoat. He was in the middle of a stretch when Robert landed in front of him. Cambrian almost laughed aloud at the dumbfounded expression on Robert's face.

"How did you beat me?" Robert asked. "I never even saw you…"

"Take off?" Cambrian interrupted. "I am not surprised. You would have needed eyes in the back of your head for that." He nodded at the sword rack. "Whenever you are ready."

Irked at being outdone by someone he considered an easy mark, Robert did not bother to stretch before taking up a sword. If it were not for the high pay, good food, and his hopes to marry well, Robert would have disdained to work for a bureaucrat like Cambrian. Even with all of those extra advantages, he could barely endure serving the artistic dolt. Whipping the training sword through the air a few times, he went quickly to a designated sparring lane.

"So soon?" Cambrian called after him. "Very well," he completed one last stretch and flew over to the lane in a leisurely style. He watched Robert's face as he approached, amused to see Robert's expression go from aloof to impatient so quickly. He decided that Robert was probably planning to make short work of him. Politely, of course—how else would a valet defeat his master? Perhaps it was time to get a new valet after all, one that was a little more complex.

An instructor stepped forward. "Present buttons," he barked. Rich or poor, in his fencing area they were all students. When he had satisfied himself that the buttons were securely fastened he ordered, "En garde. Commence!"

Cambrian knew the rules of fencing. And he had a cardinal rule of his own—never make the first move. That allowed him to study his opponent. In this case, it made Robert even more agitated. Cambrian parried Robert's predictably over-extended lunge. Carefully, he avoided making a point on his return blow.

The swords flashed in the mid-afternoon sunlight, carrying on a conversation in their own language. *Are you fast enough to stop me?* one blade challenged, darting forward. *Fast enough for that and more,* hissed the other, blocking and returning the challenge. *Are you really paying attention?* the first blade mocked, switching mid-lunge to a cutover. *Attention is the price of living,* sang the second blade as it moved to block high, *and I always pay my dues!*

"Point!" cried the instructor, indicating Robert. It was a fair point, so he added nothing to his call, but he had his own opinion about whether or not Cambrian had given it away.

The two opponents circled each other, looking for a weakness. If one of them so much as blinked…Robert lunged. Cambrian parried, but too late and with insufficient force.

"Point!" the instructor cried again, adjusting his shoulder sash and feeling vaguely amused. He should have stopped the match and drilled them both for hours—but more especially Robert, who was apparently not even aware that Cambrian was toying with him. "Two for Robert. En garde. Possible match point!" He added that last for the benefit of the gathering crowd. He hoped that the prince would see fit to gain at least one point, if only for the benefit of the Post's morale!

Cambrian made a little more effort this time. Truth be told, he was already bored with this game. Almost bored enough to become careless and let Robert see how good he really was.

"Point! Match point!" barked the instructor, glowering at Prince Cambrian. "Would his highness care to take a few lessons while he is here?"

Cambrian plucked a kerchief from his belt and dabbed at his forehead, wishing he had chosen to exercise before the day had gotten so warm. "Not today, thank you, sir." Tossing his sword to Robert, who caught it deftly, Cambrian added, "I suppose you have had enough of me for one day." Closing the gap between himself and Robert so that he could speak more quietly he went on, "And I suppose you would rather not endure another official dinner. Would you care to take the rest of the day off?"

"You are too kind, Highness," Robert bowed from the waist. After working off his ire, redeeming himself in his own eyes in the process, he was back to his carefree self. Besides that, there was the prospect of an evening off—and the hope of doubling his month's salary with a little skillful wagering.

"Very good," Cambrian nodded. "While you are out I would have you ask some questions." He watched Robert carefully but saw only bored resignation on his face. "About Major Layton. Find out everything you can." He was taking a chance, entrusting such a delicate task to an increasingly insubordinate aide, but Robert had a talent for obtaining such information. It would be useful to have his version to compare with the official records. At the moment, all he knew for certain was that however Major Layton had come by his promotions, someone had signed the papers.

"As you wish. Will there be anything else, Highness?" Robert tucked the blades under his arm to keep from twirling them impatiently.

"No, that will suffice. See you tomorrow, then." Tossing the instructor a cheery salute, Cambrian retrieved his things and flew off in the direction of his rooms. He became so absorbed in his thoughts that his flight grew slower and slower until he dropped to the ground and began walking.

"A grain for your thoughts, Prince Cambrian," suggested a familiar voice.

Cambrian blinked and looked around. Surprised to find himself approaching the docks, he smiled at the woman-fairy who had hailed him. "Captain Kimberlite," he smiled, recognizing her at once from his time aboard the Falcon, a Kestrel-class windship. She had been reassigned after the battle to the Nadauld, a larger, more heavily-gunned Gyrfalcon-class windship. Recalling her offer he asked, "Would that be a grain of gold or a grain of silver?"

"Silver, Highness," she answered, smiling apologetically and trying to forget that she was wearing a bicorn hat as part of her dress uniform.

The front point jutted out over her forehead, making her feel like she had an extra nose positioned just above her eyebrows. "I am just a humble officer in the King's Fleet."

Cambrian offered his arm and was pleased when she accepted it. "An officer, I will grant. But humble?" he teased as they began walking toward the docks together, that being her apparent destination and he having nowhere else to be. "Are there two Captain Kimberlite's?" He instantly regretted his jest when he saw a subtle change in her facial expression, almost like a door closing. "Forgive me, Captain," he apologized without delay. He stopped walking so that he could face her. "It was a poor joke."

"I," she paused, "have heard worse." She tried so hard not to care what others said, whether it was about her or to her. She looked away while she consciously smoothed out her expression.

"And I hold myself to a high standard," he forestalled any excuse she might have made to leave him. "Unfortunately, I am not always able to maintain it." He stood quite still while she turned back to him and examined his face for any hidden meaning. This was a very different woman-fairy from the cool, efficient Captain Kimberlite he had observed during the pirate offensive. He wondered briefly what had made her so suspicious of men-fairies, but supposed she had just cause.

"You meant no harm," she agreed at last, relaxing again.

"If you have really forgiven me," he placed her hand tentatively back on his arm, "I shall admit that I have no thoughts at the moment."

"Oh," she frowned in confusion. "You certainly appeared pensive."

Cambrian resumed his walking. "Brooding would be a better term, I fear." He felt a curious freedom with her, perhaps because he could so readily empathize with her reaction to his earlier insensitive remark. He doubted she would be interested in his rather harsh assessment of his own life up to that day. It would be only natural for her to pity him his loneliness, but he did not want her pity.

"Hmm." She was silent for several seconds. "Did you know that my father was also a windship captain?"

"No," Cambrian shook his head. "Did you say was?" he added gently.

She nodded, the tear-shaped crystal button on her bicorn sparkling in the sun. "He was on the training ship Illepidam when it went down over North Point."

"A tragedy," Cambrian said after a moment, sternly repressing a shiver. Even with their safety gear, the majority of the crew had fallen victim to the sub-zero temperatures. The handful of survivors had resorted to dismantling the windship and burning it to keep warm.

"Yes, but what I was going to say," she rejoined lightly, "was that whenever he saw thunderclouds hanging low across the horizon, he would say that they were brooding."

"Ah." Cambrian was not sure how he felt about being compared to a weather phenomenon.

"He also said that was why he never worried about me when I brooded," she continued seriously, "because sooner or later the storm would break and my skies would be clear again."

Cambrian looked closely at her, no longer seeing an officer but an individual. She was, he realized, rather fetching. He could not remember the last time he had considered a woman-fairy's appearance with more than the hope of producing an appropriate compliment. Certainly not since Princess Joanna had died.

"Your father was very wise," he said abruptly, hoping he had not been staring at her.

"Yes," she agreed. She looked away, out over the docks, fearing that she was about to blush. Was there a smudge on her cheek or something? "Yes, he was."

Hearing a change in her tone, he turned to see where she was looking. Things were busy this time of day, and at first he saw nothing that should have caused her to frown. Except…

"She is coming in at an angle," he observed, taking a half step forward.

"A very steep angle," she corrected. Without another word, she began flying toward the dock.

Cambrian followed her instinctively. "What are you doing?" he asked her when he caught up.

"Something is wrong," she answered. She halted suddenly beside a small, unoccupied sideboat. Glancing back at the oncoming windship, now recognizable as the schooner Dispatch, she pointed at it and shouted an alarm, "Beware!" Hearing other voices take up the cry, she nodded in satisfaction. Untying the hitch knot deftly, she shoved the sideboat off the dock and stepped aboard as it dropped away.

Cambrian dropped his notebook on the dock and dived after her. Landing beside her, he lent a hand with unfurling the sails.

"Highness," she exclaimed in surprise. "You should not be here!"

"Where should I be?" he asked, moving to the stern to take the tiller. "Can you sail this by yourself and help her at the same time?" Besides, he wanted to be there, actually in the action for a change.

He looked up sharply as a loud cracking sound split the air. While he watched, her starboard wingtip appeared below the Dispatch's belly. Slowly it fell away, down into the emptiness beneath them. "She has lost a wing," he said through stiff lips.

"At least two more are failing." Captain Kimberlite frowned but yielded the tiller to him. There was not time to turn back now. Moving to the middle of the tiny sideboat, she ordered,

"Keep us pointed straight at her!"

Cambrian obeyed, but that took only a fraction of his mental energy. He applied the rest of it to trying to deduce how she was going to use a six-twig sideboat to stop a schooner from crashing.

"Ahoy the Dispatch!" a man-fairy's voice floated out from the dock. "Steer for the crevice!"

"It is too late for that," Kimberlite said through clenched teeth as she knotted a line about the base of the mast. "She has already overshot it." Straightening, she caught hold of the mast to keep from being blown overboard. Her bicorn tumbled off her head and kept falling, buffeted about by the crosswinds that plagued the canyon. If only there was time to don a weathervest and safety line!

"Careful!" he called, then told himself he was a fool. Of course she was being careful. His grip tightened on the tiller. As they closed on the Dispatch he could see the sailors scrambling along her deck, presumably trying to free their lifeboats.

She tossed him a grim smile. "When I shout," she began loading the sideboat's harpoon into the launcher, "find something and hold on tight. Understand?"

Cambrian gave a short, sharp nod. He was still mystified as to what she was planning, but he certainly understood what she wanted him to do.

While he watched, she aimed the harpoon toward the Dispatch. He was about to protest when he realized that she was aiming just ahead of the schooner's keel. He knew what she was going to do. He glanced about the sideboat, but there was no rope close enough for him to reach. Desperately, he began fumbling with his belt buckle.

"Ready," Kimberlite shouted, lining up her shot. "Now!" She slammed the lever forward and watched the harpoon streak in front of the Dispatch's bow before it sank into the hull of the moored Watcher. She had a death grip on the mast, but it was not enough. The Dispatch's sudden impact against the end of the now-taut harpoon line shook her feet out from under her. She was falling forward…and then something heavy hit her, knocking her to the bottom of the sideboat.

"Leaving so soon?" Cambrian gasped down at her. He managed to get his arms underneath his body and raised himself so that she could breathe. She really did have the most perfect mouth…he forced himself to focus on what she was saying.

"Who, me?" she asked, wincing as she tried to move. "I was just testing the wind."

"Did I hurt you?" he asked when he noticed her wincing again.

"I will take bruised ribs over a military funeral any day," she responded cheerfully.

He looked up to find that they were on a final approach for a cliff face. Without thinking, he dropped back on top of her, using his arms to cover her head. Nothing happened. Then there was a splintering, tearing sound as the sideboat made its rendezvous.

Learn more about the author at
leacarterwrites.wixsite.com/wholesomefantasy